This is a work of fiction. Names, characters, businesses, places, events and incidents are either the products of the author's imagination or used in a fictitious manner. Any resemblance to actual persons, living or dead, or actual events is purely coincidental.

As ever, for Suzanne & the Two Terrors ...

INTO

THE

DARK

C.J. LOUGHTY

'I don't like it.'

Those were the first words out of my brother's mouth when we pulled up outside the house. We had come to view it with our parents. Or, to be more precise, they had come to do a second viewing and dragged us along with them – against our will. This was never going to go well (not for my brother and me, anyway).

'I don't like it,' Kieran repeated.

Sat next to him on the back seat, I voiced my agreement. 'Nope,' I said, shaking my head. 'I don't like it either.'

My mum was sitting in the passenger seat at the front. She turned around and glared at both of us. 'Now why did I know you were going to say that,' she said in an icy tone.

'It's not like you haven't seen pictures of it on the Internet before,' my dad said from the driver's seat. Killing the Astra's engine, he regarded me in the rear-view mirror with an expression I couldn't gauge.

'I don't know why you brought us with you,' I said. 'You've already made up your minds about wanting to buy it. Nothing we say is going to change that. If this is an attempt to convince us what a great home it's going to be, then don't bother. We're not interested.'

'Err,' Mum said with thunder in her blue eyes. 'I'll hear less of the attitude, little miss! I won't be spoken to like that by an eleven-year-old.'

I stared sullenly out of the side window, not saying a word.

'And you can dispense with the grouchy look as well,' Mum said to me. She focused her attention on Kieran. 'That goes for you, too. You're two years older than your sister, so you should know better.'

Kieran said nothing. He just pushed tumbles of thick brown hair away from his fringe whilst sporting the same sullen expression as me.

'It looks even spookier than it did on the Internet,' I muttered.

'Sorry,' Dad said, chiming in again, 'what did you say?'

'I said that we may as well go in and have a look around then.'

'Really?' Kieran said, shooting me a confused sideways glance.

I shrugged. 'At least we can check out the bedrooms. I'm having first dibs on the biggest.'

'I'm the eldest,' Kieran informed me, 'so if anyone's having dibs, it'll be me.'

'Actually, it'll be me and your father who get first choice,' Mum said. 'Seeing as we're the ones who'll be paying the mortgage.'

'Okay,' I said, 'what are we waiting for?'

'The man from the estate agent,' Dad said, checking the time on his watch. 'He should be here by now.'

As if on cue, a green Volvo trundled down the long driveway and pulled up in front of us. A man wearing a grey suit got out and approached us with a spring in his step.

'Okey-dokey,' Dad said, reaching for the door handle. 'It's all systems go.'

Dad went and shook hands with the man, so we all joined them.

'If you're back for a second viewing then I'd say that sounds promising,' the man in the suit said. He flashed a smile which featured a perfect set of white teeth.

'It could be,' Mum said, not giving much away. 'We'll have to wait and see, Bob. Another look around the place will sway our minds one way or the other, I'm sure.'

It won't sway mine, I thought miserably.

I looked up at the house, shielding my eyes from the sun with my hand. It loomed large and impressive in front of us. It was a lot bigger than the house we were currently living in and that was for sure. The roof had green moss crusted to its tiles and the chimney was canting slightly to one side like a drunkard. Some of the windows had paint peeling away from the timber. Each one was fitted with decorative shutters mounted to the sides, which also had paint peeling away. With one of the hinges missing from the door, the garage to the side was also in a dilapidated state. The front garden had rubbish strewn here and there.

'It's a wreck,' Kieran said, taking it all in.

'It does need a lot of work,' Mum conceded. 'But that's why it's so cheap.'

'Our house is a lot nicer than this,' I said. 'I really can't see *why* you'd want to move here.'

'This place is twice the size of our house,' Dad said. He inhaled deeply and then exhaled, smiling. 'Can you smell that fresh country air? And what a great area this would be to live in, out in the sticks like this, away from it all. It'd be a real move up the social ladder for our little family if we can turn this house into the gem I know it can be.'

'It is a lovely rural area,' Bob agreed, nodding enthusiastically. He pulled some keys from his pocket and jangled them.

'Are we ready to look inside?'

'We most certainly are,' Dad said.

He and Mum accompanied Bob to the front door.

Meanwhile, Kieran and I lingered on the pavement. I looked at him and he looked at me. We communicated a message to each other without speaking. It was not a positive message.

'D'you think there's any way we can put them off buying this place,' Kieran said.

I replied, 'Probably not. But we can always live in hope. Who knows, maybe the place is haunted. Now *that* would put them off.'

'Oh, I don't know. It'll take a bit more than ghosts and ghouls to frighten Mum. Dad, perhaps – but not Mum.'

'The ghosts and ghouls would probably be frightened of her.'

4

'You're right there,' Kieran said, joining the others. Lingering on the pavement, I looked upon the house again, squinting because of the sun. I scanned every bit of the place with a keen eye. Then, in the top window to the right, I was sure I saw movement. I looked towards the front door, expecting to see that the others had gone inside, but they hadn't. They were still standing there, waiting for me.

'Come on,' Mum said, gesturing for me to hurry up. 'Get a move on!'

Before I went to join them, I cast one more glance towards the window. I saw nobody there – no sign of movement. *Just a shadow caused by the sun*, I convinced myself. *Or my imagination playing tricks on me*. But that was not to be the case.

The inside of the house was just as run-down as the outside. The hallway was long and wide, the walls decorated in sickly green wallpaper. Floorboards that'd once been polished to a dark sheen, but were now faded and scuffed, creaked underfoot as I shifted to the side to make way for the adults.

'This will make quite a reception room with a bit of TLC,' Bob declared.

'A *lot* of TLC, you mean,' I muttered.

Mum glared at me.

'Right,' Bob said, 'I'll leave you to it, then. Any questions, just give me a holler. I'll be hovering around, hopefully not getting in the way.' He flashed his toothy smile, then disappeared through a door at the end of the hallway.

When I was certain he was out of earshot, I said, 'He's from the estate agent, so I wouldn't take any notice of him. He just wants you to buy the place so his company can get some money.'

Dad ruffled my hair and told me to keep my voice down. 'We're not daft,' he said. 'We know how to make up our own minds, me and your mum – and we won't be swayed by anyone else.'

Not even your own children, I thought. *Because our opinion doesn't count for anything.*

'Why don't you kids go and check out the bedrooms upstairs,' Mum said, 'while me and your father have a gander in the kitchen again.'

Kieran smiled at me, then shot up the stairs like his bum was on fire.

I took off after him, saying, 'Hold up – wait for me, will you!'

Catching up with him just as he reached the landing, I put a hand on his shoulder and brought him to a halt. 'We can't call dibs on any of the bedrooms until we know which one is Mum and Dad's,' I said.

'I know that,' Kieran said, 'I just wanted to get up here and look around. This place is kind of creepy, don't you think? I really wouldn't be surprised if it was haunted.'

I considered telling him about the movement I'd seen – or *thought* I'd seen – in the upstairs window, but I decided against this. I figured he wouldn't have believed me anyway. And he would have thought I was pulling his leg, just so I could scare him.

I decided to investigate. The room was at the end of the landing. Beckoning Kieran to follow me, I went inside and had a look around.

'Err,' Kieran said, appearing at my side. 'There's black mould everywhere. This can be your room.'

'No thanks,' I said, shivering. 'Brr – it's cold in here.'

'You know what they say about cold spots in houses, don't you?'

'What do they say?'

'It's ghosts that cause it.' He pursed his lips together and waved his arms in the air. '*Woooo!*' he said, doing his best ghost impression. He spotted a dirty, old white cover in the corner of the room, on the floor. Picking it up, he put over his head and resumed his impression. '*WOOOOOOOO!* The headless spook is coming to *get you*, Ella!'

'Oh quit it,' I said, jabbing him in the side with my finger. 'You don't scare me.'

And he wasn't scaring me, either. It takes a lot more than a goofy kid with a sheet over his head to put the frighteners on me.

Kieran tossed the sheet aside. 'That mould was in the downstairs hallway as well. I bet it's all over the house. And the whole of this place is cold, not just this room.'

'I wonder how long this house has been empty,' I said, my voice echoing into the emptiness of the room.

'A long time, from the looks of things.'

I went to the window and looked out towards the trees.

'We'll be able to have some fun playing in the woods,' Kieran said, joining me. 'Think of the dens we'll be able to build.'

Building dens was not something that interested me, but I had no doubt I would get roped into constructing one. Kieran had a habit of nagging me until I went along with what he wanted me to do. Quite often, I thought of myself as being his substitute brother. He told my mum once that he wished I'd been born a boy. And I told her that I wished he'd been born a girl, so I had someone to do some girly things with. She told us both to shut up.

'I wonder if the other bedrooms are as big as this one,' I said.

'Let's go and find out,' Kieran said, leading the way.

The next room we entered was a lot bigger. It had a walk-in wardrobe and an en suite shower.

'Bagsy this one for me,' Kieran said, getting excited.

'Oh come on, you just know this one is going to be Mum and Dad's.'

'Yeah, probably.'

This room had a view of the back garden, which was surprisingly long and spacious. It was much bigger than the one at our house in Rivington. And there was even a pond, too, which was a bonus. Beyond the garden, trees stretched to the horizon.

'You'll be able to play football on that lawn,' I noted.

'No I won't. Look how overgrown it is. The whole garden is like a jungle. The grass looks like it hasn't been mown in years.'

'It's a chance for us to earn some pocket money, clearing it up.'

'Good point.'

We continued exploring the upstairs.

The bathroom was disgusting. Everything was dirty and there was black mould all around the ceiling. Even if the room had been cleaned from top to bottom, it would still have been disgusting. Someone had thought it was a good idea to install a pink bath, with matching sink and toilet.

'I will *never* use this room,' I said. 'I'd rather go to toilet in the garden.'

'No way am I ever taking a bath in here,' Kieran said. He ran his finger along the inside of the tub and showed me some gunk. '*Eek!*' he screeched, wiping his hands on his jeans. '*Grrrross!*'

We had seen enough.

We moved on, exploring the remaining rooms upstairs. I found a small one which I thought would be a good match for me (I like nice, compact spaces that are easy to manage). Kieran found one that was spacious enough for all his toys and other clutter. It was as we were leaving this room that we heard the noises.

I looked at Kieran and he looked back at me. Then we both looked towards the ceiling, where the noises seemed to be coming from.

'What d'you suppose that is?' I said.

Kieran shrugged. 'I dunno. A bird, probably.'

'What if it's a ghost?'

Kieran chuckled. 'Well, I guess we'll be in for a scary time when we move in, then, won't we?'

'*If* we move in,' I said, correcting him. 'Nothing's been finalized yet. Mum and Dad haven't even put an offer in.'

We heard movement again.

'Sounds like wings flapping,' Kieran said. 'It's got to be a bird. I'll bet there's a nest up there. Either that or it's got trapped.'

There was a door to our left. It was the only one we hadn't been through.

'I bet this leads up to the attic,' I said, pushing the handle down.

Upon opening the door, I revealed a steep wooden staircase which led up into darkness.

'Why don't you go and take a look,' Kieran suggested. 'I'll stay here and keep an eye out.'

'Hah-hah,' I said, reaching inside the doorway, probing the wall with my fingertips, trying to find a light switch. 'Very funny.' Finding the switch, I flipped it – but nothing happened.

'Bulb must have gone.'

We heard the flapping again. And another noise as well. I turned my head to the side, listening intently. To me, it sounded like a clicking noise. Edging a little farther into the darkness, I placed my foot on the first step and continued to listen. And that's when I saw the eyes glaring down at me. Glowing, baleful eyes. Retreating backwards, I slammed the door shut.

'What's up?' Kieran said. 'What did you see?'

I told him.

'D'you think it was a bird?' he said, looking terrified.

'How many birds do you know that have glow in the dark eyes?'

Mum called up to us: 'Ella and Kieran, are you okay up there?'

No, I thought, *we are most* definitely *not*.

Kieran and I raced back across the landing. At the top of the stairs, we wrestled briefly for who would go down first. Kieran pushed me aside with ease.

'Thanks,' I said, scurrying after him. 'You're a real gentleman.'

Mum and Dad were now in the living room, talking to Bob. When we came bursting through the doorway, Dad held his hands up and said, 'Whoa – whoa! Hold up, you pair. What's the rush? What's got your feathers ruffled?

'Upstairs!' I said, out of breath. 'In the attic! There's something in the attic!'

'There is,' Kieran said, backing me up. 'We heard a flapping and a clicking noise. And Ella saw some glowing eyes!'

Mum regarded us both as though we'd gone mad. 'Don't be silly,' she said. 'I'm sure there's a perfectly rational explanation.'

'The noise is just a bird that's got trapped, I'm sure' Bob said.

'But I opened the door that leads up to the attic and saw glowing eyes – glaring at me!'

'It was probably just chinks of light coming through the rafters,' Bob said.

'It wasn't chinks of light,' I responded, beginning to get annoyed. 'I *know* eyes when I see them.'

'Please calm down,' Dad said. 'Getting hysterical about this isn't going to help matters, now, is it?'

'She's only getting hysterical because no one believes her,' Kieran said.

'Okay,' Bob said, easing past me, 'there's one easy way to put an end to this.'

'Where are you going?' I asked him.

Pausing in the doorway, he said, 'Why up to the attic, of course. I'm going to take a look around and put an end to your worries.'

'There's really no need,' Mum said, her red lips tightening to a thin line as she gave me a harsh stare. 'Honestly, Ella, why bother this nice man with such silliness?'

'I am *NOT* being silly!' I said, stamping my foot down hard.

Mum levelled the dreaded finger at me. 'Another raised word from you and you'll sit in the car until we're done. Do you understand me?'

Given what I'd seen, the idea of sitting in the car didn't seem such a bad idea. But I kept my mouth shut anyway, just to stop mum from glaring at me.

'The light for the attic doesn't work,' Kieran said to Bob, 'so you won't be able to see where you're going.'

Bob reached into his trouser pocket and pulled out a small torch. 'Always pays to be prepared,' he said, winking at Kieran and then disappearing from the room.

After he'd gone, an uncomfortable silence descended in the living room. Nobody knew what to do with themselves. Dad kept pacing back and forth, clicking his fingers. Mum stood still as a statue, with her arms folded and a look of thunder on her face. Kieran kept glancing at me and I kept glancing at him.

Any second now I was sure that Bob would scream out and come bounding down the stairs to tell us what he'd seen. But there was no scream. And when he did come back down the stairs, it was at a controlled, leisurely pace.

'Well,' he said, looking neither happy nor unhappy, 'I've got some good news and ... some bad news. The good news is that I didn't see any glowing eyes or any creature that might *have* glowing eyes.'

'And what's the bad news?' Mum said, looking concerned.

'There appears to be some form infestation in the attic. I found droppings. From bats, or birds, or rats, something like that. Probably bats, judging by the noises your children heard. '

'I hope it isn't rats,' Mum said, aghast. 'I hate rats! And I'm not keen on bats, either.'

'Ah,' Dad said. 'That's not good. This could be a game-changer. No wonder the place is cheap.'

'I'm just guessing as to what's caused these droppings,' Bob said. 'I'm not an expert in infestations, but I do know droppings when I see them.'

'We'll need to discuss this in-depth,' Mum said to Dad, who nodded solemnly.

An overwhelming feeling of hope washed over me. *Looks like we might not be moving in after all*, I thought.

'What are you pair looking so happy about?' Mum said to Kieran and me. 'Go on, get yourselves out in the garden or something. Your father and I need to talk – *alone*.'

'We've already seen the garden from upstairs,' Kieran said.

Dad pointed to a door at the far end of the room. 'Go and explore through there, then. It's where we were hoping you could put all your games and stuff.'

Intrigued, I followed Kieran through to the room. I was just about to shut the door behind us when it slammed in my face.

'Charming,' I said.

'I think that's scuppered their plans,' Kieran said, smiling.

'We hope,' I replied, turning my attention to the spacious room we were now standing in. 'Crikey, this is supposed to be our playroom. It's huge. We could get loads in here.'

'What about a pool table? I've always wanted one and now we'll have room.'

'That's all good and well, but it's looking less likely that we're going to live here, remember. And then there's the small matter of the glowing eyes in the attic.'

'Are you sure you saw glowing eyes? Bob's explanation about the chinks of light through the rafters does sound plausible, I must admit. Or it could have been a rat or bat or whatever it is that's living up there, making those droppings.'

'Rats don't have eyes that glow in the dark (and I'm pretty sure bats don't either). I know what I saw and it wasn't like anything I've seen before. Maybe it hid when Bob went up there.' I changed my mind about telling Kieran about the movement I thought I'd seen behind the window when we'd arrived. 'I'm sure someone was watching us.'

'Why didn't you mention this before?'

'Because I didn't think you'd believe me. And from the look on your face, I'd say you don't believe me now.'

'I don't doubt that you *thought* you saw something at the window. And I don't doubt that you *thought* you saw something in the attic ...'

I threw my hands up in exasperation. *Even Kieran doesn't believe me now*, I thought.

He put his ear to the door. 'Hey,' he said, gesturing me to do the same, 'come over here – I can hear every word they're saying.'

I copied him, putting my ear to the door as well. What we heard was not good news. Bob was doing his best to convince my parents that they should still buy the house.

'Even if you have got vermin in the roof,' Bob was saying, 'it doesn't matter – not really. There are plenty of companies that specialize in remedying such a problem. Granted, it won't be cheap – but you've got a real opportunity for this to be a positive thing rather than a negative one.'

'How can having vermin in the roof be a positive thing?' Mum asked him.

Bob explained: 'This property is already a bargain – even factoring in the cost of dealing with vermin – but you can get the vendor to go even cheaper by mentioning the cost of having to deal with the problem.'

'He has got a point there, dear,' Dad said to Mum.

'I don't believe it,' I said to Kieran. 'They're still going to buy this hellhole.'

'Nothing's certain,' Kieran replied. 'Mum could still take some convincing.'

'We need to think long and hard about this,' we heard Mum say.

'I do understand,' Bob said. 'But I wouldn't dilly-dally too long. Others have expressed a keen interest in Selby House and it won't be long before it sells, in my opinion.'

'Even with the infestation?' Dad said.

'Yes,' Bob replied, 'even with the infestation.'

Sales patter, I thought. *What a load of hogwash!*

'Looks like we'll be having a long talk later on this evening,' Dad said to Mum.

'Lots to ponder,' she said in a thoughtful voice.

'Lots to ponder, indeed,' Bob concurred.

'Right,' Dad said, 'I suppose we better get the kids back in here and let them know what's going on.'

Kieran and I darted away from the door, then pretended to still be checking out the room that was meant to be our playroom.

'Right,' Dad said to us, 'you can come back in now.'

We did as we were told.

'So,' I said, 'is this going to be our new home, then, or what?'

Mum looked at Dad and he looked back at her. I was trying to gauge what message they were trying to communicate. Then Bob chirped in.

'What do you reckon, then?' he asked Kieran and me. 'Putting aside that there's vermin in the attic, is it a winner?'

'No,' Kieran said miserably, 'it isn't.'

'Absolutely *not*,' I agreed. 'This house is damp and cold and creepy.'

'Oh,' Mum said. 'Not exactly the response we were hoping for, but it's to be expected, I suppose.'

'Ignore the vermin and decor and general state of the place,' Dad said, trying to sound chirpy and enthusiastic. 'Just think of this house as being a blank canvas.'

'A blank canvas that's covered in black mould,' I said. 'It's all over the house.' I pointed to the far corner of the room. 'And it's even in here, look.'

'That's caused by damp,' Bob explained. 'Because the place hasn't been lived in for some time, there's been no fresh air moving through the rooms. The best thing to get it off is bleach – *neat* bleach. And once you've got rid of it, make sure you keep the place ventilated by opening windows regularly; especially when you're doing things that make steam: like having a bath or cooking. Most older properties do suffer with black mould problems, to be honest. Investing in a dehumidifier might be a good idea. I've got one and you'd be amazed at how much moisture it sucks out of the air.'

'It's nothing that some elbow grease won't take care of,' Dad said. 'And we'll certainly consider getting a dehumidifier, Bob.'

'That's assuming we move in,' I said.

'Please – *no no no no*,' Kieran muttered.

'We really do have *lots* to discuss tonight,' Dad said, 'me and your mother.'

After a short silence, Mum said, 'Okay, I think we've seen enough. Thank you, Bob, for your assistance. The information you've given us will certainly go a long way in aiding us to make up our minds.'

Bob flashed his smile, his pearly whites. 'Just doing my job. But it's always a pleasure to be of assistance to potential buyers. If you have any questions, just call me. I'm always eager to help.'

As we were all leaving, I developed a sudden need to wee.

'What's up with you?' Mum asked me as we were about to go through the front door. 'Why are you pulling that funny face?'

'I need the toilet,' I said, crossing my legs.

'You'd better go before we get back on the road, then, hadn't you?' Mum said.

'What – in that pink nightmare of a room upstairs?' I said, aghast at the thought. 'I'd rather go in the bushes, thank you very much.'

'You are not going in the bushes!' Mum hissed. 'Get yourself upstairs now. Go on – skedaddle! Bob is waiting for us to leave so he can lock up.'

'It's okay,' Bob said, nice as ever. 'When you've got to go, you've got to go. And there's no need to use the pink nightmare, as you called it (and rightly so); there's a loo at the end of the hallway.'

'Oh yes,' Dad said. 'I forgot about that one. That's convenient. I've always wanted a house with one of these small downstairs lavs.'

I didn't like the idea of going anywhere in this house on my own. Not even down the hallway a short way. So I looked at Kieran, hoping that he would come with me.

'I don't think you need an escort, Ella,' Mum said, shooing me away. 'Go on – *skedaddle!* – we haven't got all day, you know!'

'Why do I have to be so desperate for a wee now,' I whispered to myself.

I walked away on rubbery legs. Down the hallway and around the corner I went. Seeing the door at the end of the hallway, I stopped. A scary thought popped into my head: *what if I open that door and the thing with the glowing eyes is in there?* Another thought replaced this, one that was spoken in my Mum's voice: *the creature with the glowing eyes is in the attic, you silly billy. Go on – get a move on –SKEDADDLE!*

Mustering up courage, I put my chin in the air and marched down the hallway. Pausing for a second with my hand on the doorknob, I wondered whether I should try to hold my bladder. The problem was that I was *desperate* for a wee. Plus, I didn't fancy incurring Mum's wrath by asking if we could pull over on the journey home so I could relieve myself (which I was pretty sure was what would happen). I wasn't sure what was more terrifying: facing a creature with glowing eyes or my Mum with a bee in her bonnet. I opted for the creature ...

The door creaked ominously as I opened it, and ... to my surprise, it was a nice, little lavatory. Stepping inside and closing the door behind me, I was also surprised to see that there was no black mould. Not a jot. Pulling my bottoms down, I set about my business. I could hear the others talking, but I couldn't make out what they were saying.

I looked down at the white tiled floor, thinking things through. I was beginning to warm to the idea that my imagination had been getting the better of me. *Maybe it was just a shadow I saw in the window*, I thought. *And maybe the glowing eyes were just chinks of light shining through the rafters.* But then I looked up and gasped ...

Above me, along the edge of the ceiling, black mould had appeared.

'What the ... *heck*,' I said, staring open-mouthed. 'That wasn't there before!'

Mum called out, 'Ella, are you going to be much longer? We haven't got all day you know!'

For a few seconds I couldn't move. My body had numbed over in shock. Then, right before my eyes, more black mould began forming. Spreading down the wall, it edged its way closer to me ...

'Alive!' I said. '*It's alive!*'

I had seen enough. Panic took over from the numbness and I got moving. Desperate to get out of the bathroom before my way became blocked, I pulled up my bottoms and yanked the door open. Then I ran from the toilet, screaming my head off.

As I darted along the hallway, the others moved to intercept me.

'What's going on?' Mum said, looking suitably worried. 'What's happened?'

I hugged her around the waist, burying my face in her chest. As a result, my response came out muffled, 'Blag mollle!' I said. 'The blag mole is aliyyy!'

Grabbing me by my shoulders, Mum forced me away from her so she could get a proper response. 'What is it?' she said. 'What have you seen?'

'Black m-mould,' I said, blubbering. 'In the b-bathroom. It's ... it's *alive!*'

Mum made a funny face. 'What? What are you talking about, child?'

I tried to get myself under control. Then I explained: 'When I went into the toilet there was no black mould. But after I'd sat down and began going about my business, I looked up and there it was – on the wall, near the ceiling. And then it started moving down towards me. Moving like it was *alive!*'

From behind Mum, I heard Bob say, 'What we have here is a prime example of an over-active imagination.'

'I didn't imagine it!' I snapped.

'Err – excuse me,' Mum said, 'you need to watch your tone, little miss.'

'But I *didn't* imagine it,' I repeated.

Dad appeared at Mum's side and said, 'Okay, okay, let's just calm down here, shall we. Clearly you believe that you saw something. And the easiest way to sort this out is for me to take a look.'

As Dad moved away, Kieran came and stood with me. He gave me a troubled look, then we all watched as Dad disappeared through the toilet door and closed it behind him.

Don't touch it, I wanted to yell. But no words would come out of my mouth. Only a small whimper.

I don't know what I expected to happen next. Part of me hoped that Dad would come tearing out of the toilet, pale as a ghost from fright. At least then I'd have known I hadn't imagined it. And, of course, no way would my parents have bought the house then. But that wasn't to be the case.

About thirty seconds after entering the room, Dad emerged and shrugged his shoulders. 'I can't see any black mould,' he said. 'None at all.'

I shook my head in disbelief. 'It was there,' I said. 'Creeping down the wall.'

'This silliness needs to stop,' Mum said. 'I can see what you're doing here and it isn't going to work. If we're going to move into this house, then we're going to move into it – and none of your made-up stories will put us off.'

'Made-up stories,' I muttered, hardly able to believe what I was hearing.

'Are you in on this?' Mum said to Kieran. 'Is this some idea you've concocted between the two of you?'

Kieran shook his head. 'No,' he said. 'No way – *don't* throw any blame in my direction!'

'First the glowing eyes and now this!' Mum said, tssking and batting her eyelids at me. 'Whatever next, hmm? Vampires in the closest? Gargoyles in the garden? Or what about werewolves in the cellar?'

'There's a cellar?' I said, perishing the thought. If ever there was a place where evil ghouls and ghosts could lurk, it was a cellar. I stamped my foot on the floor. 'I'm not trying to put you off buying this hellhole; I'm just telling you what I saw – and I *DIDN'T* imagine it!'

'*Ooh,*' Mum said, seething. 'You just wait 'till I get you home, little miss. Your feet won't touch the ground ...'

'Right, *right!*' Dad said, holding his hands up like a preacher about to give a sermon. 'That's enough – I don't want to hear another word. We're leaving. Bob, please lead the way.'

Bob led everyone outside and then locked the front door.

'I can only apologize for the trouble we've caused you,' Mum said to him. 'My daughter isn't normally like this, I can assure you.'

'It's okay,' Bob said, cool as ever, flashing his pearly whites. 'Don't worry about it. It's not a problem, really. Not a problem at all. As I mentioned before, if you have any questions, please don't hesitate to ask. And, remember, others have expressed an interest in this house – so don't delay too much if you're going for it.'

Poppycock, I thought.

'We won't delay,' Mum assured him amiably.

Bob said goodbye and then drove away.

I could feel Mum's eyes boring into me, so I marched sullenly to the car with my bottom lip pooched out. Whilst I waited in the back for the others, I cast occasional glances towards the upstairs window where I thought I'd seen movement. Any second now I was sure something would happen. Either a shadow would be cast on the wall at the back of the room, or a face would appear at the glass or something like that ...

'*BOO!*' Kieran said, suddenly appearing at the car door.

My heart nearly jumped up into my throat. '*You idiot!*' I blurted, clutching at my chest. I took a few seconds to compose myself, then said, 'I can't believe you did that. After everything that's just happened! Are you for real, or what?'

Shrugging, he offered an apologetic smile. He got in the car and gave me a playful punch on the arm.

'Please,' I said, 'I'm not in the mood.'

'What was that all about in the house? You didn't really see black mould creeping down the wall, did you?'

'No, I just thought I'd come screaming out of the toilet babbling like a whacko for the hell of it. And before you ask again: no I didn't imagine it. One second there was nothing there and then there was.'

'Just like with the glowing eyes.'

This time it was me who did the punching. But there was nothing playful about it.

'*Ow!*' Kieran said, rubbing his arm. 'What did you do that for?'

Mum and Dad were still outside the house, talking. I pressed my ear against the glass, trying to hear what they were saying.

'So, d'you think this will be our new home?' Kieran said, still rubbing his arm.

'Hopefully not.'

'What are they saying?' Kieran said, leaning across me. 'Can you hear?'

'No,' I replied, pushing him back. 'But they are now looking over here and Mum looks like she might throttle me.' She also had her arms folded across her chest, which was never a good sign.

'If I was you, I'd keep your trap shut on the way home.'

This seemed like sound advice to me. Although I figured it would be difficult to do, given what had happened.

A few minutes later, when Mum and Dad had finished their talk, they got in the car and not a word was said. It wasn't until later that day that the shouting match would occur.

As we were pulling away, I cast one last glance towards the house, towards the window in the top right-hand corner. I saw no movement there. It was the one to the left of it that caught my eye this time.

I caught a glimpse of a shadow moving. A shadow shaped like a person.

When we got home I continued the silence. I went to my bedroom because I knew that was where Mum would send me anyway. I stayed there for hours, flat out on my bed. With my hands behind my head, fingers laced together, I was lost in my thoughts when Mum finally called me down to dinner in the kitchen.

Normally I would devour a Toad in the Hole (my favourite!), but not this time. I picked at the food on my plate, moving it around with my fork.

'Not hungry?' Dad said. He was seated across from me, sporting a concerned look.

'I've lost my appetite,' I replied.

Mum was in her usual place, next to Dad. She did not look impressed.

'Well you better eat some of it,' she said, 'because you know how much I hate food wastage.'

How could I not, when she had lectured me on the subject so many times.

I spooned some into my mouth and chewed unenthusiastically.

'This loss of appetite,' Mum said thoughtfully, 'it wouldn't have anything to do with your shenanigans earlier on, would it, by any chance?'

Here we go, I thought. 'If you'd seen what I'd seen, then you'd be off your food, too.'

Mum rolled her eyes. 'I thought some time in your bedroom might help you get a grip on reality,' she said, 'but obviously I was wrong. You're still persisting with the silliness – and to what end? This is the sort of behaviour I expect from your brother, not from you.'

'Oh, right, thanks,' Kieran said from beside me. 'Since when have I gone whacko and pretended to see things?'

I took a sideways swipe at him with my foot.

'*Hey!*' Kieran said, taking a swipe back.

'*Quit it!*' Mum snapped. 'I will not tolerate mucking around at the table.'

'She kicked me,' Kieran moaned.

'I don't care who hit who,' Mum said. 'Just quit it!'

I don't know what came over me next. I should have kept my mouth shut. That would have been the smart thing to do. But instead I blurted, 'You don't care – that's your problem! It's all about what you and Dad want and to hell with us. We don't want to move! Our friends are *here* in Rivington. Our school is *here* in Rivington. But that doesn't matter, because it's all about what our parents want. Mine and Kieran's opinions count for nothing. Like always.'

Silence descended.

Kieran pursed his lips together to form a perfect O of surprise.

Mum looked ready to explode.

Dad looked like he wanted to climb under the table and hide.

Part of me wanted to do that, too. And another part of me – the *stronger* part – wanted to have my say. And that was what I was going to do.

'Now is not the time for this,' Dad said calmly. 'Not while we're eating our dinner, Ella.' A spoonful of mash on his fork dropped onto his plate with a *plop*.

'I don't want to hear *that* at any time,' Mum said, seething. 'Not in *that* tone.'

'And it's not like we'll be moving to the other side of the world,' Dad said. 'The new house is just twenty-five minutes away in the car, so you'll still be able to see your friends.'

'But it won't be the same,' I said. 'Dawn lives at the end of our road. If I want to see her, I can just nip around and I'm there in seconds. If we move to the hell house, I'll be lucky if I see her once a week, because you won't want to ferry me back and forth, will you?'

'If you're so desperate to see your best friend,' Mum said, 'then there's always the bus.'

'Thanks,' I said. 'That's really helpful.'

Before Mum could scold me, Kieran joined in on my side.

'I'm going to miss my friends, too,' he said. 'And I'm *really* not looking forward to going to a new school. It won't be nice being the new kids. Neither of us will have any friends.'

'You'll make friends,' Dad said.

'We'll probably get picked on for being the new kids,' I said.

'I'm sure you won't,' Mum said. 'But if you do, just let me know and I'll sort them out.' As she took a sip of water, I could see that her hands were shaking.

'If we do have any problems, please don't get involved,' Kieran said. 'It'll look *really* bad if our mother shows up, shouting the odds.'

'Plumpton Sudsbry is a nice town,' Dad said, 'so I'm sure you won't have any problems fitting in. We'll all have to adjust and make concessions if we do move. Both me and your mother will have longer commutes to work. And with regards to moving, things are a long way from being sure on that front. There's the vermin situation, which we haven't had a chance to discuss yet. We'd have to put an offer in and it would have to be accepted. We'd have to find a buyer for this house. Then, if things got that far, there's the survey to consider. Plus a heap of other things that I can't think of off the top of my head.'

All the things Dad had mentioned gave me hope that the move wouldn't go ahead. His words calmed me. Made me less on edge. But in the back of my mind I couldn't stop thinking about the black mould and how it'd appeared out of nowhere. And then there were the eyes – the *glowing* eyes. My imagination was alive, speculating what could be living in the attic. Last but not least, of course, was the movement at the window. Who had that been, if anyone at all? Why would someone be in a house that was supposed to be empty? And if there was someone there, why hadn't any of us come across the person while we were viewing the place?

I didn't bother mentioning the movement to my parents, because I knew what reaction I would get. They hadn't believed me about the mould and the eyes, so why would they believe me about anything else?

Making a token effort, I spooned peas into my mouth and pretended to enjoy eating them.

Now it was Kieran's turn to play with his food, manoeuvring peas around his plate like he was playing some game. I could see this was annoying Mum, but she didn't say anything. She was probably just glad that quiet had descended and was prepared to let this slide.

Thanks to Dad's little speech, the rest of the meal continued without any further incidents of protest.

Later that evening, when Kieran was playing on his XBOX in his bedroom, I went to him. I sat on his bed, next to him. Then I told him that I'd seen movement behind the upstairs window as we were leaving.

Pausing his game, he regarded me with the look I'd expected. One that conveyed a simple message: are you for real, or what?

'I know you think I'm going mad,' I said, 'but I did *not* imagine it. Just like I didn't imagine the glowing eyes, or the mould coming down the wall.'

'Okay,' Kieran said, humouring me, 'so you saw movement at the window again. There must have been a person there, I take it? Was it a man or woman? Boy or girl? Old or young? Tall or small? Fat or thin?'

I shrugged. 'I don't know what I saw,' I said, wondering why I'd bothered to tell him. 'I just saw … something. A shadow.'

Kieran rolled his eyes. 'If there was someone in that house we'd have come across them while we were looking around the place.' He nodded towards his TV screen. 'I'm on level forty-two and I need only ten more points to get to the next bit. I've never done it before and I need to concentrate. So, if you don't mind ...' He flicked his fingers, gesturing for me to leave.

'Thanks for nothing,' I said, slamming the door as I swept from the room in a huff.

I'm not normally afraid of the dark. But that night, as I lay in bed, the absence of light troubled me. The street light outside my bedroom window cast the same shadows it always did: on the ceiling, and on the far wall. But somehow those shadows seemed different tonight. More alive. I was tempted to switch on my bedside lamp when I heard my parents talking in the kitchen. Kieran and I had gone to bed an hour before, so they would have assumed we were asleep.

Easing myself out of bed, I moved closer to the door so I could listen. But I couldn't make out what they were saying, so I moved onto the landing. Above the noise of Kieran snoring in his bedroom, I could now hear every word that was being said.

'The survey will be the key to everything,' Dad said. 'And we'll have the most expensive one done – the all bells and whistles one. That way, if there's anything majorly wrong with that house, we'll know about it.'

'Does vermin count as majorly wrong?' Mum replied.

'No, of course not. That shouldn't be too much of a problem to solve. But if the roof is about to collapse ... now that *would* be a problem.'

'So you think I'm overreacting when I say that the vermin is a potential deal-breaker?'

'Yes, dear, I would say you are overreacting.'

After a short silence, Dad said, 'The only thing that concerns me is the kids. Ella's antics earlier, when we were viewing the house ... she's not the sort to make things up. The prospect of moving must really be concerning her for her to react like that. And both her and Kieran are so worried about starting at a new school. I can empathize with them, I must admit.'

'So can I – but this house, if we decide to go for it ... it's an investment. And you know how much I've always wanted a big house in the countryside. Who knows how long it'll be before another opportunity like this comes along.'

Oh Please, I thought, not liking where this conversation was heading, *pleeeease don't put an offer in.*

'I take it the vermin problem isn't such a problem anymore,' Dad said, 'now you've had a chance to think things through?'

'It's something I can look past, as long as the problem is sorted *before* we move in. The thought of something scurrying or flapping around in the roof ... ooh, it gives me the creeps. But like you said, it's not a major concern. I just need to concentrate on that fact and nothing else.'

'So does this mean we're going to be putting an offer in?'

'I think it does.'

NOOOOOOOOOO! I thought, grimacing. I wanted to run down the stairs and scream at them. I wanted to tell them they were making a mistake that they would regret – that we would *all* regret. I wanted to tell them that the place was haunted. But I knew there was no point. First, I'd get told off for being out of bed and earwigging their conversation. Second, I'd get told off for making things up. The only thing I could do was creep back to bed, so – after a few minutes of just sitting there in a dazed stupor – that's what I did.

Lying in bed with the covers pulled over my head so I wouldn't have to look at the shadows, I reassured myself that a move was still far from certain. As Dad had pointed out, there were many stumbling blocks that could throw a wrench in the wheels. *I just need to be patient,* I thought, *and see how things pan out.*

Because I felt so restless and on edge, I was sure I wouldn't be able to sleep. But it didn't take me long to nod off. That night I had a nightmare. I was in the new house, sleeping in my bed in my new bedroom when something woke me. Peeking out from under the covers, I looked around, taking in my surroundings. Moonlight was shining through the curtains, illuminating the wall above my head. One second there was nothing there – and then black mould appeared at the top of the wall, near the ceiling. I tried to move, but I couldn't. It was like I had been glued to the bed by an invisible force. Then the mould began moving down the wall, edging closer towards me. I wanted to scream, but I couldn't. I opened my mouth – but nothing would come out. The mould kept getting closer, closer, *closer* ...

When I woke I was covered in sweat. Instinctively, I looked up at the wall behind me – checking for black mould. There was none, of course. The mould had only been in my dream. Never, in my whole life, have I been so relieved to be in my own bed, in my own home.

The alarm clock on my bedside table began sounding its monotonous bleep, telling me it was time to get up for school. During breakfast, when my parents were out of earshot, I mentioned what I'd overheard to Kieran. He was sitting opposite me, eating a bowl of Cornflakes. He dropped his spoon, which clunked into the bowl, making milk slosh over the sides.

'But what about the vermin?' he said. 'I thought that had put Mum off big time.'

'I hoped it had, too. But Dad has persuaded her that it's not such a problem.'

Kieran pushed his bowl away. 'Great – I've lost my appetite.' His chair scraped across the tiled floor as he got up and left the table. 'I'm going,' he said, leaving the room.

I didn't feel hungry myself, but I still managed a few mouthfuls of toast before leaving.

At school, after assembly, I told my best friend Dawn that we might be moving house. She got really upset. She did brighten slightly, however, when I said I'd only be a twenty-five-minute drive away. For the briefest of moments, I considered telling her about what I'd seen at the new house: the mould, the glowing eyes, the movement at the window. I decided against this, though. Everyone else I'd told had thought I was being delusional, so why should Dawn be any different? *Because she's your best friend*, came a reply in my head. *If you can't tell your best friend, then who can you tell?* This was true, but I still didn't want her to think I was losing my marbles. With that in mind, I decided to give her a different version of events – a more *believable* version. I told her that I suspected the place was haunted.

'Haunted?' she said, aghast. 'How come? Did you see something?'

'Erm, no – not exactly,' I said. 'I just got a bad vibe while I was there. I felt like ... like I was being watched.' This was not a lie.

'I've had that feeling before,' she said, tying her long, straight brown hair up in a ponytail. 'It's just your imagination. You have to be brave and tell yourself that there's nothing there. Ghosts don't exist. Or, at least, that's what my dad tells me. He says that you need to worry about the living and not the dead because they're the ones who can hurt you.'

I hoped that this was the case.

'Hey, if you do move in,' Dawn said, 'perhaps I'll be able to stay at your new house for a weekend. That'd be cool, wouldn't it? We could go on a ghost hunt. You know, like they do on that program: Most Haunted. It could be a scarily cool sleepover.'

'Yeah,' I said, trying to sound enthusiastic. 'Cool.'

Mr Blake, our form tutor, asked us why we were mooning around in the corridor, so we hurried off to our first lesson.

On Mondays, after school, I went to dance class, so I didn't get home until later. When I walked through the front door, Mum and Dad greeted me with nervous smiles, which made me wonder what'd happened.

Putting his arm around Mum, Dad said, 'We've got some good news, sweetie.'

'Some *very* good news,' Mum said, positively glowing.

I said nothing. Just waited for them to tell me what it was, with a deep sense of unease stirring inside me.

'We've put an offer in on the house,' Dad said.

'And it's been accepted,' Mum said, finishing his sentence.

I dropped my bag. It hit the polished wooden floor with a thud. Hardly able to believe my ears, I was stunned to silence.

'Now, we realise that this may not seem like good news at the moment,' Dad said, 'but in time, you'll come around. Sometimes, in life, what seems like a disaster at one point can actually turn out to be a blessing later on down the line.'

A blessing! I thought. *Are you kidding me?*

'But what about the vermin?' I said. 'Has that been forgotten about?'

'Absolutely not,' Mum replied. 'The vendor lowered the price substantially because of that.'

'I bet they did,' I muttered.

'Look, nothing is certain,' Dad said, stepping away from Mum and putting a hand on my shoulder. 'There's the survey to consider. If that pulls up something bad, we won't be moving. Simple as that. Plus, we've still got to find a buyer for this place, which could take time. We haven't even put it up for sale yet.'

All my hopes now hinged on the survey. Our house was small, but it was nice and modern, well decorated in neutral colours. And we lived in a decent area, as well. I couldn't see there being any problems with finding a buyer.

'And when is the survey being done?' I asked.

'We were just about to ring up and arrange it when you came through the door,' Mum said.

'Fine,' I said, pushing past them.

'Err,' Mum said, gesturing towards my bag, 'aren't you forgetting something?'

Retrieving it off the floor, I threw it in the cupboard under the stairs and went into the living room before they could say another word. Kieran was sitting cross-legged on the footstool in front of the TV, engrossed in a cartoon episode of the Avengers. I tried to engage him in conversation, but all I could get out of him were grunts and groans. Eventually, sick of me interrupting his program, he held up a finger, appealing for quiet.

As I headed for my bedroom, I heard Dad on the phone in the kitchen, arranging the survey.

'... as soon as possible, really ... yes, this Thursday would be great ... Um, um ... the full survey, yes – not the cheap one ...'

I'd heard enough. I went upstairs and crashed out sulkily on my bed. What could I say to my parents to make them change their minds? How could I put them off buying a house that was clearly haunted? I kept asking myself these questions and failing to come up with a solution. I wanted to punch the wall. I wanted to kick the door. And, most of all, I wanted to give my brother a whack around the lughole for not listening to me. All right, he hadn't seen the things I had seen. He didn't believe me about the house being haunted. But if we moved house, he would still have to go to a new school and make new friends, just like me. I imagined myself being a cartoon character with steam coming out of my ears from anger. That brought a ghost of a smile to my face for a few seconds. And then it was gone.

On Thursday, Dad heard back from the surveyor, and it wasn't good news (not for me or my brother, anyway). The house had been deemed structurally sound, which did not come as a surprise to me. Somehow, I just knew this was going to happen, and I *knew* we were going to end up moving into that haunted house. The only obstacle now was the sale of our current home. Or so I thought ...

My parents called both Kieran and me into the living room to give us the final, fatal bit of news. Mum and Dad took centre stage, standing on the shaggy rug, whilst Kieran and I sat huddled together on the settee.

'It's going to be all go in the next few weeks,' Dad said, pausing for dramatic effect, '... because we're going to be moving into the new house.'

I felt Kieran stiffen next to me. '*What!*' he said, aghast. 'You've found a buyer for our house already? But it's not even on the market yet, is it?'

'No, it isn't,' Mum confirmed. 'But it will be soon. There'll be a sign up in the next few days ...'

I said, 'I don't understand. How can we be moving if you haven't even sold this place yet?'

'Well, if you don't interrupt us, you'll find out,' Dad said. 'A friend of mine knows someone who wants to rent a house for a few months. He's from America, visiting relatives. This place is small and compact, just right for him. It'll give us some extra income *and* time to generate some interest in this place from prospective buyers.' With an enthusiastic curve to his eyebrows, he looked at Kieran and me, waiting for us to say something. 'You can talk, you know. It is permitted.'

He wanted us to talk, so we did. Kieran went first, voicing his dissent ...

'I don't know why you're looking at us like we should be happy,' he said, close to tears, 'because we're *not*.'

'Oh, come on,' Dad said, 'don't get upset, son; it's not like this has come as a surprise. You knew there was a good chance that the move would go ahead.'

'Yes, we knew,' I said, looking suitably upset. 'But you seriously can't expect us to be happy about this.'

'No,' Mum admitted, 'we can't. But we're moving house – and that's that. The sooner you deal with that fact, the better. I'm sorry if that sounds a bit harsh, but this opportunity is too good to pass on. You must understand that, yes?'

'What about the vermin?' Kieran asked. 'You're okay with having bats flapping around in the roof, are you? Because I'm not.'

'The seller has lowered the price quite a bit because of that,' Mum said.

'And you're right,' Dad informed us, 'it is bats.'

Do they have eyes that glow in the dark? I thought. I could feel a Google search coming on ...

Kieran shook his head and folded his arms in disgust. 'Best start saying goodbye to my friends, then, hadn't I?'

'There will be no need for that,' Dad said. 'We've already discussed this with Ella. The new house is only a relatively short drive away and it's on the bus route.'

I have never felt so frustrated in my life. I *knew* there was something wrong with that house – I *knew* it was haunted – but there was no way I could convince my parents of this (or Kieran, either). They would just think I was losing my mind. All I could do was roll with the situation and deal with what came next.

It was two weeks later when we moved in. We arrived at the house at the same time as the removal men and we all mucked in to help them. By the time we had carried everything in, I was exhausted. The hallway was filled with boxes of items that would need to be unpacked and each room was littered with stuff that needed to be sorted. Whilst Dad and Mum assembled the beds upstairs, Kieran and I crashed out on the settee in the living room.

'Well, here we are,' Kieran said.

'Yep, here we are,' I replied. I spied a patch of black mould in the corner of the room, just below the ceiling. 'Dad promised me that he'd scrubbed the house clear of that stuff,' I said, pointing.

'He didn't do a very good job. I saw some in the hallway, as well.'

'Let's just hope those bats are gone.'

An expert had been called in and he'd cleared the loft of infestation. I asked Dad if the expert had seen anything unusual whilst he was up there and Dad had said no. I'd always believed that bats were blind, but a Google search revealed this to be a myth. They actually have good eyesight, and the bigger ones can see better than humans. Not surprisingly, my search also revealed that they don't have glowing eyes, either. So what had I seen in the attic?

When my parents had finished putting the beds together, they called for us to come upstairs. They were in Kieran's new room and greeted us with smiles.

'It's going to be chaos for the next few days,' Mum said, 'but at least we've got the weekend to sort ourselves out. If you want to bring some boxes of your stuff up and start unpacking them, please feel free. You can begin arranging your rooms as to how you want them then.'

If I wasn't so certain that the house was haunted, the prospect of arranging my new room would have excited me. As it was, all I felt was this ever-present need to be on the lookout for something out the ordinary to happen (like some black mould coming to life and trying to swallow me whole, for instance).

'You told me that you'd cleaned that stuff off,' I said to Dad, pointing to a patch near the window.

He squinted at it, looking confused. 'I did. I cleared the entire house.'

'You obviously missed a bit,' Mum said.

'No, I'm pretty sure I didn't,' Dad replied. 'I can remember – *very* vividly – cleaning around that window and I didn't miss a spot. It all came off easily enough with neat bleach.'

'Perhaps it's grown back since you did it,' Kieran suggested.

'What, in two days?' Dad said, scratching his head in confusion. 'I've never known mould be able to form that quickly.'

'Me neither,' Mum said.

I have, I thought. *I saw it forming right in front of my eyes – creeping down the toilet wall towards me.* The memory of it gave me shivers.

'I'm sure there's a reasonable explanation for this,' Dad said. 'What we have to remember is that no one has lived in this house for a while, so it's been quite neglected. The whole place needs a good airing, for starters.' Dad opened the window, letting in a blast of fresh air. 'Bob suggested that we get a dehumidifier, so that's what we'll do tomorrow.'

'And what if that doesn't cure the problem?' I said.

'I'm sure it will,' Mum said.

'Look, you pair just concentrate on shifting some boxes up here and arranging your rooms,' Dad said. 'I'll check the house and scrub off any mould I encounter.'

'Very good,' Mum said with an approving smile. 'And then you can help me in the living room, dear.' She looked at all of us. 'If your arms aren't hurting by the end of the day, then you haven't been pulling your weight.' She clapped her hands together. 'Let's all get busy. Chop, chop ...'

After Mum and Dad had gone downstairs, Kieran said, 'When I've sorted my room, I'm going for a look around in the woods. D'you wanna come?'

'Not too sure Mum will like that. We've only just moved in here and we're supposed to be "pulling our weight", remember?'

'We will be pulling our weight – out of this house and into the woods. C'mon, sis, don't be a party pooper. I heard Dad say to Mum that we've got neighbours not far from here. We can check 'em out. See if they're axe-murderers or something. It's gotta be better than mooching around here.'

'Mum won't give us permission.'

'We won't be asking for *permission*.'

I gave it some thought and then nodded. 'Okay.'

I must admit, I was quite eager to have a nosey around the area.

'Cool. Let's get on.'

Kieran began unpacking his belongings from boxes, so I went to my bedroom and did the same (I had been careful to choose one of the bedrooms at the back of the house, whilst Kieran had opted for one at the front (my reports of movement and shadows hadn't put him off his selection)).

I put my clothes away in my set of drawers, which Dad had positioned at the end of my bed. I didn't like it there, but the room was too small for it to fit anywhere else. I kept busy for the next ten minutes or so, until the door creaked open – and Kieran appeared.

'You ready?' he said, eager.

'There's no way you've put away all your stuff yet. Not even if you were rushing like your life depended on it.'

'I've done enough. The rest can wait 'til later.'

'Mum *really* is going to do her nut if she knows we've gone out without her permission.'

'I just heard her say to Dad that she was nipping to the shop for a few things and that she'd be gone for about half an hour, so now is our chance. We'll be back in twenty minutes. We'll just take a quick look around, that's all.'

'Has she gone yet?'

'Yes, I just heard the front door click shut. If we're going, then we need to do it now.'

'But what about Dad?'

'He's busy putting some shelves up in the living room.' We could hear him drilling holes in the wall. 'If we're quiet, he won't know we're gone. You know what he's like. Half the time he doesn't even know where he is, never mind anything else.'

'Talk about exaggeration; he isn't anywhere near that bad.'

'Whatever!' Kieran said, getting frustrated. 'Are you coming, or what?'

'Yes,' I replied, knowing full well that there was a good chance we'd get caught out. 'Anything to shut you up.'

As we crept down the stairs, Dad was still drilling in the living room, which meant we were able to sneak out of the front door without being noticed.

When we were clear of the house, I said, 'Okay, where are we going?'

Kieran looked left and right, the wind ruffling his hair. 'On the way here, I noticed a cottage set back from the road. I think we should investigate. Who knows, there might be some kids who live there. We can't be the only kids who live around here, right?'

Sounded like a good idea to me. Although, at the time, I wouldn't have been surprised if we were the only kids in the area, given that there weren't many houses near ours. The nearest town, Plumpton Sudsbry, was a two-minute drive away and was where Mum had gone to do her shopping.

'To the cottage it is then,' I said. 'Shall we walk along the road?'

'What fun would that be? Nah, let's go through the woods.'

'But what if we get lost?'

'We won't get lost. It's over there,' Kieran said, pointing. 'In that direction. And it's not far.'

He set off and beckoned me to follow him. As I did, I glanced over my shoulder, back towards the house. My eyes were immediately drawn towards the upstairs windows: the ones where I'd seen the movement. I didn't see anything this time. Just the sun reflecting off the glass, making me squint.

'Come on, slowpoke!' Kieran called out. 'We haven't got all day, you know.'

When I caught up with him, I said, 'I can see why Mum and Dad like it here. It's tranquil in these woods and quite beautiful.'

'Moving here does have some positives, I must admit.'

And some negatives, I thought. Big *negatives*. Ones *I've tried to tell you about, but you won't listen. Nobody will LISTEN!*

'We should try building a treehouse at some point, don't you think?' Kieran said, taking in the big oak trees around us, looking for a suitable one. 'That'd be even cooler than a den, wouldn't it?'

'Yeah,' I replied, brimming with false enthusiasm. 'That'd be grrreat.'

We walked for a few more minutes, twigs crunching under our feet, until we finally came upon the cottage. It was a pretty place, with white walls and a thatched roof. A lot nicer than the house we'd just moved into.

'There's no one around that I can see,' I said. 'So what do you want to do? Go knock on the door and ask if there's any kids who want to come out to play?'

'Don't be daft. We need to move a bit closer so we can get an idea of who lives here. If we could just peek through one of the windows. Might give us some clues as to whether it's an axe murderer or not.'

'Oh don't start on about axe murderers again, will you.'

We stood there for a few seconds, listening to a bird chirping in a nearby tree. And then Kieran began walking towards the cottage. When I stayed rooted to the spot, he stopped and beckoned me to follow him.

'What are you waiting for?' he said. 'Come on!'

'I don't think this is a good idea.'

'Why?'

'Because we might get caught.'

'We won't be doing anything wrong.'

'We'll be trespassing. And it'll look really dodgy if someone catches us looking through the windows.'

'If anyone does challenge us, we'll tell 'em we're the new neighbours, come to say hello.'

After waiting a few more seconds, Kieran rolled his eyes at me and then kept moving towards the cottage. Sure that I would regret it, I hurried along after him.

'You're a typical boy, do you know that?' I said, catching up with him. 'No common sense at all.'

'And you are your typical girl,' Kieran replied. 'Nag, nag, nag.'

The well-tended garden was enclosed by a white picket fence. Reaching the gate, we opened it and proceeded up the footpath. There was no car on the driveway, which could only be a good thing.

'Perhaps we should knock,' I said as we approached the front door. 'That would be the sensible thing to do.'

Ignoring me, Kieran made straight for a window and peered through. He cupped his hands to the side of his head, cutting out the glare so he could see better.

'Not good news,' he said. 'I think an old person lives here.'

'An old person *does* live 'ere,' a gruff voice said.

Startled, both Kieran and I turned to see an elderly man approaching. Hunched over and moving with the aid of a walking stick, he did not look glad to see us.

Kieran backed away and positioned himself behind me. My brave brother.

'Sorry, sir,' I said, 'but we're not robbers or anything. We've just moved in next door and were hoping to acquaint ourselves with our new neighbours.' I smiled to emphasize that we had friendly intentions.

The old man gave me a searching look. He had one eye bigger than the other, so it was quite an unnerving experience.

'Lookin' teh acquaint yehselves, are yeh?' he said. 'Well, nosyin' through someone's window ain't the best way teh go 'bout it, jus' so yeh know.'

I apologized again, then said, 'You'll have to forgive my brother; he has no manners at all. I told him to knock on the door, but he wouldn't listen.'

'Sounds like yeh're the brains of the outfit,' the old man said to me.

'I am,' I replied. 'For all the good it does me.'

'Hey, I'm not exactly a dumbo, you know,' Kieran said, still hiding behind me.

'Yeah, right,' I said. 'Whatever.'

A moment of awkward silence followed, during which the old man kept a close eye on us, weighing us up. Then he hobbled a few steps closer and said, 'Now my lugholes don't work anywhere near as well as they used teh, but did I jus' 'ear yeh say that yeh've moved into Selby 'ouse.'

'Yes, sir,' I said.

The old man's big eye widened even further. 'I'd be careful in that place, if I were yeh,' he warned. 'Careful as careful can be.'

'Why?' I said. 'Are you talking about the fact that it's haunted?'

The old man nodded. 'Ayuh, haunted is what it is.'

'Ah, please,' Kieran said, rolling his eyes. 'Don't tell her that; she's paranoid already.'

'And well she should be,' the old man said, spittle flying from his lips as he spat the words in anger. 'Yeh parents wouldn't 'ave bought that 'ouse if they knew what I know, I can assure yeh!'

'Can you tell us what you know?' I said.

The old man considered this for a moment, then said, 'Not standin' out 'ere on the doorstep, no. My legs are tired an' I need a sit down, so if yeh wanna hear what I've got teh say, yeh goin' teh 'ave teh come inside, so yeh are.'

Kieran whispered in my ear: 'No way – he could be an axe murderer. Remember when our parents told us never to trust strangers?'

The guy can hardly move, I thought. *Give me a break.*

'We'd love to hear what you've got to say,' I said to the old man.

'Right-e-o yeh are then,' he said, hobbling towards the front door with the aid of his walking stick. He let himself in and we followed him over the threshold. Me first and brave Kieran right behind me, like a shadow.

'If yeh want a cup of tea,' the old man said, 'then you'll 'ave teh make it yehselves. Sorry if that sounds rude, but I need teh sit down 'fore I fall down. Kettle's over there,' he said, pointing towards the sideboard with a crooked, knobbly finger. 'Teabags an' sugar are in the pots next to it an' milk's in the fridge, of course. An' I take two sugars, jus' so yeh know.'

Seeing as I was going to be making a brew anyway, I thought I'd have one myself. I glanced towards Kieran, who shook his head.

A wooden chair scraped across the tiled floor as the old man pulled it out from under the table and seated himself. Clearly glad to be off his feet, he gestured for Kieran to sit down.

'No point standin' on ceremony 'ere,' the old man said, gesturing again. 'Rest yeh bones, lad.'

Reluctantly, Kieran seated himself across from the old man.

I busied myself making the cups of tea.

'Bes' introduce meself 'fore I start blabbin', I s'ppose,' the old man said. 'Me name's Reginald – but yeh can call me Reg for short.'

'I'm Ella,' I said, getting some cups from the cupboard, 'and the annoying one over there is my brother, Kieran.'

'You're the one who's annoying,' Kieran said, sticking his tongue out but managing a smile.

'All brothers an' sisters annoy each other,' Reg commented. 'It's always been that way, as far as I know. There's biscuits in the barrel next teh the bread bin, if yeh want some. Chocolate digestives. Very nice.'

Now Kieran was interested because they were his favourites. 'Don't mind if I do,' he said, rubbing his hands together.

I put some on a plate, ready to be served.

When the kettle had boiled, I poured water into a white pot. Then I put everything we needed on a tray and took it over to the table. As soon as I put the tray down, Kieran grabbed a biscuit and began scoffing it.

'Don't eat them all,' I said to him, 'because that would be rude.'

'I'm not going to eat them all,' he replied indignantly.

Reg poured some tea into a cup and took a slurping sip. 'Sergeant Major's brew, nice an' strong – jus' how I like it.' Now that he'd got some tea down his neck, he looked ready to commence with explaining why our parents had been fools to buy Selby House. And then he did: 'Right-e-o, let's not beat 'round the bush, shall we. Let's get straight teh the point. That place yeh've moved into: a woman called Maud Bellingham used teh live there. Teh say she was odd would be a bit of an understatement. Don't get me wrong or anythin', she was always polite enough teh me, always said 'ello when I saw 'er. Not that I saw 'er that often, of course. As yeh've noticed, there's a good distance 'tween my house an' yours.'

'It's not that far,' Kieran said.

'Tiz when yeh're old an' decrepit like I am,' Reg replied.

I chastised my brother: 'Don't interrupt someone when they're explaining something.'

'S'okay, don't worry 'bout it,' Reg said. 'When yeh young, yeh impulsive. Yeh gob seems teh work before yeh brain can engage. That's how it was feh me, back when I was a whippersnapper. Although I struggle teh remember back that far, if the truth be told ... Anyways, where was I? Ah, yes, like I said, I never really spoke teh Maud very much, but she *was* an odd one, that's feh sure. I remember the first time she moved in: abou' nine years ago, this was. And I remember that it wasn't long 'fore other neighbours began talkin' 'bout her. The Bradleys, who used teh live further up the road – a bit closer teh Maud than me – they told me that they'd noticed some strange things. Like plants in Maud's garden growin' at unbelievable speeds. Graham Bradley told me 'bout a row of trees that suddenly appeared in 'er back garden. Anyone who knows anythin' 'bout trees knows that they should take years teh grow. An' yet there they were, large as life, twenty feet tall in less'n a week. I had teh see it with me own eyes teh believe it. An' it wasn't just the trees that caught me attention as I was gogglin' over 'er back fence. There was weird plants growin' in that garden as well: ones I've never seen 'fore, an' never seen since.'

'So she's a fantastic gardener,' Kieran said, through a mouthful of biscuit. 'So what? Am I detecting a touch of the green-eyed monster here? Perhaps you've got it in for old Maud because your garden wasn't as good as hers? Hmm?'

Reg said to me, 'Yeh're right; 'e's not that clever, is 'e?'

I gave Kieran a look filled with daggers. 'I can only apologize for him again and would like you to know that I can give him a few slaps, if you want me to? It's not a problem.'

'I'm sure that won't be necessary,' Reg said. 'But if 'e could keep 'is gob shut feh for more'n thirty seconds then that'd 'elp.'

'If you don't keep it shut then you can wait outside,' I said to Kieran.

'All right, all right,' he replied, 'there's no need to get shirty.' He motioned for Reg to continue, so Reg did (after a sip of tea).

'Okay, so as I mentioned, the Bradleys noticed some strange goin's-on where Maud was concerned. But they weren't the only ones. There was the Smiths, as well. They lived a stone's throw from the Bradleys. They had some strange tales teh tell 'bout Maud, as well. There's a particular one that sticks out in me memory (very disturbin' business, it was, by all accounts). Rosa and Peter 'ad only jus' moved in an' wanted teh acquaint 'emselves with their new neighbours, so of course they went around teh introduce 'emselves teh Maud. They knocked on the front door, but couldn't get any joy. They were jus' 'bout teh give up when Peter 'eard somethin': a loud moanin' sound. 'e tried the front door an' it was open, so 'e an' Rosa went inside feh a look around. (They were worried that someone had been

'urt; they had visions of 'em lyin' on the floor, needin' 'elp).
Peter an' Rosa searched the 'ouse, but they couldn't find anyone.
Then they 'eard the moanin' again, an' realised it was comin'
from the cellar. Rosa was scared, so Peter went teh investigate on
his own. An' that's when he found Maud. She weren't 'urt nor
nothin'. She was kneelin' 'fore some weird five-pointed drawin'
on the floor that'd been done usin' chalk. 'er head was bobbin'
up an' down, an' she was moanin' away, sayin' some sort of
prayer in a language Peter couldn't fathom. 'e was jus' 'bout to
turn tail an' get the 'eck out of there when somethin' 'appened.
A ghostly figure began teh form in front of Maud, shimmerin' in
an' out of existence. Well, as yeh can imagine, that scared the
'eck out of Peter. 'e ran out of that cellar like 'is pants were on
fire, I can tell yeh.'

'That happened in *our* cellar?' Kieran said, looking like he'd
seen a ghost himself.

'Ayuh, that it did,' Reg confirmed. 'As yeh can imagine, it
didn't take long feh the Smiths teh put their 'ouse up for sale an'
move away from the area. But not 'fore they'd told me an' the
Bradleys wha' they'd seen in that cellar. Good job it wasn't me
that saw that ghost, 'cause I think me ticker would 'ave given
out.' Reg shuddered, perishing the thought. He steadied himself
with a big gulp of tea.

'Just exactly what are you trying to tell us here?' I said. 'Was
this Maud a psychic or something? Did she summon a ghost to
haunt Selby House?'

'She were summonin' somethin' all right,' Reg said. 'But
psychic isn't the term I'd 'ave use teh describe Maud; I'm
thinkin' more along the lines of *witch*.'

'A witch!' Kieran said, aghast. He'd forgotten all about the
biscuits now and was too busy being scared. 'As in like an old
croon who rides a broomstick, wears a pointy hat and can turn
someone into a toad. You mean *that* sort of witch?'

'Ayuh,' Reg replied, nodding. 'Although I must admit, I never saw 'er wearin' a pointy 'at or whizzin' 'round on a broomstick. That's fairytale stuff, that is, I'm sure.'

'Why didn't the Smiths call the police after they found Maud in the cellar?' I asked Reg.

'Peter did,' Reg said. 'As soon as 'e got back 'ome, 'e was on the phone to 'em. But 'e didn't tell 'em what 'e'd seen; 'e just told 'em that 'e'd 'eard some weird noises comin' from the 'ouse and that someone sounded like they were in distress, that's all ...'

'Why didn't he tell them about the ghost?' Kieran said.

I answered the question. 'I'd have thought that was obvious. If you were a police officer, would you believe someone if they rang up and told you they'd seen a ghost? No – and neither would I. The coppers won't investigate a spook, but they will investigate a report of someone being in distress.'

'Spot on,' Reg said, giving me a toothless smile.

'I'm guessing that when the coppers showed up, they didn't find anything amiss,' I said. 'They just found a kooky old woman alone in her house, wondering why the police were on her doorstep.'

'Spot on again,' Reg said.

'Why do you suppose she was summoning up a ghost?' I asked him, rewording the question I'd asked before in the hope I'd get an answer this time.

Shrugging his bony shoulders, Reg said, 'I 'ave no idea. Your guess is as good as mine, so it is.'

'Perhaps she was getting the ghost to do the gardening,' Kieran suggested. 'Maybe that's how she managed to transform her garden and grow weird plants.'

'You just can't help yourself, can you?' I said to him. 'Forever the joker – forever the fool.'

Kieran's brow furrowed and his bottom lip pooched out. 'I am *not* a fool. A joker, yes – but not a fool.'

'Stop acting like one, then,' I fired back at him.

It suddenly occurred to me that my brother was probably scared witless and that acting silly was just his way of dealing with the situation. I was about to apologize to him, but then Reg continued talking ...

'Anyways,' he said. 'Keepin' things movin'. As I was sayin' 'bout the Smiths: they moved out pretty fast when they knew what was goin' on next door to 'em. An' the Bradleys didn't last much longer neither. They got sick of seein' strange things in the windows an' hearin' strange noises carryin' across to 'em. An' no one that's lived there since 'as lasted long either.'

'Is anyone living in either of those houses now?' I said.

'One's got a feh sale sign up outside of it,' Reg said, 'an' t'other's owned by some young business type called Rufus, who's hardly ever there. Now that Maud's dead, there's nothin' teh put people off, yeh see.'

'My sister reckons she's seen some weird things in our new house,' Kieran said. 'Glowing eyes in the attack, movement in the upstairs windows when there should be nobody there, and black mould coming alive on the walls in the toilet. I thought she was imagining it all – or going a bit crazy – but now I'm beginning to wonder.'

'She's not goin' crazy,' Reg said. 'I don't doubt feh a second that she's seen some hair-raisin' things. An' it'll only get worse, if yeh ask me.'

'Why?' I said.

Reg took a big gulp of tea, readying himself for what he was about to tell us.

Cupping my hands around my mug of brew, I took a gulp as well. I found it hard to swallow, though, because a big knot was forming in my throat. I had a feeling that what Reg was about to tell us would not be something I wanted to hear.

'A few years ago, Maud got 'erself in some financial difficulty,' he said. 'I don't know how, exactly. All I know is that debt collectors started turnin' up at Selby 'ouse, demandin' money, and Maud didn't 'ave the money teh give 'em. I used teh 'ave a dog called Timmy and I wasn't so decrepit back then, so quite often I used teh walk Timmy – bless 'is little paws – through the woods. A few times, when I was out strollin' with 'im, I witnessed a couple of unsavoury incidents. Bruisers on 'er doorstep, clutchin' paperwork an' lookin' mean. Then more bruisers turned up one day – in a van this time – an' they cleared 'er out of all 'er valuables, so they did. And that's when I went around teh see 'er, teh find out what were goin' on.'

'After everything that'd happened and knowing that she was a witch, you *actually* went round to see her,' I said. *You're braver than I am*, I thought. *Or more foolish.* I was about to find out which.

'Ayuh,' Reg said. 'An' d'yeh know what, I don't think that woman 'ad ever been so pleased teh see a friendly face in 'er whole life. She was in bits, so she was. 'er 'ouse was nearly empty, 'cause of those bailiffs, but that weren't the worst of it. She'd been issued with a judgement feh repossession of the 'ouse, so she was set teh lose everythin' if she couldn't find a large amount of money in one month.'

Reg paused so he could take a sip of his tea, whilst Kieran and I stayed silent, waiting in anticipation to know what happened next.

But then Reg shook his head and just said, 'I wish I could 'ave 'elped 'er, I really do. But I'm not a rich man, as yeh've probably noticed. Any money I could 'ave loaned 'er wouldn't 'ave even scratched the surface in terms of clearin' Maud's debts. I knew that from lookin' at all the bills an' final demands on 'er kitchen table.'

'Didn't she work?' Kieran said. 'Or was being a witch her full-time job? A job that paid *nothing*. And if she was this really great witch, why couldn't she just conjure up some money? If she can make a tree grow in a week, then why couldn't she pull some notes out of a hat?'

'If she could have,' I said, 'I'm sure she would have.'

'Clearly, magic isn't the answer teh everythin',' Reg said. 'Anyways, back teh what I was sayin'. Maud knew there was no chance of 'er raisin' the money she owed. So durin' 'er last month in Selby 'ouse, 'er 'ealth deteriorated dramatically. She jus' couldn't bring 'erself teh terms with the fact that she was goin' teh be 'omeless. One thing she did tell me was that no one would live in that 'ouse after 'er. I remember the look of grim determination on 'er face when she said it, an' it chilled me teh me bones, so it did. She told me that Selby 'ouse would be cursed, an' that anyone who moved in there would regret it.'

'You see!' I said to Kieran. 'I told you that I wasn't imagining things. That place *is* haunted! It *is*! *Now* do you believe me?'

Kieran mulled things over for a second, then said, 'I must admit, I am beginning to worry. But ... I only believe what I can see with my own eyes and so far I haven't seen or witnessed anything unusual.'

'I have!' I said. 'I'm your sister and you don't believe me?'

'I don't doubt that you *think* you've seen something,' Kieran said.

Shaking my head, I turned my attention back to Reg. 'How can I convince my parents that we need to move out of that place?' I asked him. 'Would you be able to talk to them? Could you convince them?'

'Now I don't know your parents,' Reg replied, 'but I'm goin' teh 'azzard a guess that they wouldn't believe me. They'd jus' think I'm some kooky ol' fool who's lost 'is marbles.'

'So what should I do?' I said. 'We can't just carry on living there and hoping that nothing bad will happen!'

'Yeh mum an' dad will realize their mistake soon enough,' Reg said. 'Yeh've jus' gotta 'ope that somebody doesn't get 'urt before the penny drops.'

'Oh, great!' I said, throwing my hands up in the air in frustration. 'Well *that* sounds like a good plan.' Closing my eyes,

I took a moment to get myself under control. And then I apologized to Reg. 'I'm sorry. I didn't mean to raise my voice, but I'm just getting so frustrated. That house is haunted and no one else in my family will believe me. Not even my berk of a brother here.'

'I am not a berk,' Kieran said in his defence. 'I'm just ... a realist. I heard Mum say that once and thought that it sounded cool.' His mouth dropped open as he remembered what I'd just remembered when he'd mentioned Mum. Kieran checked his watch. 'Oh my God, our parents are gonna kills us!'

'How long have we been gone?' I asked him.

'Twenty-five minutes,' Kieran replied.

'Oh, no!' I screeched. The chair I was sitting on scraped across the floor as I stood up. 'We need to go – and we need to go *now*.'

'Ayuh,' Reg said. 'I'm gettin' the impression that yeh pair ain't got permission teh do anythin' today other'n unpackin' an' 'elpin' out around the 'ouse.'

'That's exactly what we're supposed to be doing,' I said. 'Look, thanks for the tea and biscuits, but we've got to go.'

'We appreciate everything you've told us,' Kieran said, trying to sound level-headed and sensible for a change. 'And we'll bear in mind everything that you've said.'

But you still don't believe, I thought about my not so level-headed brother.

'You jus' be careful now,' Reg warned us. His big eye expanded as he looked from me to Kieran and then back again. 'If anythin' 'appens ... if you see anythin' strange ... yeh run teh yeh parents. And if yeh can't run teh 'em, get out of that 'ouse, d'yeh understand me?'

I nodded because I truly did.

Kieran nodded as well. 'We will,' he assured Reg.

We headed for the door, but Reg had one more thing to say before we left. 'Don't go yappin' teh yeh parents 'bout what I've told yeh, now, will yeh? As I told yeh before, they'll jus' think

I'm a crazy ol' kook. An' they'll probably ban yeh from comin' anywhere near me, so they will. I'd do the same if I was in their position, if the truth be told.'

I pinched my forefinger and thumb together, then ran them across my lips, mimicking a zipping action. 'We won't yap,' I assured him.

Kieran said, 'Thanks for your hospitality, mister.'

'S'all righ',' Reg said, 'it was nice teh 'ave some visitors feh a change.' He flicked his wizened fingers towards us, shooing us off with a gummy smile. 'Go on, yeh pair – skedaddle – get movin' an' yeh might make it back in time.'

We didn't. When we got back, our parents were waiting for us at the front door. Dad looked worried more than anything. Mum, on the other hand, looked ready to release a tirade of verbal abuse in our direction. And then she did ...

'Where have you been?' she hissed as we approached. 'I gave you explicit instructions not to leave the house until you'd unpacked and we'd got ourselves sorted. And yet here you are, the pair of you, gallivanting around like you haven't got a care in the world.'

'We just went for a walk around,' Kieran said. 'I'm sorry. It was my idea. We lost track of time, is all.'

'No, it's *not* all right!' Mum seethed.

'This isn't a very good start to our first day here, is it?' Dad said, more to himself than anyone else.

Things are only going to get worse, I thought. *You just don't know it yet.*

Mum stepped to one side of the door and Dad stepped to the other, making space for Kieran and me to pass.

'Both of you get upstairs now,' Dad said in an unusually harsh tone. 'Your mother and I have got a lot to do, so we don't want to hear from either of you until you've unpacked all your stuff and got your rooms in tidy order. You're grounded for the next few days.'

'*What!*' Kieran protested. 'But it's the weekend and we want to explore the area!'

'Should have thought about that before you went swanning off, then, shouldn't you?' Mum said. 'Perhaps next time you'll engage your brains, the pair of you, before you act.'

Bowing our heads, Kieran and I did as we were told. As I was about to disappear into my new bedroom, I sniffed at the air, which smelled of bleach.

'I think Dad's cleaned off all the black mould,' Kieran said, sniffing as well. 'Let's see if it stays away this time.'

'I'll wager you a hundred quid that it doesn't,' I responded.

'You haven't got a hundred quid.'

'I know. I'm just trying to make a point.'

Mum yelled up the stairs, '*STOP YACKING AND GET UNPACKING! I DON'T WANT TO HEAR ANOTHER WORD!*'

Kieran rolled his eyes at me and I did the same back to him. Then we both disappeared into our bedrooms and set to work.

Later that evening, when we were settled in and had finished our chores, I asked Dad if he would reconsider the punishment he'd imposed on Kieran and me. The answer was a resounding no. I knew there was no point in asking Mum. If I couldn't persuade Dad to reconsider, what chance would I have stood with her? None. Zilch. Nada. Don't waste your breath Ella.

By 9pm, Dad had collapsed onto the settee in the living room from exhaustion. His head was tilted back and he was snoring loudly, which made it difficult for Kieran and me to hear the TV. I was sitting on one side of him and Kieran was slouched next to him on the other.

'If I stick one finger up his nostril and you stick one up the other,' Kieran said, 'maybe it'll stop.'

'You can try it,' I replied, flicking through channels with the remote control, 'but I'll give that a pass.' I found an episode of Goosebumps that featured a spooky old house that was haunted.

'Seriously, you'd watch *that* after what the old man told us,' Kieran said. 'You'll be on your own with that one, sis.'

'I thought you didn't believe what he'd told us. I thought you didn't believe what he'd said.'

'Believe what who'd said?' Mum enquired, entering the room. 'Who are you talking about?'

'Oh, err, nobody of interest,' I replied, doing some quick thinking. 'Just ... someone at our old school trying to convince us to believe something we know isn't true.'

'And what's that?' Mum enquired.

Time for some more quick thinking, thanks to Mum's usual dogged persistence. 'It was the ... world record for bunny hops done in thirty seconds. Jude, who was in Kieran's form class, tried to convince him that it was one hundred and thirty-five. Kieran thinks that's impossible and I agree with him.'

Mum gave me a sly look for a second, weighing me up. 'You're about as good at lying as your brother,' she said. 'Do you know that?'

I did. But telling the truth wasn't an option. Reg's last words to me and Kieran were still fresh in my mind: about how we shouldn't tell our parents what he'd told us. The problem was that I couldn't think of another plausible lie. Not at such short notice. My brain just couldn't work that quickly; especially when Mum was giving me her hard stare.

'Hey,' Kieran said, pretending to look offended, 'how dare you, Mum? I'm a *much* better liar than she is.'

'The only thing you need to be good at is getting yourselves to bed,' Mum said, gesturing us to leave the room. 'Come on, let's have both of you upstairs now. And get your teeth cleaned, please. Kieran, remember that you've got to be up early in the morning for football.'

He was excited (and nervous) about a tryout Dad had arranged for him with a local team. (Being grounded didn't exempt Kieran from "the beautiful game", apparently).

Normally Kieran and I would negotiate to stay up for a little longer, but we'd already been grounded so we didn't want to push our luck. We did as we were told. Kieran darted off like it was a race between him and me. I followed behind slowly, not caring if I lost the race.

On my way through the hallway, I glanced towards the closed door of the downstairs toilet. I hadn't been in there since the viewing and I had no intention of going in there again. It was the Pink Nightmare upstairs or nothing, as far as I was concerned; even if it meant crossing my legs and grimacing until I could get in there (Mum had cleaned the room from top to bottom, so it wasn't looking so bad in there now).

After everything Reg had told me about the cellar, I was nearly as fearful of venturing there as I was of going into the toilet. Nevertheless, feeling a surge of bravery, I opened the door. I looked down the stone steps and into the darkness below. There was a light switch on the wall, but flicking it resulted in nothing more than a clicking sound. I was tempted to get the torch from the kitchen and use it, just so I could take a peek from the safety of the top step. No way was I brave enough to go down there. Not yet. Not on my own.

The front door opened and Dad stepped into the hallway, making me jump.

'What's up with you, sweetheart?' he said. 'You look like you've seen a ghost.'

I'm sure I will, I thought. 'You startled me,' I said.

'Sorry,' Dad said.

I closed the cellar door, then Mum came through from the living room.

'Oh, you're finally home,' she said to Dad. 'And stinking of beer, I might add. You told me you weren't going to drink alcohol and you told me you'd only be gone for an hour at the most. So what time do you call this, hmm?'

'I only had one beer,' he said, trying to appease her with a defensive smile that he must have known wouldn't work. 'I didn't realise the time. Me and Dave got carried away playing dominoes. Next thing we knew, I looked up at the clock and gasped. It's a genuine mistake.'

'Of course it is,' Mum said with a heavy air of sarcasm. Then she turned her attention to me. 'Why are you still lingering? Are you going to offer up some wishy-washy excuse, or are you just going to take yourself off to bed like I asked you to?'

I went with the latter option.

Upstairs, in Kieran's bedroom, I expressed my concerns to him. 'I'm worried about being on my own,' I said. 'Can I sleep in your room?'

'No way,' he replied. 'I'm not sharing my bed with you.'

'I won't be in your bed. I'll sleep on the floor, so you won't even know I'm there.'

'What if Mum sees you? How will you explain that?'

'I'll just say ... that I thought it would be good to crash out on your floor for the first night, because ...' I shrugged, '... that's the cool thing to do in a new house.'

'D'you think she'll believe that?'

'Probably not. I suppose I could tell her the truth. Just say that I'm scared out of my brains because this place is haunted and that we're all in grave danger until we move out.'

Kieran shook his head. 'You don't need to be in my room. You're only across the landing from me and if you scream, I'm sure we'll all hear. If it'll make you feel better, I'll leave my door open. Is that okay?'

Looks like it'll have to be, I thought. 'I'll leave mine open as well,' I said.

Whilst we were cleaning our teeth, Kieran kept flicking water at me, trying to get me to smile. It was no good, though; I just knew something was going to happen during the night. I just didn't know what. Would black mould creep down the wall and smother me whilst I slept? Or would I see glowing eyes in the dark? Or would the shadows come alive and reach out for me with cold, clammy hands? I shook my head, trying to banish these thoughts.

As Kieran was leaving the room, I said, 'You will keep your door open all night, won't you? And you'll come to me if you hear me scream, yeah?'

'*Yesss*,' he said, rolling his eyes. 'I'll jump up like I've been spring-loaded.'

I bet you won't, I thought, watching him as he disappeared into his room.

Hearing footsteps on the stairs, I darted into my bedroom and slid under my bed covers. A few seconds later, Dad stuck his head around the door and bid me goodnight. Then he went to turn off the light.

'No,' I said, 'leave it on, please.'

'Why?' he said, looking puzzled. 'You're not normally afraid of the dark ... are you?'

'No, of course not. I was just ... hoping to do some reading before I nod off.'

'Really? So when did you start reading in bed? And where's your book?'

'Err ...' I said, cursing myself for not getting one off the shelf before I laid down. 'I haven't decided which one I want to read yet.'

My dad was daft, but not daft enough to believe such an obvious lie. 'It's because of what happened before, isn't it?' he said. 'It's because of the things you thought you saw? The eyes in the attic. The black mould coming alive in the bathroom.'

My silence was answer enough.

Dad seated himself on the edge of my bed. He took one of my hands and clasped it firmly between both of his. Then he told me that everything was going to be okay.

'After we've settled in,' he said, 'all these jitters will go away. You'll wonder why you were so spooked and I bet you'll even be able to laugh about all this in a few weeks.'

I'm pretty sure I won't, I thought. But I went along with what he was saying, just to make him happy.

'I'm sure you're right,' I said. 'Once I get through the first night, I'll feel a lot better. And getting my first day at the new school out of the way will help a lot. The closer Monday gets, the more nervous I'm feeling.'

This wasn't a lie. I *really* was getting worried about my first day.

'I can remember my first day at big school,' Dad said, 'and I can remember being so worried that I had the shakes. But do you know what, come the afternoon, by home time, I'd made some great friends and realised there was nothing to be concerned about.' He gave my hand another reassuring squeeze, then looked towards the books I'd arranged in a pile on the floor. 'Reading really is great for taking your mind off things, you know. Getting yourself lost in a good story ... ah, you can't beat it.' Dad got up and began sifting through the pile of books, which were mainly children's fantasy. 'What about this?' he said, holding one up which had a picture of a purple dragon on the front. 'It looks good. Want to give a try?'

I decided that I did.

Dad smiled as he handed me the book. Then he ruffled my hair and kissed me on the cheek.

'Don't stay up too late reading that,' he said. 'No matter how good it is.'

'I won't.'

As Dad was leaving the room, he went to close the door.

'No,' I said, 'don't shut it; I want it left open, please. And can you make sure you leave Kieran's open as well?'

Dad looked at me for a second, his brow furrowing with worry. And then he said, 'If it'll make you feel safer, sweetheart, then that's fine.'

After he'd gone downstairs I read the book for a while. It turned out to be a good read, but not good enough to prevent me from falling asleep.

When I woke I was greeted by darkness. Someone – probably Mum or Dad, I assumed – had turned off the light. And the door was shut. Panic set in as I pushed the covers back and reached out to turn on my bedside lamp. Then my hand clipped it and it fell to the floor with a thump.

'*Grrrr!*' I said, picking it up and putting it back on the table. Fumbling, I located the switch and pressed it. The room filled with reassuring light.

With Mum being a light sleeper, I was concerned that the noise might have woken her, so I listened for the sound of her stirring. Any second now, I was sure she'd burst into my room and demand to know what the noise had been. But she never stirred, never came. All was quiet as everyone else slept on.

My attention turned to the ceiling. In the corner of the room, near the door, I saw a splodge of black mould that I was *sure* hadn't been there before. Panic seized me as every muscle in my body seemed to freeze.

'*Oh no no no,*' I mumbled. But then I realised it wasn't mould after all – it was just a patch of dirt. *Good job I didn't scream the house down*, I thought. Never mind me being scared, imagine how the rest of my family would have reacted to being woken by an ear-piercing screech. My ear-drums would have taken a beating from Mum and that was for sure.

Slipping out of bed, I tip-toed across my room and then across the hallway. Floorboards creaked beneath my feet no matter how carefully I trod. It came as no surprise to see that Kieran's door had been closed, too. Pushing it open, I peeked into the darkness of his room. He was fast asleep, snoring lightly underneath his duvet. I really didn't want to go back to my room and be on my own at this point. I had an overwhelming feeling of being watched again. No matter where I went in that house, I always felt like someone was scrutinizing my every move. But I knew that Kieran would have a hissy fit if he found me asleep on the floor beside him, so that was no more of an option than it had been earlier. The only option open to me was to make sure Kieran's door was left open and then go back to my bedroom. So that's what I did.

Back under my bed covers, I reached towards the lamp with the intention of switching it off. My fingers hovered over the button, however, as I considered whether I wanted to plunge the room into darkness. I decided that I didn't and withdrew my fingers.

As I puffed the pillow up and got myself comfortable, I wondered how I could ever get back to sleep again. I felt completely awake. Not in the least bit tired. Never mind getting some shut-eye, I wanted to go downstairs and watch TV. But that would have been a bad idea. If Mum heard me, she'd have gone to DEFCON 5 in an instance and that would have been that, as they say.

A noise from above made me focus my attention on the ceiling. A flapping sound. The same flapping sound I'd heard before: when I'd first been viewing the house and stared up into the darkness of the attic. A few minutes past, with me lying prone beneath the covers, icy shivers racking all my muscles. Then I pitched myself up onto my elbows and listened intently. Did I actually hear the flapping sound, or did I imagine it? I did wonder ...

Dad told me that all the bats were gone, I thought, trying to reassure myself. But then I remembered the glowing eyes and knew it could never be that easy. I never heard any more fluttering after that, though (or any clicking sounds either). Not that night, anyway. The real problem with bats would come later.

I don't know how long it was before sleep took me again – an hour, maybe two – but when I woke it was pushing 4am. Darkness greeted me (again!). Someone – or some*thing* – had turned off the light (again!). And the door was closed as well (*again!*). Had Mum or Dad got up for a late-night trip to the bathroom and done the dastardly deeds? This could have been the case. But somehow I didn't think so. Once again, I was seized by a powerful feeling that I was being watched.

As I reached out to switch on the bedside lamp, I imagined a hand would appear out of the darkness and seize my wrist. Nothing happened, though. Once more, after being plunged into unexpected darkness, light filled every corner of the room. I briefly considered getting out of bed to open the door, but I changed my mind. My imagination was in overdrive now and I was sure that some ghoul or ghost would seize my ankle from underneath the bed as soon as I placed a foot on the floor. So I remained still for a time, trying to think happy thoughts and take my mind off things like bats and witches and black mould. This was easier said than done. But I managed it eventually and was woken at 8am by the sound of Kieran's heavy footfalls on the stairs.

'Come on, you're going to be late!' Dad called up to him. 'Get a move on, will you!'

'I can't find my football boots!' Kieran hollered back. He was crashing about in his bedroom now, moving stuff and cursing. 'I'm sure I saw them in here somewhere.'

Mum joined in with the yelling: 'They were by the back door the last time I saw them! You were supposed to clean the mud off them, remember! I take it you haven't bothered?'

'Err ...' came the reply. And that was answer enough.

As he darted downstairs, Mum gave him a roasting.

Shortly after that, Dad popped his head round my bedroom door and said, 'Right-o, we're going to get going. Don't stay in bed too long and make sure you eat up that bacon your mother's cooked for you. You know how she gets when we don't eat food she's cooked for us.'

'What!' I said, springing up like I'd been electrified. 'You're going out and leaving me on my own?'

'Yes. We told you yesterday that we were taking Kieran to football training this morning.'

'D'you both have to go with him? Why can't Mum take him and you stay here?'

'He's excited about joining his new team. Honestly, Ella, I *did* tell you this yesterday. You need to pay attention when people are talking to you. And then you won't end up having conversations like this.'

'Oh,' I said, beginning to panic. The thought of being in the house on my own was a frightening prospect.

'You're more than welcome to come with us,' Dad said, 'but you'll have to get a move on because we're about to go out of the door.'

Stay in the haunted house on my own, or be bored out of my skull watching my brother play football? What a choice!

'I'm coming,' I said, springing out of bed and getting myself dressed.

Before we left, I grabbed the book I'd been reading the night before. Sticking my face in the pages had to be better than watching a bunch of immature boys kick around a ball for an hour and a half. Anything had to better than *that*.

It was a good day for it, though. The sun was out and not a cloud could be seen in the sky.

Because I was in such a rush to leave the house, I didn't get a chance to eat any of the bacon. As a result, my tummy was rumbling with hunger. What didn't help matters was that there was a food van parked in the car park. The smell of sizzling bacon carried to me on the light breeze as Dad slung a large sports bag over his shoulder and we made our way towards the pitch.

Mum saw me looking wistfully towards the van and said, 'You should have grabbed something to eat before we left, like your father told you to.'

'There wasn't time,' I responded.

'This'll be a good chance for you to make some new friends,' Dad said to Kieran as we approached the pitch.

'I hope so,' Kieran replied.

We found a spot near the touchline, then Dad pulled out a blanket from the bag and laid it on the grass. I sat cross-legged, book in hand, watching the players on the pitch. Mum perched herself next to me and pulled out a book of her own (an Agatha Christie murder mystery). Both teams were practicing their passes and peppering their goalies with shots. Kieran looked hesitant about joining in with them.

'Go on, son,' Dad said, beckoning him forward. 'Have at it, then.'

'What if no one passes to me,' Kieran said. 'What if no one wants to be my friend.'

'They'll pass to you, I'm sure,' Mum said.

'But what if they *don't*,' Kieran persisted.

'Well then they'd be fools,' Dad said, 'because you're a heck of a player, yeah. Now get yourself over there and show 'em what's what.' He ruffled Kieran's hair and told him to skedaddle.

'Yes, go on and skedaddle,' I chirped in. 'And show them who's boss.'

Kieran gave us a forced smile and then ran onto the pitch. As he did, a man in a red tracksuit emerged from a ruck of players and greeted him.

'That's Andy,' Dad said to me. 'He's the coach. Nice guy. He'll look after your brother.'

Andy gave Dad a thumbs up and Dad returned the gesture.

Then Kieran was off and running, making his way towards his teammates. He weaved in between two boys, then someone passed him the ball and all his worries disappeared. He weaved through some more players and slotted it past his own goalie with ease. The other boys on his side looked impressed.

'There you go,' Dad said. 'Just like I told him: nothing to worry about. *WELL DONE, KIERAN – NICELY DONE, SON!*'

A few minutes later, the referee appeared and the game began.

I tried to read my book, but I found it hard to concentrate because of the noise that was going on all around me. There were screams from players, shouting out things like, 'Space, space! I'm free, pass it to me!' And: 'Down the wing! Get it down the wing!' And: 'Hit it! You're clear! Hit it, you div!'

Dad was really getting into things, pacing back and forth along the touchline, barking out encouragement to Kieran and his team members.

But the person who was making the most noise was a huge, barrel-chested man standing farther along the touchline. He was dressed in sports clothes – a red tracksuit with matching red trainers – but he didn't look like he'd done a day of exercise in his life.

'Go on, Gareth!' he was yelling. '*Tackle him! Get in there, lad! That's it – now take the shot! ... Oooh, just over the bar. Unlucky, lad – unlucky!*' He clapped his shovel-like hands together and gave a lonely round of applause. 'Keep it tight out there, you guys. Don't give 'em any space! Shut 'em down and shut 'em down quick!'

Dad followed my gaze and commented: 'Anyone would think he's the coach. That's an overenthusiastic father right there. If I ever yammer on like that, please feel free to kick me in the shins.'

'I would,' I responded, smiling, 'but I think Mum would beat me to it.'

'I certainly would,' Mum put in.

The smell of bacon was making me really hungry now: so much so that my tummy was rumbling.

Mum noticed me glancing towards the burger van and said, 'You can have something this time, but this is just a one-off. Next time make sure you get yourself up earlier so you can have breakfast at home and save me some money.' She produced a ten-pound note from her purse and handed it to me. 'I want the change.'

'Thanks,' I said, springing up and taking off towards the van.

Inevitably, there was a queue. Nothing makes a queue form faster than the smell of delicious food cooking. As I joined the back and waited patiently, a group of girls queued behind me. At first, they didn't seem to acknowledge my existence. They were talking amongst themselves, mostly about which songs they liked and boys. But then they turned their attention towards me.

'Hello,' a small blonde girl said, 'I've not seen you around here before.' She was talking more to her friends than me, but I responded nonetheless.

'I'm new to the area,' I said, a bit sheepishly. 'Only moved in a few days ago.'

'Only moved in a few days ago,' another girl said, mimicking me.

I should have walked away right there and then. Never mind the annoying comments, I could tell from the way they were looking at me that they weren't going to be friendly. And speaking of dirty looks, there was one particular girl who was *really* giving me daggers. She was much bigger than the others and much meaner looking. She didn't like me from the moment she clapped eyes on me. I have no idea why. Maybe it was the way I was dressed, or how I'd done my hair, or perhaps she just wasn't keen on my face for some reason. Who knows? All I do know is that she was still staring at me like I'd done something bad to her. I couldn't bring myself to look at her, so I stared at the ground.

'Move up, then,' she said to me. 'Come on, dumbo; the queue's moved on and you're just standing there.'

The queue had advanced, so I did too.

They moved up next to me. I turned my back on them and tried to think happy thoughts.

One of them whispered something to the others and they all giggled.

'Look at how she's standing,' the blonde one said. 'What a retard.'

Happy thoughts, I thought. *Just ignore them. Ignore, ignore, ignore ...*

'Hey, don't you know it's rude to turn your back on people,' the big girl said.

'Yeah, it's rude,' one of them agreed. 'Didn't your parents teach you good manners?'

'Didn't yours teach *you* any?' I replied, turning around and glaring at one of them.

I regretted it almost immediately. I should have taken my own advice and ignored them. They were insulting my parents, though. Throw all the insults you like at me – but don't say anything bad about my mum and dad. That's always guaranteed to get me angry.

'*Wheeew!*' the big girl said, pursing her fat lips together and sucking in air. 'Looks like we hit a raw nerve there, you lot. I do believe Little Miss Prim and Proper is offended.'

'Ha-ha!' the blonde girl said. 'Little Miss Prim and Proper – I like it. Nice one, Emma. *Niccccce!*'

'I am not prim and proper,' I protested.

'Could have fooled me,' Emma, the big girl, said.

'Well, that wouldn't take much doing, now, would it?' I said.

Emma stared at me for a second, her top lip curling to form a snarl. Then she said to the blonde girl: 'I think someone's cruising for a bruising, don't you, Lisa?'

Lisa, the blonde girl, agreed.

Half of me wanted to turn tail and run, get back to my parents. But the other half – the more *determined* half – wanted to get busy with my fists. Even if it meant I took a beating. I'm no toughie, so I was under no illusion that I could fight off all four girls, or maybe even one of them. But I was determined to hurt at least one of them, if things got rough. Oh yes, I was confident I could at least do *that*.

'The queue's moved up again, dumbo,' one of the girls said.

'Well why don't you all just barge past me anyway,' I said, 'if you're in so much of a hurry?'

They all looked at each other and then at me.

'Okay,' Emma said, shrugging her shoulders.

She was the first to push past me. And then came the others, each one giving me a death stare.

Other people were taking an interest in what was going on now. An elderly couple behind us was looking on with concern.

'Are they giving you any grief?' the man asked me. 'You wanna go and tell your mum and dad if they are, you know.'

I'm not running back to my parents, I thought.

The old lady leaned in close to me and said in a hushed tone, 'They look like a rum bunch. I'd watch yourself, if I were you.' Her breath smelled of a mixture of peppermint and tobacco. I found the combination quite sickly. 'And I'd definitely give that big girl a wide berth. I saw her picking on some little kids earlier. Most unsavoury business, it was. Unsettling to watch.'

'Thanks for the advice and concern,' I responded, not bothering to lower my voice, 'but I can look after myself just fine, thanks.'

The nasty comments and stares didn't let up as the queue continued to advance. I tried to tune myself out of the situation by taking an interest in the match, but it was no good – their words were too hurtful to ignore.

I don't feel ashamed to admit that I breathed a huge sigh of relief when the girls walked away after being served. They moved over to the touchline and sat together whilst eating cobs full of hot food. And, I have to say, I wasn't surprised that they were with the man in the red tracksuit: the barrel-chested one with the big gob. I figured he was a father to one of the girls. And I was right. You can probably guess which one.

After I'd ordered a jumbo bacon cob, I made my way back to my parents and plonked myself down next to my dad.

'What's up, sweetheart?' he asked me, looking concerned. 'You look like you've lost a pound and found a penny.'

I've found something all right, I thought. *A bunch of nasty little rats who've taken a dislike to me just because I was unlucky enough to be in the wrong place at the wrong time.*

'I'm fine,' I said, trying to sound chirpy. I considered telling him about the girls but decided against this. He would ask who they were, then Mum would get involved and she'd feel the need to have a go at them, which would be embarrassing. 'Just can't wait for this football match to be over, is all.'

'It will be before you know it,' Mum said, sipping juice from a plastic cup. 'Want some?'

I shook my head. Then I set about making my cob disappear before my parents asked why I wasn't eating.

'Kieran nearly scored while you were gone,' Dad said to me. 'Did you see? He got behind their defence and was clear on goal. His shot must have scraped some paint off the post, it was *that* close.'

'That's good,' I said through a mouthful of food, trying to sound enthusiastic and doing a bad job of it, no doubt. 'I'm sure a goal or two would make him popular with his new teammates.'

'That's a good point,' Dad said. 'I never thought of that.' He turned his attention back to the match. '*Come on Kieran – you can do it, son! Belt one in for the boys!*'

Keeping my back to the girls, I tried to read my book but I just couldn't get into it. Even though they were some distance away for me, I could still hear their chatter and laughter, which was putting me off. I wondered what they might be saying and imagined they were laughing at me. I couldn't wait to get away from there.

Towards the end of the match, Kieran found himself clear of the last defender and was bearing down on goal. *Don't fluff this*, I thought. *Just keep your cool and slot it past the goalie.* And that's exactly what he did. Kieran ran towards the corner flag, then clenched his fist and punched towards the sky.

'*YESSSS!*' he said as his teammates swarmed around him, celebrating.

'Nice one, bro,' I said, feeling happy for him.

'Nice one indeed,' Dad said, clapping.

'Ah, I'm glad that's happened,' Mum said, looking very proud. 'That'll settle his nerves.'

But then all hell broke loose as the guy in the red tracksuit stormed onto the pitch, shouting, '*Offside! He was offside!*' first he vented his fury at the referee and then the linesman. '*Are you blind, mate! He was offside by a good few feet!*'

I couldn't hear what the linesman was saying, but a shake of his head was enough to convey his response. This infuriated the guy in the red tracksuit even more. He straightened himself up and thrust out his barrel-like chest, making himself look as big as possible. A mean expression spread across his craggy face. And then his shovel-like hands balled into fists.

'Oh my goodness,' Mum said, 'would you look at this guy; talk about a gross overreaction. You don't think he'll hit that poor man, do you? He's quite small and skinny and really doesn't look like he'd be able to defend himself.'

But as small and skinny as the linesman was, he wasn't backing down. He continued to shake his head as the aggressor squared up to him.

'Okay,' Dad said, 'somebody needs to put a stop to this.'

He walked towards the trouble, but Mum sprang up and grabbed him by his arm.

'Err,' she said, 'what do you think you're doing? There's no way you're getting involved. You'll get punched in the eye, or end up with broken ribs.'

'Well someone needs to do something because that brute is out of control,' Dad said.

'The ref is coming over, look,' Mum said, gesturing. 'He'll put a stop to this.'

Doubt it, I thought. *He's even smaller and skinnier than the linesman, so he's not putting a stop to anything.*

But this turned out not to be the case. After another bout of fury from the man in the red top, the ref put an arm around him and led him to one side.

'Brian,' the ref said loudly, appealing for calm, 'raging is not the way to go, my good friend. The decision has been made and it shall stand. There was no offside.' He began coaxing him farther away, still appealing for calm. And, amazingly, it seemed to be working (I figured the ref must have been friends with him or knew him quite well). But then someone else chirped in from the sideline. The big girl, Emma: the one who'd been giving me a hard time with her friends at the burger van.

'Don't let him fob you off, Dad!' she yelled. 'It WAS offside! I saw it!'

'Oh my God,' I muttered. 'That's *your* dad. Why does that not surprise me.'

Emma's outburst fired up her father again. He pushed away from the ref and continued his protest. This went for at least another five minutes, with Emma continuing to chirp in and egg her father on, before other adults began getting involved (including Andy and the coach of the opposing team). I was beginning to think that the match would have to be cancelled due to this one loud, obnoxious man. But then, all of a sudden, Brian must have realised that he wasn't going to get his own way and he backed away from the trouble. He went to his daughter: the only person who'd given him any support. They moaned to each other about the linesman's decision but there were no further attempts to disrupt play. The match resumed.

There were no more goals, which made Kieran the star of the show. When the final whistle blew, it was the sweetest sound to my ears. Just like after he'd scored the goal, Kieran got swamped by his teammates, who celebrated as if they'd won the World Cup.

This was an awkward moment for my parents, who wanted to celebrate as well, but they were still worried about Brian and how he might react. I, however, was more worried about Emma and the fact that she was staring at me like she wanted to kill me. She had obviously put two and two together and figured out that I was something to do with Kieran. And of course her friends were giving me the deadeye too, which made me feel even more uncomfortable. Mum noticed what was going on and asked me if everything was okay.

'Yes,' I replied. 'Everything's fine.'

'Really?' she replied, looking at the girls and then back at me. 'Are you sure about that?'

'They gave me some trouble at the burger van,' I said, shrugging my shoulders. 'It's nothing I can't handle.'

Mum's brow furrowed. 'Hmm,' she said, obviously not sure whether this was the case. 'And they're all with that obnoxious man. Now why does *that* not surprise me.'

'If he comes over here, just ignore him,' Dad said, all jittery, snatching glances in Brian's direction. 'It takes at least two people to have an argument and he can't engage us in one if we don't acknowledge him. I have a feeling that Kieran will be wanting to come here every week. I hope the same can't be said about *him* over there.'

Well I certainly won't be coming here every week, I thought.

Suddenly appearing in front of us, Kieran bounced up and down like he was on hot coals with bare feet. 'Did you see that finish?' he asked me. 'Did you see how I slotted the ball past the keeper and into the corner like a pro?'

'Yes, I did,' I replied. 'You're going to be the next Ronaldo, for sure.'

'Ha-ha,' Kieran said, still beaming. 'Very funny, sis.'

'You played very well,' Mum said to him. 'Well done.'

She leaned in to kiss him on the cheek, so he edged away from her.

'Not here,' he said, worried someone might have seen. 'Not in the middle of a field.'

'Oh,' Mum said, giving an indignant shrug of her shoulders.

'Dad, are you all right?' Kieran enquired. 'You seem a bit worried.' He glanced in the direction that Dad was looking and noticed the problem. 'Oh, him. That's the guy who was certain that my goal was offside. Which it wasn't. Anyone with decent eyesight could see that.'

'We know,' Dad said. 'But we'd rather not have to discuss it with him; so if you could just say goodbye to your new friends, then we can get on our way and avoid any unpleasantness, thank you very much.'

'I specialize in dealing with unpleasantness,' Mum said with a steely glint in her eyes.

'I know you do,' Dad said. 'That's half the reason I'm so eager to get out of here. You pair clashing is a scary thought. Are you still here, Kieran? I thought I told you to say goodbye to your teammates.'

Kieran did as he was told. He exchanged high fives and fist bumps with everyone, including Andy, whilst my parents and I lingered around, twiddling our thumbs, so to speak. Then Brian began walking in our direction with a mean look on his face. He had his daughter with him and the boy named Gareth (who I assumed was his son). Emma was also sporting a mean look, which was directed right at me.

Oh here we go again, I thought.

'If they want an argument,' Mum said, turning to face them, 'then they've come to the right place.' She cracked her knuckles in a way that made me cringe. 'Bring it on.'

This could be embarrassing, I thought, shooting Dad a quick gander. As expected, he did not look quite so up for trouble as Mum. But he stood his ground, bless him. As scared as he was, there was no way he would leave Mum and me to deal with what was coming. He showed me how to be truly brave when I'm truly scared. My Dad: the coward with a streak of steel in his blood.

When Brian and the other two got close to us, however, they veered to the right and headed towards the car park.

He put his arm around the boy's shoulders and said, 'C'mon, laddo, let's get you back to your parents.'

Not his son, then.

'Well thank God for that,' Dad said, relaxing a little. 'I thought we were in for a good bout of nastiness there.'

Mum looked almost disappointed. 'So did I,' she commented. 'They're still giving us filthy looks as they get into their car, though. Some people just need to get a grip, they really do.'

'I think your unflinching stare put them off, dear,' Dad said. 'Perhaps that oaf has a little more common sense than I thought.'

'Doubt it,' I said.

Somehow I knew this wouldn't be the last time encountered Emma and her father. And not because we were now living near a small town where everyone most likely knew everyone. In life, I've noticed that when you come across hateful people, you end up crossing paths with them again at some point. Usually when you least expect it and you could least do without the hassle.

After we got back home and Kieran had showered, he suggested we have a look in the garden.

'Really?' I said. 'You want to go snooping after what Reg told us about the weird plants that are out there?'

'He told us they were weird; he didn't say anything about them being dangerous.'

I just know that they will be, I thought. 'Think I'll pass,' I said. 'I've already had enough weirdness in the last few days, so I don't want to tempt fate.'

Kieran shook his head. 'So what are you gonna do? Never go out there? You know you're gonna get curious and want to take a look at some point, so you may as well do it now while you've got your big bro to protect you. Curiosity is a beast that cannot be tamed, you know.'

'That's probably the most intelligent thing you've ever said to me.'

'Really?' he replied, all smiles.

'I'm talking about the "curiosity is a beast" part, not the "my big bro will protect me" hogwash. Since when have you ever protected me from anything?'

'There's always a first time.'

'Yeah, right.'

Mum noticed us heading towards the back door and said, 'Eh, where do you pair think you're going? You're grounded, remember? That means staying in the house and not going anywhere ... remember?'

'Surely we can go in the garden,' Kieran said. 'Surely we can do *that* much.'

'Oh, right ... yes,' Mum said. 'I suppose we can stretch to that.' Then her eyes narrowed to fine slits as she levelled a finger at us and issued a warning: 'Don't go getting any ideas about sauntering off anywhere, though. You will be in so much trouble if you do. Are we clear on this!'

'Crystal,' I said.

'Yeah,' Kieran said, following my lead, 'crystal.'

'Good,' Mum said. Just before we went outside, she added: 'Oh, and watch yourself out there; it's like a jungle. It's so overgrown down the bottom. It'll take me and your father a good few weeks to tidy it all up. With a little help from you two, I hope.'

'Yeah,' Kieran said, unenthusiastically. 'Of course.'

On the patio, at the back of the house, I looked towards a line of trees that ran along the left side of the garden, near the fence. Kieran followed my line of sight and guessed what I was thinking.

'They're the ones Reg told us about, aren't they?' he said. 'They're the ones that grew really fast.'

'I remember him saying that they were by the fence, so I'm pretty sure they are.'

'They look pretty normal to me. We did about trees at school not long ago and I'm pretty sure those are oaks.'

'They look like oaks, yes. But the leaves are round, so they can't be.' Something about them just didn't look right. Some of the branches reminded me of slumped arms and their knobbly ends made me think of fists. I could imagine them crashing down on anyone who dared get too near.

As Kieran shot off across the patio, he tripped over a jutting slab and nearly went down.

'Careful,' I said. 'I'm sure your new football team won't want to lose their star player after just one game. And I wouldn't be so eager to get near those trees. I'm going to keep a safe distance and you might want to do the same.'

'Oh come on,' Kieran said, eager to get closer to them. 'What's the worst that can happen?'

What's the worst that can happen? I thought. *Are you kidding me!*

I could see he was concerned about the trees himself, but curiosity was a force he couldn't resist. He went down the steps and along the overgrown path.

'Kieran!' I said, beginning to worry. 'No, please don't. Have you already forgotten what Reg told us, or are you being deliberately ignorant?'

Either he didn't hear me, or he *was* being deliberately ignorant. Knowing my brother, it was probably the latter. He sauntered towards the nearest tree. Leaves rustled and dropped to the ground as he yanked on one of the branches.

'Oh my God,' I hissed under my breath, 'what *is* he doing!'

'You see,' he said, giving it another tug, 'nothing to worry about, sis.'

'Don't do that!' I pleaded. 'I really don't think that's a good idea.'

He gave the branch another tug. 'Like I said, nothing to worry about.'

I stood rooted to the spot, cringing. Any second now I was sure that one of those branches with the fist-shaped ends would spring to life. I imagined it giving Kieran a good whack and sending him flying (perhaps knocking some sense into him – although I'm not sure even a good whack from a tree could have achieved that minor miracle). Or, even worse, maybe it would grab hold of him and twirl itself around his body, crushing him like a boa constrictor.

'I'm being serious now,' I pleaded again to Kieran, 'please move away from there.'

Letting go of the branch, he finally did as I told him. He moved a safe distance away, then threw his hands up in frustration.

'Honestly,' he said, 'if anything weird was going to happen, I think it would have happened by now, don't you? Or is it just you that weird stuff happens to?'

'It feels that way at the moment,' I said, making my way down the steps and joining him.

We both stood looking up at the trees, in awe of their size and girth. They towered over us like wooden giants, their thick boughs and leafy branches silhouetted against the darkening skyline full of grey clouds.

'It was like a summer's day a few hours ago,' Kieran said. 'Now it looks like it's gonna tip it down with rain. The weather in this country is so unpredictable. No wonder people go abroad for their holidays.'

'It's not the weather that concerns me; it's the house we've moved into and the garden we're now standing in. I'm going to get a plaque made for the front door which reads: Creepy House.'

'Oh yes, I'm sure Mum and Dad would *love* that. And speaking of creepy, check out those weird things down there.' He nodded towards a bed of spidery-looking plants which were situated around the base of each tree.

'Now I'm no expert gardener, but who the heck would plant anything at the base of a tree where it'll get no light. Perhaps they're weeds.'

'Maybe. But they look too well arranged to be weeds. And have you ever seen a weed that looks like that?'

Kieran shook his head.

'No, neither have I.'

Kieran walked forwards and bent down to give one a closer inspection. As he did, a branch from the nearest tree began rustling. Then the branch creaked as it slowly moved backwards – like it was winding up to take a swipe at my brother.

'*Watch out!*' I said, grabbing him by the shoulders and pulling him clear of danger.

As we both fell backwards, Kieran landed on top of me, knocking the air out of my lungs.

I tried to push him aside, but couldn't budge him. 'Get ... off of me!' I gasped, trying to shift his heavy weight. 'Get ... OFF OF ME!'

Rolling to the side, Kieran pulled himself up to a kneeling position, then threw his hands in the air. 'What did you do that for?' he raged. 'Why did you pull me over?'

I glanced towards the tree, expecting to see the branches reaching out for us, or taking a swipe at us. But none of them was. They were just hanging limp and lifeless, like they should have been.

'The tree,' I said, still struggling to breathe. 'It came to life. One of the branches ... It ... It was about to hit you.'

'What?' Kieran screwed his face up in disbelief. He regarded the tree with an unnerving look, then focused his attention on me. 'Are you for real?'

'Yesss!' I said, deadly serious. 'I'm not mucking around.'

Tipping his head to one side, Kieran continued to regard me with a sceptical expression.

'I'm being serious here!' I hissed. 'That thing would have grabbed you or hit you if I hadn't intervened.'

BANG! BANG! BANG!

Both of us jumped in surprise as we saw Mum glaring down at us from an upstairs window. Then she opened the window and scolded us: 'What are you doing down there in the dirt? Get up, both of you! You'll end up in a right mess!'

Kieran and I got to our feet. Acting sheepish, we brushed ourselves off.

Credit to Kieran, he came up with an excuse straight away. 'I tripped over,' he said without hesitation. 'Ella tried to stop me from falling, but I dragged her down as well.'

It was Mum's turn to sport a sceptical look. She waved a cautionary finger at us (yes, she loved her cautionary finger-wagging, did my mum), then shut the window and continued doing whatever it was she'd been doing.

'That's twice in the last few days that you've surprised me with your quick thinking,' I said to Kieran. 'I'm beginning to think that you do have a brain after all.'

'Thanks,' he replied, brushing himself off again. 'So maybe I should let you come up with a good excuse next time.' He looked genuinely insulted, which made me feel a little guilty.

'I'm sorry,' I said. 'I was just joking.'

'Of course you were.'

'I was,' I assured him. Even though I wasn't, if I'm honest.

'Yeah, well, the next time I'm about to do something, please don't grab hold of me and drag me down into the dirt. It's really not funny.'

'I wasn't trying to be funny; I was trying to save you from ...'

'A tree that came alive,' Kieran said, finishing my sentence. 'Can you just quit it with the crazy stuff, please; it's getting old now. And annoying.'

I wanted to grab hold of Kieran and scream in his face: that's how frustrated I was getting. Instead, I just shook my head and mumbled to myself: 'I give up; I really do.'

'Yeah – and so do I.'

'Do you want to look around the rest of the garden, or shall we just go back inside?'

'You think this tree came alive, took a swipe at me, and you want to *continue* exploring? Seriously? Who's to say there aren't other plants ready to grab hold of us – ready to eat us alive.'

That was a fair point. What was I thinking!

Spots of rain dappled my cheeks as I turned my face towards the ever-darkening sky and then looked towards the upstairs windows. I half expected to see a flash of movement or a shadow behind one of the glass panes, but I saw nothing more sinister than reflections. Never in my life have I felt so alone as I did at that moment. Yes, Kieran was with me and the rest of my family were close by, but I was on my own against this house of horrors and the grounds it laid in. *What can I do to make them see sense? I* thought dismally. Then I averted my gaze from the windows and saw that Kieran was crouched down next to one of the spider plants.

'Crikey,' he said, giving one of them a stroke with his fingers, 'these things really *are* weird.'

'Get away from there!' I said, panic seizing me.

But Kieran ignored me. He continued to stroke the plant with his fingers ...

I heard a rustling sound and caught a glimpse of movement in the tree above him.

'Please listen to me for once in your life and get away from there,' I begged my brother. I knew he wouldn't listen, the pig-headed fool. But still I continued to beg, hoping that a small amount of sense might penetrate his brain. '*Please* get away from there, Kieran; I've got a bad feeling that something scary is about to happen.'

Then something scary *did* happen. A branch swooped around, low and fast, whooshing through the air. Before either of us could react, the fist-like end connected with the top of Kieran's arm and sent him flying. Landing at my feet, he let out an 'Ooomph!' of surprise and pain. He looked up at me, wide-eyed and disbelieving.

I bent down to drag him clear of danger, but there was no need; he was up on his feet and scrambling for cover. I scrambled away with him.

'Are you hurt?' I said. It was a silly question. He was holding his shoulder and grimacing, so of course he was hurt. I just felt the need to ask, because I couldn't think of anything else to say. 'Can you answer me? Are you badly hurt?'

'Of course I am!' he said, still sporting that wide-eyed and disbelieving expression. 'Did that tree just hit me? Or did I imagine it?'

'You didn't imagine it. It swiped at you like you were an annoying fly.'

Kieran touched his arm lightly and let out a low moan of discomfort. 'Ouch ... ow ow ow ... I think it's broken.'

'Let me see.' I tried to roll up the sleeve of his jumper, but he was having none of it. 'Let me see, will you.'

'You'll prod it – and it'll hurt.'

'I won't prod it. I just want to see.'

Kieran shook his head. He continued to hold his arm and wince.

'Just roll your sleeve up so we can take a gander.'

'Don't need to take a look,' Kieran said with tears forming in his eyes. 'It's broke. I can *feel* it!'

'Try raising your hand.'

'What?'

'I said, try raising your hand.'

'But it'll hurt!'

'I know it will, but just do it anyway.'

He gave me an indignant scowl, then did as I told him. It was painful for him to do all right, but he did manage to get his hand all the way over his head. As he slowly lowered his arm, he finally succumbed to fits of tears.

'Oh come on,' I said, 'it's really not that bad.'

Kieran glared at me like I was his worst enemy.

'It's not broken,' I assured him. 'You wouldn't be able to raise your arm if it was.'

'How would you know? Are you a doctor?'

'No, I'm not. But I'm quite confident of my diagnosis. You wouldn't be able to raise your arm if it was broken,' I said again. 'I saw something similar on a program once and that was what a doctor told some kid.'

Kieran focused his attention on the tree that'd hit him. 'Did that thing really come alive and just knock me for six? Or was it the wind?'

I couldn't believe my ears. 'The wind? Are you serious?' I shook my head. 'As if the wind could make that thick branch move enough to launch you like it did. It would take a hurricane force to do that, not the breeze that's barely ruffling my hair at the moment.'

'I'm just trying to think of a rational explanation as to what happened.'

'There is no sensible explanation. You got hit by a tree. I saw it happen, so just accept it.'

The only thing that my brother accepted at that moment, however, was the fact that he was in a lot of pain. Tears continued to roll down his cheeks as he rubbed his arm and winced in discomfort.

Then the heavens opened up and the fine rain turned to a downpour.

As we rushed for the house, I said, 'Mum's going to ask us what happened. Just tell her that you tripped over and fell on a rock, okay.'

'She can spot a lie a mile off; especially when I'm the one telling them.'

'Be convincing then. Or tell her the truth. I'm sure she'll believe you.'

As it was, she believed the lie – but only because I was the one who told it. Mum once told me that people who can't look you in the eye when they're talking to you are probably not telling the truth, so I was careful to hold her gaze as she quizzed me.

In the kitchen, she got Kieran to take off his top so she could get a good look at his arm, which was red at the top and beginning to bruise. She asked him to raise his arm, so I told her that I'd already got him to do that.

'Just do it anyway,' Mum insisted.

'But it'll hurt,' Kieran protested. 'I nearly passed out last time.'

'Oh don't be such a sissy,' Mum said. 'And just do as you're told.'

Reluctantly, Kieran did as he was told. And it did hurt. So much so that he screeched like a dog that'd just had its paw trodden on.

'Right, well, I don't think there's any need for A and E,' Mum said. 'Nothing's broken as far as I can tell.'

'There you go,' I said to Kieran. 'Told you so.'

'Okay doctor know it all,' he replied in a silly voice.

'Honestly, you pair,' Mum said, 'all you've been is trouble since we moved into this house. I hope this sort of behaviour isn't going to continue. My patience only stretches so far, you know.'

We heard the front door open and then Dad stepped into the room holding a big box.

'What's in there?' I said, seizing the chance to change the subject. 'Anything nice? Anything for me?'

'Nothing particularly interesting, I'm afraid,' he replied. 'Just the dehumidifier I said that I'd buy. We won't be troubled by black mould ever again. Or, at least, that's what the man in the shop assured me.'

I wouldn't be so sure about that, I thought. Then I pointed out a blotch of mould on the wall, in the corner of the room, near the ceiling.

'But I scrubbed all that off,' Dad said, confused. 'I didn't miss any; I'm *sure* I didn't.'

And I'm sure you didn't either, I thought.

'Brr! It's cold in this house,' Dad said. 'What's up with you?' he asked Kieran. 'Why are you holding your arm and looking so sorry for yourself, kiddo?'

Mum explained what'd happened, so then Dad insisted on taking a gander at Kieran's shoulder as well (despite Mum's assurances that his injury wasn't serious). I left them to it because there was something I wanted to check.

Starting upstairs, I went from room to room, checking walls and ceilings for black mould. I found a patch in my room, near the window and a long splodge on the ceiling above Kieran's bed. Downstairs, I found a small smudge in the hallway, above the door and some more in the kitchen. I was tempted to take a peek in the toilet – the speediest peek ever – but I gave it a miss. The memory of what I'd seen in there was still fresh and gave me chills. Pausing outside the cellar door, I considered opening it and taking a look down there as well (again, just a peek – no more than a peek). But I once again remembered what Reg had told me about the neighbours and how they'd found Maud performing a weird ritual down there.

'Are you all right?' Dad said, coming up behind me and making me jump. 'Intrigued by the cellar, are we?'

Yes, I am, I thought – *and troubled*. 'Have you been down there?'

'Of course I have. I wouldn't buy a house without checking out every room. Even the cellar. There's quite a bit of old junk down there that needs removing. Another job for us to do, but not one that's pressing.'

'What sort of junk?'

'Just furniture and stuff. Nothing interesting.' Dad gave me a searching gaze. 'Why do you ask?'

'Just curious, that's all.'

'Well, don't go getting too curious and playing down there. The air is quite damp and fusty. It'll irritate your lungs if you're exposed for too long, sweetheart.'

'I have no intentions of playing down there,' I said, aghast at the idea. 'Was there any black mould?'

Dad sighed and gave me a concerned look. 'Yes, there was. But I cleaned it all off. You're not going to go weird on us again and insist that the house is haunted, are you? I thought we were getting past that.'

'I wasn't being weird. I was just telling you what I saw.'

'What you *thought* you saw.'

I rolled my eyes and took an interest in the wall.

'Oh dear,' Dad said, giving me another concerned look. 'Do you know what, I think you should start thinking about school and nothing else. You've got a big day tomorrow. It's your first day, so make sure you get an early night. And I want you up early, too – all bright and eager.'

Yeah, right, I thought. *I'll be early but I won't be eager. And neither will Kieran.*

As if on cue, he let out an anguished moan in the kitchen and then told Mum to stop touching his arm.

'I'll be surprised if he doesn't use his shoulder as an excuse to get out of going to school,' I said.

'Well, he has taken quite a knock. It's going to leave a nasty bruise.'

'I'm sure his ego is bruised more than his arm.'

'I have a feeling you could be right.'

Five minutes later, Dad was busy scrubbing off any black mould he could find. He'd also set the dehumidifier running in the hallway, which was making a lot of noise.   By this time, Kieran had seated himself in the living room and was watching telly. He'd shut the door in an attempt to block out the noise, but he could still hear the drone of the machine even after he'd turned up the volume on the TV.

'Can you please turn that thing off,' Kieran moaned to Mum. 'Or run it upstairs or something.'

'It's a noise you're going to have to get used to,' she insisted. 'We have a problem with damp in this house and that needs to be addressed.'

'Fine,' Kieran said with some attitude. 'I'll just do this then.' He fingered a button on the remote and cranked the volume up even higher.

'Turn that down,' Mum said loudly, so she could be heard above the din.

Kieran ignored her.

Then Mum stood in front of him, blocking his view. She gave him one of her icy stares.

'Okay, fine,' he said, dropping the volume, but not dropping the attitude. 'I'll just sit here and stare at the wall, shall I? I may as well because I can't hear the telly!'

'Cut out the back-chat,' Mum warned him, 'or you'll be in your room for the rest of the night.'

'I probably won't be able to hear my telly in there either,' Kieran said.

Mum's eyes narrowed to slits as she brandished a finger at him. 'You won't *have* a TV in your room if you keep on moaning. Or an XBOX, for that matter. I'll confiscate both of them!'

That got through to Kieran. A threat to take away his XBOX was always guaranteed to make him back down.

'I give up!' he said, springing up out of the armchair like he'd been electrocuted. 'I *hate* this house and I *hate* you!' Huffing and puffing in frustration, he held his arm in discomfort, then disappeared through the door that led to the playroom.

Mum looked at me with a surprised expression. I shrugged at her and then followed Kieran, making sure I shut the door behind me.

Standing by the window, Kieran was staring out towards the garden, towards the trees that lined the fence. His eyes were tearful as he rubbed his arm and shook his head in dismay.

'Is it still hurting you?' I asked him as I came up behind him. 'Sorry, that's a daft question, I know. You wouldn't be rubbing your arm if it wasn't.'

'I've taken some painkillers, so it's not too bad,' Kieran said. 'It's throbbing more than anything.'

A moment of silence descended. I wasn't sure what to say next. I was about to say something – some token effort of small talk to assure him that Mum did care about him despite what'd happened – but then Kieran spoke up.

'That tree,' he said, nodding towards the one that'd hit him, 'it did take a swipe at me, didn't it? It did knock me to the ground ... didn't it?'

'Yes,' I replied without hesitation. 'It did.'

He continued rubbing his arm, his expression unblinking as he kept staring at the tree. 'Why? Why do you suppose it did that? And how is that even possible? I remember what Reg said and I know the woman who lived here before us was supposed to be a witch, but ...' he shook his head again, '... I just can't get my head around this, sis. Trees don't attack people. It doesn't happen. Not in real life.'

'It *did* happen. Everything Reg told us is the truth. The black mould in this house is alive and it's going to keep coming back. Dad can run that machine of his for as long as he likes because it won't make a difference.'

'And then what? Why do you look so worried? It's not like it'll reach out and grab you or anything. Mould can't do that ... can it?'

I looked at Kieran with raised eyebrows. 'And trees can't give you a good whack either – but one just did. Maud cursed this house and everything on this land, so anything is possible here. We both need to be careful and we need to watch each other's backs. And we need to watch out for Mum and Dad, too. We know that something's happening here, but they don't. Unless they see it for themselves, they'll never believe a word we tell them about a witch or a curse.'

Kieran mulled things over for a few seconds, then let out a troubled sigh. 'When we first viewed this house, you told me that you saw movement in the upstairs windows.'

'I thought I saw something move, yes.'

'Did you see someone?'

'It could have been someone. It could have been shadows.'

'Or it could have been the witch.'

'She's dead. Reg told us so.'

'But she's a witch. If she can curse this place – make trees and black mould come alive – then surely she can come back from the dead.'

What my brother was saying made perfect sense. The idea of her roaming from room to room as we slept tonight was a thought that chilled my heart. Kieran must have been thinking along the same lines because the colour had drained from his face and he looked a ghostly white.

'Tonight I'm sleeping in your room,' he said. 'On the floor.'

'Mum won't allow that.'

'I'll sneak in after her and Dad are asleep.'

'She'll hear you. You know what she's like: a pin drops and it'll wake her.'

'I'll be stealthy like a ninja.'

'There's nothing ninja about you.'

Kieran shrugged, then winced a little as he held his arm. 'Yeah, I'll give you that one, sis.'

I noticed a small splodge of black mould near the window.

Kieran reached out with his hand to touch it.

'No, *don't!*' I said. 'That would *not* be a clever thing to do.'

He hesitated, his fingers mere inches from the splodge – then he withdrew his hand.

I coaxed him away. 'D'you know what, there's one room in this house that I'd really like to explore, but I'm too afraid.'

'The cellar?'

'Yeah.'

'I can explore with you. We can take a look now, if you like?'

'Dad told me not to go down there.'

'If it was Mum who'd said that then I might be more worried. We could sneak down in a bit, like ninjas, and take a quick gander.'

'Don't start with the ninja thing again. We're already grounded, so if we get caught, we'll be for it, for sure.'

'We won't get caught.'

'Ha-ha – you said that last time.'

'I know, but this time we won't. Why don't you just trust your big brother for once. You know it makes sense.'

Kieran smiled. It was nice to see his expression brighten after his ruck with Mum.

'Okay, I'll trust you,' I said. Even though I didn't.

'Do you think I should apologize to Mum?'

'I think that would be a good idea. I'd rather have her in a good mood than a bad one. Wouldn't you?'

Kieran nodded. 'Don't you think I was right to complain, though? That machine makes too much noise. They should run it in the day, when we're at school.'

'It is annoying, I'll agree. But we both need to get used to it for now. Once they realize it isn't working – that the mould isn't going away – they'll stop using it.'

'How can you be so confident that it won't work?'

'I'm sure Dad's machine will work wonders getting rid of regular mould, but this isn't regular mould; it's part of the curse that Maud put on this house. And he can scrub and scrub 'till his arms feel like they're about to fall off. It won't make any difference, because, as I've said before, it'll keep coming back.'

Kieran mulled things over for a few seconds, taking in everything I'd said, then he turned his attention back towards the tree that'd hit him.

'Don't worry, it can't hurt you now,' I said. 'Unless it can uproot itself, which I'm pretty sure is impossible.'

'Trees coming alive and hitting people is impossible, but it happened. Do you think it was protecting itself when it swiped me? Or something else? What about those spidery plants that are growing beneath it – beneath all of them? Maybe it was protecting those?'

That's possible, I thought. 'Definitely possible. But whatever the case may be, I wouldn't go anywhere near there again. I think we're probably better off just not going in the garden at all, to be honest. Who's to know what other surprises could be waiting out there for us. I wish I could avoid coming in this house, but that isn't an option.'

'I'm going to be too afraid to sleep at this rate.'

'Me too. I think things will start to get really weird really quick from now on.'

And, oh boy, was I right ...

Later that evening, when our parents were settled down in the living room, watching TV, Kieran and I sneaked down the stairs from our bedrooms. Thankfully, either Mum or Dad had turned off the dehumidifier, but Kieran was still tempted to give it a kick. Pausing outside the cellar door, we both looked at each other with blank expressions.

'Sure you want to do this?' Kieran said in a low voice.

No, I wasn't. But curiosity was eating away at me too much for me to back down now. 'Yes,' I replied, also keeping my voice low. 'And what about you? Are you brave enough?'

'Not really – I'm scared as hell. So I think we better just get on with it before we both bottle it.'

Sound advice, that.

As I reached for the brass doorknob, I noticed that my hand was shaking. Kieran noticed, too. I withdrew my hand.

'Either you're cold or nervous,' he said.

'Both. But I'm shaking more because I'm nervous than anything.'

'Yeah, this house always seems chilly. Even when the heating is on full blast.'

The door-knob felt icy cold as I finally plucked up the courage to grab hold of it again. I attempted to turn it but it wouldn't budge. I tried again – but no joy.

'Let me have a go,' Kieran said, muscling me out of the way. His face turned red as he clasped the knob in both hands and gave it a good go. 'Grrr! It won't budge. The mechanism must be jammed or rusted. And I can't really grasp it that well because of my arm injury.'

'Keep your voice down. Mum and Dad are in the next room, remember. And speaking of Dad, he told me that he'd been in the cellar to scrub off the mould down there. So how can he have done that if the mechanism is broke?'

'Maybe he ... lied. He might have said that to keep you happy because he knows how worried you are about the mould.'

'But the door opened fine before. I took a peek down the steps earlier.' I was about to say something else – but then the door clicked open.

'O...kay,' Kieran said, taking a step back and looking at me with wide eyes. 'Now that's weird.'

'That thing was definitely jammed. I couldn't budge it and neither could you.'

'Well, it's not jammed now.'

Steeling myself, I pushed the door open and stared down into the darkness. I fingered the light switch on the wall, expecting it not to work, but it did. Down below, at the bottom of the stone steps, a bulb attached to a wooden beam flickered to life.

'That didn't work before,' I said. 'After you, then.' I gesturing Kieran to go first.

'Oh, no,' he replied, gesturing back. 'Ladies first.'

Rolling my eyes, I positioned myself in the doorway and looked down the moss-covered steps.

'Either Mum or Dad could come out of the living room at any moment,' Kieran said, 'so if we're gonna do this, then we need to just do it.'

'Okay, okay,' I replied, descending the steps.

There was no railing to hold, so I put my hands on the walls either side to steady myself. Like the steps, the walls were covered in moss and were damp to touch.

Hearing the door click shut behind me, I turned around to see what was happening.

'If either of them sees it open,' Kieran said, 'they'll know we're down here.'

'But what if we can't get out? We had problems opening it, remember?'

'Well then we're gonna be in a lot of trouble, I suppose.'

I understood why he'd done it, but I would have still preferred he left it open.

'Keep moving,' Kieran said, giving me a prod.

'Please don't do that,' I replied as I continued to descend.

Reaching the bottom and making my way past the cobweb-covered bulb, I looked around, taking in my surroundings. Various pieces of furniture were scattered here and there, all covered in dust and moss. More cobwebs hung from the ceiling like scary decorations. The cobblestone floor was slippery to walk on. And it didn't take me long to notice some black mould.

'Dad told me he'd cleaned all the mould off,' I said, pointing to various splodges on the walls. 'I bet he hasn't even been down here.'

'Like I said, he probably just told you that to keep you happy, so you won't worry. There's a lot of it here. Perhaps Dad should run his annoying dehumidifier down here. At least then we won't have to hear that constant droning noise.'

'We'd probably still be able to hear it because it makes such a racket.'

The cellar was big and spacious. As we moved to the far end, I knew that we were right beneath where our parents were sitting in the living room. I could hear the murmur of the TV above us.

'It's so dank and fusty down here,' Kieran said, coughing a little too loud for my liking. 'It's beginning to irritate my throat.'

Putting my index finger over my lips, I made a shushing gesture. 'They'll hear,' I said in a small voice as I raised my eyes towards the wooden ceiling.

Kieran noticed a large, black, metal cauldron in a recess in the corner. 'Check this out,' he said, lifting it up so he could have a good look at it. 'It weighs a tonne.'

'Put that down. You don't know what's been in it.'

'Witches have cauldrons. Everyone knows that.'

'Another good reason to put it down, then, isn't it?'

Kieran did as I told him. 'What next? A broomstick? There's gotta be a black cat around here somewhere. Witches always have them in the movies.'

'Yeah, well, this isn't the movies.'

Continuing to poke around, Kieran decided to investigate a dark wood cupboard which had lots of little drawers in its bottom half. He brushed some cobwebs away, then opened the top one.

'There's lots of small jars in here,' he said, picking one up and examining it. 'Says on the label that this is Essence of Venomshade.'

I didn't like the look of this – did *not* like the look of this at all. I had a good idea of what my brother had stumbled upon and I wanted to get out of the cellar before weird things began happening.

Kieran put the jar down. He picked up another and read the label: 'Fermented Moonsickles.'

'I've no idea what they are,' I said, my voice full of jitters, 'but I think we know who they belonged to.'

'And what about this?' Kieran said, pulling out a thick hardback book. He wiped the dust off the cover and read the title. 'Dark Spells for the Dark Mind.'

'Yes, and we don't need two guesses as to who the dark mind belongs to, now, do we?'

'This is her spellbook,' Kieran said with a look of wonder spreading across his dopey face. 'This is actually *her* book of spells.'

'Amazing conclusion there, Sherlock.' I folded my arms across my chest and waited for him to draw his next conclusion.

Finally, his brain got into gear and he said, 'If she's cursed this place ... if she's still here somehow, as a ghost ... I don't think she'll like us touching this.'

'*Bingo!*' I said a little too loudly. 'The penny has dropped.'

'But still ....' Kieran said, flicking through the pages. 'I'm really curious to have a gander.'

So was I, if the truth is told. But not so curious that I wanted to jeopardize my safety.

'Let's go back up,' I said. 'Before Mum and Dad notice that we're not in our rooms.'

Kieran stopped on a page titled: **Bad Luck Curse**. 'I can think of a few people I'd like to cast this upon,' he said with an evil glint in his eyes.' He ran his finger down the list of needed ingredients. 'We've already got some of these in the house and some will be easy to get hold of: salt, white candles, chicken bones, blood, brown leaves. There's others that I wouldn't know where to get 'em from, though: Bergamot, High John, Wolfsbane (I mean, what the heck are they!).'

'There's a magic shop in Pickleworth, not far from here. I bet the kooky old woman who runs the place would know.'

'Yeah, I bet she would. I've been past there a few times, but I've never been tempted to go in. What's it called?' Kieran clicked his fingers together as he tried to remember. 'The Magic Cove, or something like that. Have you ever been in, sis?'

'It's The Mystic Cove. And, no, I've never been in either.'

I wanted to go in now, though. I had questions I wanted to ask the old woman. Questions about curses and black mould and trees that come to life and hit you.

I thought I saw something move to my left, which made me snap my head in that direction. The light flickered, creating shadows that morphed and merged.

'Erm,' I said to Kieran, 'I really think we need to get out of here now.'

But he still had his nose in the book, thumbing through the pages, oohing and ahhing at all the different spells.

'There's one here for good luck,' he said excitedly. 'Gotta be worth a try, don't you think?'

All of a sudden, the temperature in the cellar dropped like a stone. My breath misted in front of me as I hugged myself and continued to urge my brother to put the book back where he'd got it from.

'God, it's getting a bit nippy down here,' Kieran said, noticing it too. 'Have you opened a window or something?'

There was only one window and it was firmly closed.

I nervously eyed the black mould on the nearest wall, sure that there was more there than there had been a few minutes before.

Kieran stowed the book away in the drawer he'd got it from.

He followed my line of sight, then edged closer to the wall. He had a curious look on his face as he eyed the mould.

'What are you doing?' I said, concerned. 'Please don't get too close to that stuff.'

Kieran stopped a few feet away from the affected area and continued to stare at the mould.

'It moved,' he said in awe. 'I'm sure I just saw it move.'

'I wouldn't be at all surprised if you're right. All the more reason not to get any closer, then, isn't it?'

He reached out with his fingers, as if he was about to touch the stuff, so I yelled at him, 'NO! What are you doing? Are you nuts!'

From above us, in the living room, I heard voices. Then the sound of footsteps moving across the room.

'Oh great,' Kieran said, rolling his eyes. 'Now we're gonna have some explaining to do.'

A few seconds later, the cellar door creaked open and Mum called down, 'Kieran? Ella? Are you pair down there?'

'Perhaps we should just say nothing,' Kieran suggested in a low voice. 'She might go away.'

'Not likely,' I said.

'Kieran? Ella? If you're down there, can you come up here now, please? *Pronto!*'

Kieran beckoned me to go first.

'Coward,' I said as I made my way towards the stairs.

Mum gave us both a look of death as we emerged from the cellar. And Dad didn't look too pleased either.

'What were you pair doing down there?' he said. 'I told you not to go down there.'

'We ... thought we heard noises,' I said. 'So we went to investigate.'

'A likely story,' Mum said, dismissing my lie straight away. 'What were you *really* doing down there?'

I stuck to my lie. I couldn't think of another good one and the truth wasn't an option.

'We heard noises,' I said, repeating myself. I knew what the next question would be, so I added, 'Clanking sounds. Like ... someone was tapping some pipes.'

Even Dad looked sceptical. 'Well, we didn't hear anything and we're sitting directly above the cellar,' he said. 'I hope you're wrong, otherwise it means we could have problems with the plumbing. And that's another problem we really could do without.'

I stuck to the lie, repeating it more forcefully, 'We heard clanking noises, so we went to investigate.'

'First,' Mum said, brandishing a finger at Kieran and me, 'take some of that bass out of your voice when you're talking to me and your father. And second, if you ever hear any clanking noises again in this house, don't go investigating. Come and tell us as we'll need to know about it as soon as possible.'

'I will,' I said, lowering my head.

'Me too,' Kieran said, lowering his head as well.

'Right,' Dad said, brushing past us, 'I suppose I better go and see what this mysterious noise is, then, hadn't I?'

'I've no doubt you won't hear anything whilst you're down there,' Mum said to him, 'but if it'll put your mind at rest, then go for it.'

Just before Dad disappeared through the door, I asked him a question: 'Did you really clean off all the black mould in the cellar? It must have all come back if you did because there's loads down there.'

'Oh God,' Mum said, rolling her eyes, 'you're not banging on about the mould again, are you? I think we need to ban that word in this house.'

'There is a lot down there,' Kieran said.

'Oh don't you start on about it as well,' Mum said.

'But there *is*,' Kieran said, reinforcing his point. 'And there's something else, too.'

He looked at me and I shook my head because I knew what he was going to say.

Don't do it, I thought. *Please don't mention the book.*

'Well,' Mum said, becoming impatient. 'What's this something else that you want to say? Come on, spit it out, for crying out loud. We haven't got all day.'

Kieran looked at me and I shook my head more vehemently this time.

'It's nothing really,' he said to Mum. 'Just that I ... saw a lot of junk down there as well.'

'Thanks for letting us know,' she said, 'but we were already well aware that the cellar needs a good clear out.'

'Okay,' Dad said, 'enough delays; I'm going to check the pipework. And the black mould.' He focused his attention on me and added: 'Just so I can keep a certain little girl happy.'

I could feel myself blushing as I said, 'I'm not little anymore.'

Dad gave me a smile, then disappeared down the stairs.

I wanted to tell him to be careful. I wanted to tell him not to touch the black mould. And I wanted to tell him to stay well away from the cupboard with the magic book and all those jars of ingredients. But, of course, I knew that any warnings would be ignored.

'Right, you pair,' Mum said, 'get yourselves upstairs and change into your pyjamas. You've got a big day ahead of you so you need an early night.'

Kieran and I didn't need to be told twice. We were thankful for a chance to distance ourselves from the situation and scurried to our rooms with eagerness. Once I'd changed into my PJs, I went to see Kieran in his room.

'If you could knock before entering, it would be nice,' he said, grimacing as he struggled to get his top on.

'Sorry,' I said indignantly, 'but you're usually quicker than me.'

'Yeah, well, my arm is still hurting so I'm not doing anything quick at the moment.'

'You need to take some more painkillers.'

'I will.'

He was still struggling to pull on the top, so I offered to help.

'Thanks but no thanks,' he said, finally managing to do it.

After a few seconds of uncomfortable silence, I said, 'We did the right thing not telling Mum and Dad about the book.'

'Really? Why is that? If we show them the book, it might go some way to making them believe that this place is cursed, that this place is haunted.'

'I very much doubt it. They'd just dismiss it as some hocus pocus rubbish and most likely throw the book in the bin. And we don't need to be brainiacs to know what sort of problems that might cause. I suppose you'd be wanting to tell them about the tree as well. They'll think you're going cuckoo, like me.'

Kieran's harsh expression softened as he took a moment to process my reasoning. And then he said, 'D'you know what, maybe throwing the book in the bin could be the best thing to do. If we anger the witch, then something big might happen. Something that'll wake Mum and Dad up to what's going on here.'

'Something that might get somebody hurt.'

'Somebody already *has* been hurt,' Kieran said, touching his arm. 'All the time we're here, things are going to get worse, no matter what happens. Why drag it out when we know there's an option to get our blind parents to see what we're seeing and feel what we're feeling.'

What he was saying made sense – to a certain degree. But I was still scared of the immediate consequences.

'I don't think it would be a good idea,' I said. 'It's a little bit too … extreme.'

'So what do we do then?'

'I don't know.'

Rolling his eyes, Kieran made for the door.

'Where are you going?'

'To get a drink. All this talk of witches and the prospect of school in the morning has got my thirst up.'

School …

I should have been a lot more worried about my first day than I was. But that worry was being overshadowed by the weird goings-on in our new house. I wondered what would happen next. What manner of strangeness would plague my brother and me? Noticing a big splodge of black mould on the ceiling, by the light, I knew it would be something to do with *that* stuff. Once again, Dad had apparently scrubbed it all away and yet here was some right above me that I was sure hadn't been there five minutes before.

No way was I going to sleep with any mould in my room, so I sneaked downstairs and into the kitchen. Mum and Dad were watching TV in the living room again, with the door partially closed. I could see them through the crack. Mum said to Dad that she wasn't surprised that he hadn't found anything wrong with the pipes in the cellar and he replied that he wasn't surprised either. Despite what they were discussing, they seemed engrossed in a TV programme and thus distracted.

After retrieving some bleach, some rags and a carrier bag from beneath the sink, I went back to my room and looked up at the mould. Just being near it gave me chills. I was tempted to ask Dad to clean it off, but I didn't want to interrupt whatever program he and Mum were watching, because she would probably get shirty about it. Nope: I had to take a deep breath and deal with this myself. And the sooner the better, before any bravery I felt evaporated away.

Positioning a chair beneath the mould, I poured a good amount of bleach onto a rag and set to work. I didn't hesitate. I just got on with it. The mould smeared across the ceiling as I rubbed the rag over the affected area. *Any second now it's going to come alive and reach out for me*, I thought. *Latch onto my arm like a leech.* But it didn't. I had to use three rags to get it all off. As soon as I'd finished, I put them all in the bag, tied it up, took it outside and dumped it in the bin.

When I came back inside, Mum was waiting in the hallway. She had her hands on her hips and a curious look on her face.

'Oh poop,' I muttered.

'And what pray tell have you been up to this time?' she enquired. 'Why were you outside?' Before I could answer, she began wrinkling her nose and sniffing at the air. 'And why can I smell bleach?'

The truth, I thought – *just tell the truth*: 'Dad said he'd cleaned off all the black mould in my bedroom, but he hadn't. There was a big splodge on the ceiling, so I've just gotten rid of it myself.'

'Bleach is dangerous stuff. If you get it in your eyes, it can blind you.'

'I know that. And that's why I was careful.'

Dad appeared behind Mum, looking inquisitive. 'What's dangerous?' he asked.

Mum told him what I'd been up to.

'I scrubbed every inch of your bedroom not more than four hours ago,' Dad said, 'so there can't be any in there.'

'Well there was,' I said, a little more forcefully than intended. 'I can show you the rag I used to clean it off, if you don't believe me?'

'No one's calling you a liar,' Dad said. 'I just can't see how there could be any when I've been so thorough.'

'You told me you'd cleaned it all off in the cellar,' I added, 'but there's loads down there.'

'Yes, I know,' Dad replied. He shook his head and gave me an apologetic look.

I knew what he was going to say next, so I said it for him: 'You haven't cleaned any of it off, have you?'

Dad shook his head and offered an explanation: 'Since we've moved in I've been so busy. Me and your mother have been run off our feet with one thing and another. You understand, yeah?'

No, I didn't. Okay, he had been busy – I appreciated that – but he knew how scared I was of the black mould and yet he'd just left it all down there to fester and spread.

'I don't like being lied to,' I said, 'especially by my parents.'

'Like you've never told a lie before,' Mum put in with a roll of her eyes.

'Yes, but I'm a child,' was my response.

'Too right you are,' Mum said. 'And that's something you should always remember. Now, with that in mind, why don't you get yourself off to bed and get an early night. You've got your big day tomorrow, you and your brother.'

Like I needed reminding.

Oh, and a nice deflection tactic there, I thought: *changing the subject.* But I wasn't going to let her change the subject that easily.

'When are you going to wake up to the fact that there's something wrong with this house?' I asked my parents. 'When are you going to realise that the black mould we've got growing here isn't *normal* black mould. It's ...' I was about to say cursed, but I knew my parents would just scoff at any such remark. Just like they'd scoff if I were to mention the word witch or that there was a tree in the garden that liked taking swipes at people with its branches. That sort of weirdness needed to be witnessed to be believed; especially by doubters like my parents.

'It's what?' Dad asked me. He cocked his head to one side and gave me a curious look. 'What were you going to say, sweetheart?'

'Nothing,' I said, shrugging. 'Nothing that'll change your mind about anything – and that's for sure.'

'Still continuing with the silliness, I see,' Mum said, shaking her head. 'The longer this goes on, the more worried I'm getting about you. Maybe some counselling will help sort out that messed up head of yours.'

'Are you trying to say I'm mad?' I said.

'No,' Mum said. 'We're not trying to say that at all.'

'People who are losing their marbles go to see head shrinks,' I remarked.

Dad said, 'That's not true. Those sorts of people are just there to help others who are struggling.'

They really think I'm going mad, I thought. Lost for words, I just stood there with my head slumped. And I would have felt very alone if it hadn't been for Kieran putting his arm around me and lending his support.

'I will have to agree with my sis here,' he said to Mum and Dad. 'Something is definitely not right with this house. Weird things are happening around us and you pair haven't got a clue about it all.'

'Oh dear,' Dad said. 'Not you as well.'

'You pair!' Mum said. She seemed more concerned about the way Kieran was talking to her and Dad than anything else. 'The madness is catching in this house. Let's hope it doesn't spread any further.'

'When you say weird things,' Dad said, giving Kieran and me a strange look, 'what exactly do you mean?'

'Well ...' Kieran said, glancing sideways at me.

My expression conveyed one clear message: be careful what you say.

'Well,' Kieran said, beginning again, 'there's the black mould for starters. You've got to admit that it's a bit creepy how it keeps coming back, even though you keep scrubbing it off.'

'I don't want to hear the words "black mould" any more,' Mum said. 'Yes, it's a little odd; I will grant you that much ...'

'Yay!' I said, clapping my hands. 'Finally, a breakthrough.'

'Please don't interrupt me while I'm talking,' Mum said, giving me an icy stare. 'You know that's the sort of thing I won't tolerate.' She composed herself, then continued. 'Now, back to what I was saying. It is odd how the mould keeps coming back, but make no mistake, me and your father are going to get to the bottom of this matter. There is a rational explanation for everything and this is no different.'

'So what's this rational explanation?' I asked.

'I don't know yet,' Mum said, getting more and more agitated. 'We'll figure it out, though. And then you and your brother will laugh about it when you realize how silly you've been.'

We won't be laughing about anything, I thought. *I can assure you of that, mother.*

'And,' Mum added, brightening a little, 'we'll get another expert out for a second opinion on the problem. Clearly the man from Bergin's either didn't know what he was talking about or he's missed something obvious.'

'I'm going to give the house a thorough check over before we go to bed,' Dad said. 'Then perhaps we'll all be able to sleep a little easier.'

I won't, I thought. 'And does this check involve removing the mould in the cellar?' I asked him.

'It's a bit late for taking on a job of *that* magnitude,' Dad said.

All I could manage to say in response was, 'Oh.'

'Right-e-oh,' Mum said, clapping her hands together and looking happy with herself, as if the conversation we'd just had would remedy all our problems. 'Why don't you and your brother get yourselves a hot mug of Ovaltine each whilst me and your father go on a mould hunt.'

Shoulders slumped and feeling deflated, I followed Kieran into the kitchen and began making the drinks.

'Well,' Kieran moaned, whilst pouring milk into two mugs, 'looks like they're both still as clueless as ever.' He put the mugs in the microwave and set it running. 'Clueless clueless clueless.'

'Couldn't have said it better myself.'

'D'you know what, I hope the walls are covered in black mould in the morning. Then Mum and Dad will be forced to admit that something supernatural is going on here. Surely they would come to no other conclusion.'

'Oh, I'm sure they'd find some "rational explanation" for it.'

'There's nothing rational about what's going on here.'

'I know you're worried about the mould, but I'm just as worried about what's happening out in our garden. I keep thinking about that tree and what it did to me.' Kieran's hand moved instinctively to his arm and he began to rub.

'Is it hurting bad?' I asked him.

'Just a little. I need to take some more painkillers before I go to bed.'

The microwave hummed for another thirty seconds, then pinged loud enough to make Kieran and me jump.

'My nerves are shredded,' I said.

'Mine, too,' Kieran said as he finished making the drinks.

For the sake of our nerves, I decided that a change of subject would be a good idea.

'I bet some of the boys from your new football team will go to the same school as us,' I said, taking a sip from my mug of steaming hot Ovaltine. 'So you'll already know some people on your first day.'

'I never thought of that.' Kieran managed a smile.

'You'll be popular before you've even started.'

My brother liked the sound of that. 'I was never one of the popular kids at our last school, so that would make a nice change.'

Neither of us was popular, I thought. *And I can't see anything being different at the new school. Not for me, at least.*

We continued talking about this and that, until eventually our parents came through and declared the house to be a mould free zone.

'I'm quite pleased to tell you that we didn't find that much,' Dad said. 'Just the odd bit dotted here and there.'

'Oh well that's good,' I said with zero enthusiasm. 'I guess we can just forget about the cellar then.'

Mum said, 'Your father already told that there's too much down there and that it's too late to tackle it. Honestly, Ella, what do you think will happen? Is the mould going to come alive in the night and start stalking you or something?'

The look on my face must have told her that that was *exactly* what I thought might happen.

'I'll not hear another word on the subject,' Mum said in a tone which suggested that any further discussion on the subject would be met with a harsh response. 'But I will show you what I can do.'

Taking a skeleton-like key from off the shelf, she marched into the hallway and all of us followed. Standing beside the cellar door, she put the key in the lock and turned it.

'There,' she said, smiling and looking pleased with herself, 'Problem solved. Now nothing can get in or out.'

'Seriously?' I muttered. Did she really think that would stop the mould from escaping?

'Yes,' Mum said. 'Seriously.'

Kieran gave a shake of his head but said nothing.

'I'll make that room a priority by the end of the week,' Dad said. 'I promise.'

That was nowhere near soon enough as far as I was concerned.

'Right,' Mum said, 'I don't want to hear another word about any of this silliness.' She clapped her hands together in a brisk one-two. 'Finish your drinks, you pair, and then get yourselves off to bed.'

Kieran gulped his down, but I left mine. Then we both did as Mum had instructed.

Before we disappeared into our bedrooms, however, we had a chat on the landing.

'No way am I sleeping on my own tonight,' Kieran said. 'After Mum and Dad are in bed, I'm coming in with you. I'll crash out on the floor.'

'Oh how things have changed in such a short space of time,' I said, smirking. 'Last night it was me begging to sleep in your bedroom and now it's the other way round.'

'Yeah well I didn't believe you then but I do now.'

'Things have a funny way of flipping around, don't they?' I said, still smirking.

'So you want to be on your own tonight?'

I most definitely did not. 'I'd feel safer with you around, I'll admit.'

'There you go then. We'll *both* feel safer.'

'Mum has a habit of getting up in the night for a wee. She also has a habit of checking on us before she goes back to bed. She'll want to know why you're on my floor. You know that, don't you?'

'I'll tell her that a witch has cursed this house and that I don't feel safe on my own.'

'Don't be silly.'

'It doesn't really matter what I say to her; she won't believe me.'

That was true. 'Best hope she doesn't get the urge then, eh?'

'Yes, let's just hope.'

Even though I had opened the window in my bedroom, the smell of bleach was still thick enough in the air to make my nose twitch. So I decided to stay up for a bit and continue on with the book that my Dad had been so eager for me to read: the one with the purple dragon on the cover.

Sitting up in bed, with some cushions behind my back, I opened the book and began to read. I got through a few pages before my progress was disturbed.

Dad stuck his head around the door and asked why I wasn't tucked up in bed with the light off.

'Because of the smell of bleach,' I explained.

'Ah, yes, it does still stink in here,' he said, sniffing at the air. 'Sorry about that. You've opened a window, I see. I should have done that myself.' He apologized again. 'How daft is your Dad, eh?'

'The daftest ever,' I said, smiling.

'Nice to see that you're still reading that book I recommended. Are you enjoying it?'

'Seems good so far.'

'Well there you go; I told you it was going to be a winner.' He looked around the room, pointing here and there. 'All clear. Spotless. Not a speck in sight.'

I wanted to make a bet with him: a hundred pounds that it would be back by morning. Not that I had a hundred pounds, of course; I was just confident that the black stuff would return quickly. *Unnaturally* quickly. I never offered the bet, however, as I knew what reaction it would be met with.

'Let's just hope it stays all clear,' I said.

Dad gave me a troubled look. One that suggested he was worried about me.

'Me and your mother are going to bed ourselves in a bit,' he said. 'We're only across the hall, so there's no need to be concerned.'

I didn't want to say that I wasn't concerned because he would have known I was lying. So I just smiled and nodded and said, 'Okay.'

'Give it ten minutes and it should be fine,' Dad said, nodding towards the window. 'Just don't go nodding off without shutting it, otherwise you'll catch a chill.'

'I won't,' I assured him.

He went to pull the door shut as he was leaving the room, then realised his mistake.

'You're going to want this left wide open, aren't you?' he said, making sure that it was.

'Yes, please.'

'Okay, sweetheart.'

After he was gone I resumed reading. And after every page I looked around the room, checking the walls and ceiling. *It won't come back yet*, I thought. *It'll wait until I'm asleep. It'll start creeping down the wall behind me and …*

'No no no,' I said, trying to banish these thoughts as I instinctively checked over my shoulder.

The longer I was on my own, the more concerned I was getting. And the more eager I was becoming for my parents to go to bed so that Kieran would come through. That was assuming he *was* going to come through, of course. Part of me was thinking that he might have changed his mind, or just nodded off as he was lying there in bed, waiting for our parents' bedroom door to click shut.

We didn't have to wait long for that to happen, though. About five minutes later, I heard them coming up the stairs, discussing something or other. After they'd both finished in the bathroom, Dad came through again to check on me.

'Still reading that book, I see,' he said.

'Yep, it's got me hooked,' I replied, exaggerating. It was good, but it wasn't *that* good.

He sniffed at the air and gave a satisfied nod. 'Smells nearly all clear in here now. Okay if I shut this?' he said, moving towards the window.

I sniffed at the air and couldn't smell much either. 'Yes, that's fine.'

Dad clicked the window shut, then kissed me on my forehead. 'Time to put this aside as well,' he said, folding my book shut and placing it on the bedside table. 'And just remember, your mother and I are just across the hallway.'

'I know,' I said. 'Thanks, Dad.'

He tipped me a wink and then switched off the light. Thankful for the glow from the hallway, I slipped down under the covers and watched his shadow disappear from the doorway. As I lay there, trying to relax, I kept expecting to hear a clicking sound and for that glow to disappear.

He knows, I thought. *He knows I'm still scared and that's why he's left the light on.*

A rush of affection spread through me as I thought about him. My good old Dad: caring and affectionate, as always. I knew Mum cared about me too, but she guarded her affections behind her tough exterior. I think her father – my granddad – was quite strict with her when she was young, which explains why she was the way she was.

Silence descended in the house as everyone cosied up in their beds. After twenty minutes passed and there was no sign of Kieran, I got out of bed so I could see what he was up to. *Most probably sleeping and snoring his head off*, I thought as I turned on my bedside lamp and tiptoed across the room.

Reaching the doorway, however, I stopped abruptly as a face appeared in front of mine, scaring me half to death. I let out a gasp of surprise as Kieran smiled at me, then gestured for me to keep quiet. He had his duvet wrapped around his shoulders and his pillow clutched in his hands.

Composing myself, I went back into my bedroom and Kieran shuffled along behind me. He looked around, checking out the walls and the ceiling.

'I've checked everywhere,' I said. 'There isn't any.'

'None in my room either. Although I can still smell the bleach, even though Dad opened the window. It's lingering in my nostrils.'

Fortunately, I don't have a good sense of smell, otherwise I was sure it would be lingering in mine too.

'Should we keep this open or closed?' he said in a low voice, referring to the door.

'You probably won't be able to keep your trap shut,' I replied, also keeping my voice low, 'so I would close it.'

Kieran pushed the door soundlessly shut.

Then darkness sucked in around us as I turned off the bedside light and got back into bed.

'You're in for an uncomfortable night,' I said, 'sleeping on the floor.'

'I could crash out on a window ledge and get a good night's kip,' he replied, stretching out on the floor and getting himself comfortable. 'Well, usually I can. But there's this small matter of our house being cursed that might get in the way of any decent shut-eye tonight. That and my shoulder still hurting me. Oh, and let's not forget about our first day at school tomorrow.'

'How could I forget.'

'Hey, do you think we should sleep with the light on? If any of the black stuff comes back in the night, we won't be able to see it.'

'If Mum notices that my light is on, she'll definitely come to investigate,'

'Yeah, yeah, that's true. But then if she gets up for a wee, she'll probably pop her head around the door anyway. So we may as well sleep with it on, right?'

I couldn't deny that it would make me feel safer. 'Okay,' I said, turning the bedside light back on.

Kieran snuggled under his duvet and said, 'In the night, if you notice anything weird, or hear anything weird, just wake me up.'

I assured him that I would.

Snuggling under my own covers, I closed my eyes and tried to relax. But then Kieran began talking again: telling me about a TV show he'd watched on Netflix that was funny.

'You should check it out,' he said. 'It'll have you in stitches.'

'I will,' I replied, turning on my side to face away from him. 'But first I need shut-eye.'

A few minutes passed before he spoke again.

'Sis, are you still awake?' he asked.

'Yes,' I replied irritably, 'I am.'

'Do you think we should take it in turns to sleep? One of us could keep a lookout while the other gets some rest. Whaddaya reckon?'

I gave this some thought, then replied: 'Sounds like a good idea in theory, but I know what'll happen. You'll fall asleep when it's your watch.'

'No I won't.'

'Yes, you will.'

'No I won't.'

'Yes, you will. And you know you *will*. You're an expert at snoring your head off, so who are you trying to fool?'

'Keep your voice down. Mum and Dad will hear.'

I agreed with him. 'Yeah, you're right; let's keep quiet.'

Another minute or so passed before Kieran spoke up again. 'Fine ... fine ... we'll just let the black mould get us then.'

'Okay, we'll do it your way. We'll take turns keeping watch. But you can go first.'

His delay in replying suggested he did not like the sound of *that*.

'How come I have to go first?' he said.

'You want to prove to me that you can stay awake, so ... prove it.'

'I can prove it after *you* prove it.'

'Ha-ha. Now it's you who needs to keep your voice down.'

'Oh God, I give up with you, I really do. You never believe me when I tell you something.'

'No I don't. I know you too well.'

Three or four minutes passed before Kieran spoke again. 'Okay ... okay, have it your way. I'll pull the first shift. Two hours and then we change over, yeah?'

'Sounds good to me,' I said, trying to hold back a smile. I noted the time on my bedside clock, then turned it so it was facing him. 'It's ten-thirty now, so you wake me up at twelve-thirty and I'll take over.'

'I will. On the dot.'

Of course you will, I thought, knowing full well what would happen.

Sure enough, a short while later, the sound of snoring filled my ears.

It was bad enough having the light on and trying to sleep, never mind having *that* racket in my earholes. But did I really want to sleep anyway? I wasn't sure. The thought of waking up with black mould creeping down the wall next to me was not something which made me want to close my eyes. But what would my first day at school be like if I had no sleep at all? I imagined myself being like a zombie: sitting in class, sporting a dazed expression and not being able to take in anything. The last thing I wanted to do, if I could avoid it, was make a fool of myself.

Turning onto my back, I stared up at the ceiling and tried to steer my thoughts away from everything that was stressing me. But it was no good. In the dead of the night, fear and worry were beginning to grip me. For a long time – or what felt like a long time – I laid there, listening to Kieran's snoring.

Part of me was glad of the noise because it broke the silence. And part of me wanted to poke him in his earhole because he was annoying the heck out of me with his constant droning noise.

I'm not sure how long I laid there before sleep finally took me. An hour, maybe two. But when I woke, darkness greeted me. For a second my thoughts were a blank canvas and I'd forgotten everything that was troubling me. Then I remembered that the light should have been on and that the room should have been bathing in a reassuring glow.

Mum must have turned it off, I thought. If that had been the case, however, then why was Kieran still snoring his head off on the floor? She would have created a fuss and most likely woke me up whilst ejecting him from my room. Had Kieran grown tired of the constant glow above his head and switched off the light himself, I wondered. Somehow, I didn't think so. It would take a lot more than that to get him out from under his duvet in the dead of night, I figured. Had there been a power cut? That was possible. The light in the hallway wasn't on either. The only thing illuminating the darkness was the dim green glow from my battery powered digital clock.

Reaching out, I located the switch on my bedside lamp and flipped it. Light bathed the room, making me blink and squint.

Not a power cut, then. If that were the case, the light would have come on when the power had been restored. So who, or what, had turned off the light? *You know the answer to that question*, I thought as I got back into bed and once again cosied up under my covers. I checked out the walls and the ceiling. No sign of any black mould. Yet. How long before it came for me, I wondered. How long before *she* brought it back?

'Me and my family have done nothing to hurt you,' I said in a hushed voice, 'so why do you want to hurt us?'

I listened and waited for a reply that didn't come.

The temperature in the room seemed to have dropped a few degrees, making it even colder than normal.

'All we want to do is live here and be happy,' I added. 'It's not our fault that you lost your house, so why punish us? *Why?*'

I waited again for a reply. And then one came ...

'Who are you talking to?' Kieran said groggily, looking up at me with half-closed eyes. 'Can you keep the noise down, please!'

'I'm *trying* to communicate with the dead. Did you turn the light off?'

'No.'

'Well somebody did.'

'Probably Mum.'

I explained why that couldn't have been the case.

'Oh, yeah,' Kieran agreed. 'Fair point.' He glanced around the room, his eyes still partly shut, no doubt checking for signs of black mould. 'So, did you get a reply?'

'A reply from what?'

'You told me you were trying to communicate with the dead. Did you get a reply?'

'No. But I bet she heard every word I said. I bet she hears everything we say. All of us. I feel like I'm being watched all the time. Do you?'

'Not when I'm asleep, I don't.'

'Oh so sorry for waking you. And speaking of sleep, you nodded off during your watch. Just like I knew you would.'

'I didn't nod off. I was just … resting my eyes.'

'Whilst making snoring noises.'

'Just for effect.'

'Yeah, right.'

'Have you had much sleep?'

'A bit. About an hour, maybe. What time is it?'

Kieran propped himself up on one elbow and squinted at the digital clock's display. 'It's five to one. Dead of the night.'

'Looks like I'm going to have to stay awake all night,' I said, sitting up in bed with my pillow propped behind my back for support. 'I don't think I'll ever sleep again, the way things are going.'

'Don't be daft. Everyone needs sleep.'

'What you need and what you get are two different things.'

'Now you're talking daft.'

'Coming from you, I'll take that as an insult.'

'Thanks,' Kieran said, feigning hurt feelings. He yawned, his mouth stretching wider than seemed possible. 'Well, good luck with getting no sleep. You'll be like a zombie in no time at all. Brrr – it's chilly in here. This house feels like a fridge at times.'

'Hmm, I wonder why that could be. How can you get any shut-eye when you know what's going on in this place?' I said, dumbfounded. 'How can you even relax?'

'Look, sis, if this witch wants to kill us or hurt us, do you think we'll be able to stop her? We're just a pair of regular kids with no idea how to battle someone with supernatural powers.'

I couldn't believe what I was hearing. 'So what are you saying? That we just do nothing and hope for the best? That doesn't sound like the intelligent option to me.'

'And what other option is there?'

'Err … I dunno … perhaps we should find a way to lift the curse that's on this place. Wouldn't that be a good place to start?'

'That's just the problem, though, isn't it? Where *do* we start?'

'That book of dark spells in the cellar might give us some answers.'

'I thought you didn't want anything to do with that book.'

'I don't. But the more I think about it, the more I'm sure that we at least need to give it a browse through. Plus, there's the magic shop in Pickleworth. I can't wait to speak to the old lady that runs that place. I'm sure she'll have some suggestions about what to do. Are you coming with me after school?'

'Yeah, of course. But what if she can't help us and neither can the book?'

'We could always burn the house down, I suppose.'

'That's illegal. And it would leave us homeless.'

'I was just joking.'

We talked for a while longer, until both of us ran out of things to say. Then Kieran went back to sleep, leaving me once again awake on my own. I was sure that I wouldn't be able to sleep myself, not after the light had been mysteriously turned off, but I did nod off again sometime later.

When I next woke, not only did darkness greet me again, but this time someone or something was poking me in the side. Through the groggy haze of sleep, I could make out a voice saying something or other. Then I realised it was Kieran.

'Wake up,' he said poking me in the side again. 'Can you hear that, sis? Wake up!'

'Hear what?' I replied, propping myself up on one elbow and looking around with concern. 'The light's off again.'

'Yeah, I know. But that's not all. Listen.'

I listened. And I heard nothing.

'What am I supposed to be hearing?' I enquired.

'Shhh!' he said. 'Be quiet or we might not hear it.'

And then we did hear it: a flapping sound, like that of beating wings. It was coming from above us.

'Oh no, not that again,' I said, looking towards the ceiling. 'I was hoping I'd imagined hearing those sounds last night. Obviously I wasn't. I thought Mum and Dad had gotten rid of those things.'

'Who says that it's bats this time?' Kieran said. I could just make out the concerned expression on his face in the glow from the digital clock. 'Could be a bird or something.'

'Could be. I don't think it is, though.'

'Why do you say that?'

'Just a hunch, based on everything else that's been happening around here.'

'Yeah, fair point,' Kieran conceded.

We heard more flapping again. And clicking.

'Sounds like there's a lot of them up there,' I said. 'Now why do I get the impression that this has something to do with you know who.'

'The witch?' You think she made them come back?'

'I'd lay money on it.'

I could feel my innards tightening at the prospect of what might happen next in our new house. How many more surprises did Maud have in store for us? And how long before things turned nasty?

'Should we wake Mum and Dad?' Kieran asked. 'I don't think they'd be angry if we did.'

'No, I can't see any point; there'll just tell us that we're not in any danger and to ignore any noises.'

'Are we in danger?'

'Not as long as they stay up there and we stay down here.'

'I have no intentions of going into the attic to see what's going on. If you want to take a gander, then that's on you – but you'll be on your own, just so you know.'

'Nice to know you've got my back, my dearest brother.'

I got out of bed and made my way across the room. Finding the light switch with my fingertips, I flipped it then squinted because of the sudden flood of brightness.

'Did the bats turn the light off, do you think?' Kieran asked.

'Anything seems possible at the moment,' I replied.

We heard movement on the landing. Footsteps coming towards my room.

Oh God, I thought, *here we go.*

Mum or Dad? Hopefully Dad ...

I shot Kieran a concerned look and he shot me one back.

Then Mum came through the doorway. Hands on hips, she glared at both of us.

'What's going on here?' she demanded to know. 'What are you up to?' she asked me. 'And what are you doing down there?' she said, directing her question at Kieran.

'Err ...' Kieran replied, lost for words. 'I'm ... err ... just bunking in with Ella because she's a bit scared.'

I wanted to say that I wasn't (even though I was). And Kieran had probably just come up with the best excuse – which wasn't a lie – so I decided to roll with it.

'Yeah,' I said, 'he's just in here with me 'cause I feel a little on edge, is all.'

'Oh what a load of rubbish!' Mum said. 'You pair are just having a laugh. And you've just woke me up with all your chitchat. Honestly, what can you possibly find to talk about at this time of the night?'

Well, there's the small matter of the house being cursed, I thought, *and everything that's happening because of that.* But I said, 'It's our first day at the new school, so we've been chatting about that.'

She pointed to the watch on her slender wrist and tapped the screen. 'It already *is* tomorrow. And you pair need to be out of bed in a few hours, so what have you got to say about that?'

Neither of us responded. Both of us bowed our heads and sported sheepish looks.

'Right, come on,' Mum said, beckoning Kieran up off the floor, 'get back to your own room now, before I lose my patience.'

Snatching up his duvet and pillow, Kieran did as he was told.

But as he was passing Mum, he decided to enlighten her about the noises in the attic.

'The bats must be back,' he said. 'Either that or something else is flapping about up there. Have you heard it?'

'No, I haven't,' Mum replied. She shook her head and sighed. 'Great, that's all we need.' She urged Kieran through the doorway. 'Well, whatever it is, we'll deal with it tomorrow; it's too late to be worrying about anything other than sleep.' She levelled a finger at me and then my bed. 'You get back in there and I don't want to hear another murmur. Got it?'

'Got it,' I said, jumping back in bed and slipping under the covers.

My heart sunk as Mum turned off the light and then closed the door, plunging the room into darkness. I heard Mum say something to Kieran and him say something back; then another click of a light switch made the glow at the bottom of the door disappear. Two doors closed shut.

And then there was silence …

Tempted as I was to switch the main light back on – or even my bedside one – I didn't bother for two reasons: one, I knew that Mum would hear the *click!* (she has superhuman hearing, I'm sure); and, two, I knew that daylight was due to break soon, in an hour or so. I figured I could hold on for that long, if I kept my wits about me.

There were no more noises from the attic that night. And at about six-thirty, when enough light had crept into the day, I got up and gave my room a thorough inspection. I found no traces of black mould, which was rather surprising given how it had kept coming back when it'd been cleaned off before.

I had a scary thought: *when things do go bad, they'll go bad quickly*. I had a hunch that this would be the case, so I needed to be ready. But before I could deal with that problem, there was the small matter of my first day at school to take care of.

Whilst I was eating breakfast in the kitchen with Kieran, Dad came in dressed in his suit, all smiling and jovial.

'So,' he said, tossing his newspaper onto the sideboard, 'are we all ready then, you pair? Raring to go?'

I was most definitely not "raring to go", but I replied, 'Yeah, it's going to be a blast.'

'And what about you?' Dad said to Kieran. 'You up for today, son?'

'Like Ella said,' Kieran replied through a mouthful of toast, 'it's going to be a blast.'

'I'm detecting a distinct lack of enthusiasm here,' Dad said.

'I'll let you know how enthusiastic I feel later on today,' I said. '*After* school.'

'I can imagine how nerve-racking it must be,' Dad said, giving us a supportive nod and smile. 'But you'll both make friends and settle in quickly, I bet you. I look forward to hearing about it all when I get in from work.'

'And so do I,' Mum said, appearing behind him, sporting a rare smile of her own. 'Just be nice to people and they'll be nice to you.'

It's never that simple, I thought. *Not at school.*

Mum began fussing over Kieran and me: badgering us to finish our food, then badgering us to get dressed in our new uniforms, then badgering us to be out of the house on time.

My parents had made arrangements to go into work a bit later so they could see us off at the front door.

Before we left, however, Dad had something to say about the bat situation. 'Your mother told me about what you heard last night. I've contacted Renshaw's, who got rid of them before, and they're going to deal with the situation, they've assured us.

You'll also be pleased to know that I've checked around the house and there's been no new black mould during the night, so perhaps we're finally getting a handle on that nastiness.'

I very much doubted that would be the case, but I just smiled and thanked him for being such an attentive father.

'Oh, and me your mother won't be back 'till later this evening,' Dad informed us, 'because we've got some business to take care of.'

'Okay,' I said.

As Kieran and I walked along the main road which ran through Plumpton Sudsbry, we talked about the previous night.

'I must admit,' Kieran said, 'I thought it was going be a lot worse than it was.'

'Lights turning off and flapping noises in the attic: that's scary enough for me, thanks.'

'No new mould, though; that's gotta be a good thing, though, right?'

'We'll see.'

'You need to try and be more positive, you know. Maybe the curse is wearing off, losing strength. Or maybe Maud has decided that we aren't the enemy and is cutting us a break by only giving us slight scares rather than hair-raisers.'

'Do you have any idea how ridiculous that sounds?'

'Which part?'

'All of it. The curse isn't going to wear off and Maud isn't cutting us a break. I think last night was the lull before the storm.'

'Really? How can you know that?'

'I don't know it for sure; it's just a … hunch.'

'Well, for our sakes, I hope your hunch is wrong.' As we continued to walk, Kieran glanced at me sideways, studying me. 'You look shattered? Did you get any sleep at all last night?'

'Not much. A few hours.'

'I'm surprised Mum or Dad didn't pull you up about how zonked you look.'

'I did my best to be alert and with it when they were around. Especially with Mum. But, still, yeah, I'm surprised she didn't say anything.'

The school loomed ahead in the distance: an old Gothic-style building with a steeply pitched roof and several square-shaped turrets. It was quite a spooky-looking place. The sort of place you wouldn't want to hang around in after dark. The sort of place that might have ghosts.

We heard footsteps behind us. And then someone tapped Kieran on his shoulder.

'Way-hay!' a boy said, appearing at his side. 'Well, if it isn't the young Ronaldo himself. Nice to see you again, mate. How's it hanging?'

'Good, good,' Kieran said. He was as pleased to see the boy as the boy was to see him. 'I'll be a lot better when I get my first day out of the way, though. That's for sure.'

'Nothing to fret about,' the boy said, walking with us. 'Don't worry; I'll look after you. You can hang around with my gang. They're all good lads and you'll know some of them from football.'

Kieran nodded towards the boy. 'This is Nick,' he said. 'Can you remember him from Sunday? He was the one tearing down the wing and whipping the ball in for me so I could get my shots in.'

'I remember,' I said, giving Nick a polite smile. 'Pleased to meet you.'

'Pleased to meet you, too,' Nick replied. He slid his rucksack off his back, then unzipped it and pulled out a football. 'Hey, d'you wanna do some passes?' he asked Kieran.

My brother didn't need asking twice. He gestured Nick to roll the ball in front of him. And then that was it: the two of them ran off ahead of me, passing the ball to one another as they went.

Wish I had a friend on my first day before I even got through the gate, I thought miserably. *Oh, and thanks for leaving me on my own, Kieran. Don't worry, I'll be all right.*

As if reading my mind, he stopped and looked back at me. He raised a hand, enquiring if I was okay, and I raised mine back, telling him that I was. Then he continued on his way, passing the ball back and forth to Nick.

A flush of guilt washed over me for being so quick to judge him. Kieran was just excited to see his friend again. He had only forgotten about me for a matter of seconds and hadn't done it on purpose. I would probably have forgotten about me too if I was in his position.

As I got closer to the school, I felt more and more nervous. Other kids were passing me now: groups of them talking to each other and laughing at each other's jokes. *Or maybe they're laughing at me,* I thought solemnly, wishing that Kieran was still with me.

I took an interest in my new black shoes as I passed through the big iron gate at the front of the school. I didn't want to attract attention to myself by catching anyone's eye.

In the playground I lingered in a corner, constantly checking my watch to see how much longer I would have to stand around looking like a lost soul. Mum had told me that we would be called in at five to nine and that's exactly what happened. Appearing from a side door, a portly woman in a long flowing floral dress ambled to the centre of the playground and began ringing a large silver bell. She did this for about ten seconds, then began urging those not moving to get themselves inside.

I kept looking around for Kieran, but I couldn't see him. Then, from the other side of the playground, I heard him call my name.

'Come on, sis,' he said, jogging towards me. 'We don't want to be late in on our first day.'

The portly woman overheard this and ambled towards us. 'First day, did you say? You'll want to make your way to the headmaster's office, if that's the case.' She gave us directions, then urged us to get a move on. 'Go on – chop, chop! Mr Williams will sort you out. Go on – off you trot!' As we did as we were told, she continued ringing her bell and calling out to any stragglers.

Inside, we made our way along the main corridor.

'Hope I'm in the same form as Nick,' Kieran said.

'I don't care who I'm with as long as they're nice.'

Boys and girls rushed past us in both directions, eager to get to their form classes before registration was called. Their voices echoed off the walls around us, up and down the narrow space, as did their footsteps.

Outside Mr Williams' office, we stopped and Kieran gave the door a rap with his knuckles. A few seconds later the door opened and a tall man with square glasses perched on his button nose looked down at us with a queer expression on his face.

'Hmm, now I don't recognize you pair,' he said, 'so I'm guessing you're Kieran and Ella, the new starters? Tell me that I'm right?'

'You are,' I said.

'Ah, good, good,' he said, walking off down the corridor. 'Follow me.'

We followed him through doors and along corridors. Up some stairs we went, struggling to keep up with the pace Mr Williams was setting.

'Come on,' he said, gesturing us to get a move on. 'I want to get you where you're going before they all file out for assembly. I would have thought you'd have turned up a bit earlier than this. You know, with you being new and all. It quite clearly stated in the letter we sent you that you should attend school fifteen minutes earlier than normal on your first day.'

Mum never said anything about that, I thought.

Up another set of stairs we went and along a wood-panelled corridor. We stopped outside room 37. Mr Williams opened the door, put a shovel-like hand on Kieran's shoulder and guided him inside. I went to follow and Mr Williams told me to stay right where I was.

What am I doing? I thought, feeling embarrassed. *Of course I'm not in the same form as him!*

Kieran was introduced to the class and his new form tutor, then Mr Williams took me farther along the corridor, to room 43. I don't think I've ever been so nervous as I was at that moment, waiting to be introduced to a bunch of kids I'd never met before. I was convinced that they were all going to laugh at me. But they didn't – only a few did.

'Come on,' Mr Williams said, coaxing me towards the front of the classroom, 'no time to waste, young lady. Get a move on, please.'

On legs that felt like jelly, I looked around at everyone. All the kids were sitting at their desks, staring at me. If a portal to another dimension had opened up next to me, I would have been tempted to jump into it to get away from the situation. If there's one thing I hate, it's being stared at.

Mr Williams introduced me to my new form teacher, Mr Brice. He was a short, stocky man with a receding hairline and the bushiest eyebrows I've ever seen.

'Right-e-o, I'll leave you all to it,' Mr Williams said, giving everyone a nod as he left the room.

After he'd gone, Mr Brice gave me a nod and a smile. Standing at the front of the room, with a black marker in his podgy hand, he told all the kids to say hello and they did. Some were more enthusiastic than others. I was about to say hello back, but then I heard a chuckle from the rear of the room.

No! I thought when I saw who was making the noise – *not you!*

It was the girl from the day before, the bully from the football match: Emma.

In the corner, crouched over her desk, she was glaring at me with a wicked smile on her face. Her friend was seated next to her: the blonde girl named Lisa. She was glaring as well.

My life is about to become hell, I thought.

'If you'd like to take a seat, please,' Mr Brice said, gesturing towards a desk at the rear, which was thankfully on the other side of the room to the nasties.

I looked at the floor as I walked in between the desks. And I would never have believed that something as simple as sitting down could bring *such* relief.

After the business of introducing me was done, Mr Brice began talking about a school trip to a farm which was taking place in a few weeks. As he was telling everyone what needed to be done so they could secure their places, I kept noticing movement out the corner of my eye. Lisa and Emma were leaning forwards, looking past the two kids seated to my left, trying to get my attention. I ignored them because I knew they were trying to goad me. This went on for about a minute or so before Mr Brice noticed what was happening and got involved.

'Emma and Lisa, what *are* you doing?' he said. 'Trying to get someone's attention, are we?' He glanced in my direction, so he must have guessed what was going on.

'We're not doing anything, sir,' Emma responded, slouching at her desk, looking sullen. 'Just listening to what you was saying.'

'Yeah,' Lisa said, backing her up. 'We was just listening, is all.'

'That'd be a first,' Mr Brice said, giving them a cool stare. 'And if you were listening, what did I just say? What did I just tell the class?'

'You was telling everyone to make sure their payments are made by the 25th,' Emma said, sporting a smarmy grin on her bloated face. 'And before that, you was talking about what we need to take with us: a showerproof coat (if we have one); a packed lunch; suitable footwear (ideally Wellington boots) ...'

'Yes, yes,' Mr Brice said, cutting her off. 'Obviously you can multitask: you can muck around *and* listen at the same time. Very good. I'm impressed.'

Emma looked suitably smug. 'Multitasking is what we girls do well,' she said. 'It's in our genetics.'

This got chuckles of laughter from some girls. The boys were unimpressed, though.

'Well I'm so glad you find this amusing,' Mr Brice said, folding his arms across his barrel-like chest. 'But if you ever interrupt me again like this, I'm going to send you home with the biggest pile of homework you've ever seen. Are we clear on this?'

Emma's grin faltered to a slight smile. 'Yes, sir!'

'*Good!*' Mr Brice said, smiling himself.

After he was finished talking about the trip, he called the register. When he said my name, I let out a shrill 'Yes sir!' in a voice that didn't seem like my own. I don't know why I did this – perhaps it was nerves – but the rest of the class thought it was funny.

'She squeaks like that bird from the old cartoon: Tweety Pie,' Emma said, lapping it up.

I tried laughing it off myself: to give the impression that I'd done it on purpose. I still felt like a fool, though.

'Give us another tweety tweet,' Lisa said, giggling away. 'Go on – you know you want to.'

Mr Brice clapped his hands together, appealing for calm. 'Okay, okay, you can all pipe down now, the lot of you.'

'Tweet tweet,' Emma said, through fits of giggles. 'Tweet tweety tweet!'

Everyone roared laughter, which echoed off the walls, seemingly making it louder. This only went on for a matter of seconds, but to me it felt like a lot longer. I wanted to tell the lot of them to shut up, then stomp out of the classroom. I just sat there instead, however, wishing so much that Kieran was with me.

Then Mr Brice smashed his fist down on his desk so hard that it made some of the items on the edge fall to the floor with a clatter.

'*QUIEEEET!*' he bellowed, his face turning a queer shade of purple. 'The next person who makes so much as a murmur will be in detention for a *week!*'

That shut everyone up.

'You,' he said, pointing at Emma, then the door. 'Get outside and I'll deal with you in a minute.'

'What!' she responded, looking confused. 'But why? What have I done?'

'I don't want *any* backchat,' Mr Brice seethed. 'Just do what I've told you to do.'

'I wasn't the only one laughing, though,' Emma protested, 'so why single me out?'

'You started it,' Mr Brice said. 'And quite frankly, I'm getting sick and tired of your behaviour. All the teachers complain about you. You're always causing trouble, you are. Always at the centre of mischief.'

'No I'm not,' Emma protested.

'I'm not arguing with you,' Mr Brice said. 'Just get out!'

Emma stood up so quickly that her chair shot out from behind her and hit the wall. Then she stomped out of the room and banged the door shut behind her.

Shaking his head, Mr Brice let out a sigh and said, 'Now there's a kid with anger issues.'

You don't say, I thought. *I bet she'll blame all that on me.*

And she did.

Later on, after assembly, she caught up with me again. As I was leaving the hall, I heard a kerfuffle behind me. I turned around and saw Emma barging her way through a crowd of kids to get to me. Lisa was with her and two other girls. I didn't recognize either of them. Things were about to get heated, so I looked around to see if any teachers were nearby. Mr Williams was talking to another teacher on the other side of the room, which was too far away for my liking.

'You've got me a weeks' worth of extra homework!' Emma said, shoving me hard enough to rock me back on my heels.

'I haven't got you anything,' I responded. 'You've done that to yourself.'

Emma clenched her hands into fists, so I did the same. I briefly considered turning and fleeing, but I changed my mind. Everyone would think I was a coward and I didn't want *that*. It was better to put up a fight and take a beating. If the worst came to the worst, I was determined to at least blacken one of Emma's eyes. Give her a reminder of what would happen if she decided to mess with me again. But the chances of me giving anyone a black eye was beginning to look slim as Emma's friends fanned out behind her, sporting their best hard girl faces.

'I'm not doing any of the homework Mr Brice gave me,' Emma said.

'Really?' I said. 'Well, you're just going to get in trouble then, aren't you?'

'No, I'm not,' Emma said with a confident look on her face, 'because you're going to do it for me.'

Lots of kids had gathered around by this time, forming a circle around us to see what all the commotion was.

'I'm not doing anything for you,' I said to Emma.

Her face hardened to a scowl. She took a step closer to me and so did her friends. They were all scowling, too.

'Do your own homework,' I said. I could feel a lump forming in my throat. I didn't swallow it down, though, because I didn't want to give away any sign of weakness.

Emma took another step closer to me. Now she was close enough for me to smell her rancid breath – but I didn't back away.

'Say no to me one more time,' she said. 'Go on – I dare you.'

'No,' I said.

A brief look of surprise appeared on Emma's face. She was clearly not used to people standing up to her.

Kieran, I thought, *where are you when I need you the most?*

As if on cue, he appeared through the crowd and muscled his way to the front.

'Got a problem have you, sis?' he said, standing next to me and giving Emma the deadeye.

'Who the heck are you?' she said, looking Kieran up and down. She obviously didn't remember him from the football match.

'Well, he's just called me sis,' I said, 'so that should give you a clue.'

'Don't get cheeky with me!' Emma said. 'I'm not stupid.'

'Could have fooled me,' Kieran said, smiling.

Emma's face went so red that I thought her head was about to explode. 'How dare you!' she said, seething. 'No one's ever talked to me like that, so how *dare* you!'

'You terrorize my sister,' Kieran said, 'and I'll terrorize you.'

'You can try,' Emma said, squaring up to my brother.

I swear she would have hit him had it not been for Mr Williams, who shouldered his way through the crowd, demanding to know what was going on.

'Nothing,' Emma said, edging away from us, 'we're just getting to know the newbies, that's all.'

Mr Williams gave her a doubtful look. 'In my experience, a circle of kids forming around any situation is not usually a good thing; especially when you're involved, Emma Price. The best thing you can do, the best thing you can *all* do,' he said, taking in everybody, 'is *disperse*. Unless you want a good dose of detention, that is.'

Nobody wanted *that*, so the crowd began moving away swiftly.

As Emma barged her way past me, she gave Kieran and me an ice-cold stare to let us know that our business wasn't concluded. And her friends did the same.

Kieran and I moved to the side, out of the way.

'That's the girl from the football match,' Kieran said. 'The one with the loony dad who was causing all the trouble.'

'I know,' I said. 'And she's well and truly got it in for me.'

'What's her problem?'

'I don't know. Think she's got a screw loose, to be honest – like her dad.'

'Just keep your distance, if you can. Come and find me if she gives you any problems.'

'Keeping my distance is going to be nearly impossible. I'm in her form and I just know that I'm going to end up in at least one of her lessons. And there's her friends to worry about as well.'

'Just stand your ground. If you show any sign of weakness, they'll be all over you.'

'I know they will. Thanks for sticking up for me.'

'S'okay sis; that's what big brothers are for.' Kieran gave me a playful tap on the arm, so I gave him one back.

'Ow!' he said, recoiling slightly.

'Sorry, I forgot about your arm.'

'It's still a bit tender,' he said, giving it a rub. 'What's your first lesson?'

'Maths,' I said, groaning.

'Mine's English,' Kieran said, showing an equal lack of enthusiasm. 'I hope today goes quicker than I think it will.'

'Me too.'

Mr Williams clapped his hands together and gestured us to leave the hall. 'Come on,' he said, 'there's no time to stand around talking.'

We moved off.

My first lesson went well. I made friends with a girl named Debra Blackwood, who kept telling me jokes and making me giggle. She helped me with my work, explaining things to me more clearly than the teacher had done (maths has never been my strong point). Next up was chemistry, which I found slightly more interesting. An experiment with a Bunsen burner and some magnesium strips was fun (although I did nearly set fire to my sleeve, which would not have been fun at all). And then came playtime ...

As I filed out through the double doors with some other kids, I noticed Debra standing with another girl on the other side of the yard. I began making my way towards them when a large figure appeared in front of me.

'Oh no,' I said, 'not *you* again.'

'Yes,' Emma said, glaring down at me with a mean look on her face, '*me* again.'

And, of course, her friends were with her too. Lisa and the girls from earlier filed in behind Emma, like groupies.

'Haven't you lot got something better to do?' I said. 'As I told you before, I don't want any trouble.'

'Trouble is what you're going to get if you don't do Emma's homework,' Lisa said.

My reply was blunt: 'The only homework I'm doing is my own.'

'But it's your fault that she's even got it,' one of the other girls chimed in.

'How do you figure that?' I said. I nodded towards Emma. 'It wouldn't have happened if she hadn't been fooling around in class, trying to get my attention so she could make fun of me.'

'We were just *trying* to be friendly towards you,' Emma said, unable to keep a straight face. 'Just *trying* to get you to look our way so we could have a laugh together, that's all.'

'Oh, just like you did at the football match, when I was queuing at the burger van,' I said. 'Were you *trying* to get my attention so you could be friendly to me then as well?'

'You're a snotty little bitch, aren't you?' one of the girls said, snarling at me like a rabid dog.

'Yeah, Little Miss Snotty,' Lisa said. 'That can be your nickname from now on. How do you like it, eh? How do you like your new nickname, Little Miss *SNOTTY!*'

I thought I was Tweetie Pie, I thought miserably.

Emma began the chant: 'Snotty … snotty … snotty …' And then the others joined in: 'Snotty … *snotty* … *SNOTTY* …'

I looked around for help, hoping that either a teacher or Kieran would be nearby. But all I could see was other kids staring at me (and some were even joining in with the chant). My new friend Debra was looking on with concern. She was staying rooted to the spot though, so I knew she wasn't going to be any help.

I'd heard enough. Turning around, I walked back towards the building with the chant ringing in my ears: '… *SNOTTY* … *SNOTTY* … *SNOTTY* …'

Once inside, I ran down the corridor and into the girls' toilet. Then I locked myself inside one of the cubicles and cried my eyes out.

By the time I came out, playtime was over and everyone was making their way to their classes. *Please, God*, I thought as I followed along behind some other kids, using them as a shield, *don't let any of those girls be in my next class*.

Next up was IT. Fortunately, only one of Emma's gang was in this class and she didn't give me any problems as I was queuing by the door. Other than the odd dirty look, she wasn't so brave without her big bullying friend around.

Debra was in this class as well. She apologized for not helping me, then warned me to steer clear of Emma.

'She's bad news,' she said, giving me a woeful look. 'Now she's targeted you, she won't stop. Whatever she wants you to do, just do it – otherwise she'll make your life hell.'

'She's going to make my life hell anyway, no matter what I do.'

'Yes, but it won't be as bad if you don't give her any lip. She wanted you to do her homework, didn't she?'

'Yeah.'

'Then just do it.'

'No way!' I said, appalled at the idea. 'If I show any sign of weakness, she'll be all over me.'

'And if you stand up to her, she'll be all over you even worse. Her *and* her friends.'

'My parents taught me that the best way to deal with bullies is to stand up to them, and I think they're right.'

'Well, okay,' Debra said, regarding me like I'd lost my marbles, 'but it could be a painful experience.'

'Right, you lot,' the teacher said, his voice booming across the room, 'get your backsides down on seats and turn to page 40 in your textbooks, please!'

He showed me to my seat, which was by the window. We were on the third floor, so I had a good view of the grounds and nearby area. As I stared vacantly out of the window, squinting because of the sunlight, I wondered what I could do about the Emma situation. Then it came to me …

He-he-he, I thought to myself, *imagining what might happen to Emma if my plan worked.*

'Is something amusing?' I heard the teacher say.

He was standing right next to me, looking down at me.

'Eh …' I said, not sure how to respond. 'I'm just … happy to be here, sir.'

'Of course you are. I know you're new here, but please pay attention in my class. Things will go much smoother for you if you do.'

I smiled and said, 'Sorry sir.'

Inevitably, later in the day, I bumped into Emma. At dinner time, as I was queuing for my meal, she appeared at my side, looking menacing as ever. And, of course, her friends were with her, looking just as menacing.

'Well well well,' Lisa said, 'look who it is. It's Little Miss Snotty.'

'Yep, it's me again,' I said casually, trying to look as unfazed as possible, even though my stomach was in knots.

'Have you considered what I asked you to do earlier?' Emma said. 'Are you going to do my homework, or do you want to fight me after school?'

I pretended to consider her options for a second, then I responded, 'I'll do your homework for you; it sounds like a less painful experience.'

A brief look of surprise passed across Emma's face. I think she was partly hoping I would fight her.

'Finally come to your senses, have you?' she said to me. 'Finally realised who's the boss around here?'

'I have,' I said, picking up a tray off the side. 'So what's this homework you want me to do?'

Emma had a rucksack strapped to her back. Shrugging it off her broad shoulders, she let it drop to the floor, then unzipped it. She pulled out a book and thrust it at me.

'The Greatness of Rome,' I said, reading the title.

'Mr Brice isn't just my form tutor; he's my teacher for history as well. He's given me a five thousand word essay to do about Rome and it's due by Friday.'

'Well, your luck's in, because I'm an expert on Rome,' I said, lying. 'I've got *loads* of books at home on this subject.' I had one, somewhere.

'I don't care how many books you've got, or how much you know,' Emma said, 'just make sure you get the essay done and have it back to me no later than Thursday.'

'Come to my house tonight and we'll do it together,' I suggested.

'I'm not getting involved,' Emma said. 'You're doing it for me – on your *own!*'

Knew you'd say that, I thought. 'There's something cool I want to show you.'

'What can you possibly have to show Emma that's cool?' Lisa said, regarding me suspiciously.

'You wouldn't believe me if I told you,' I said.

'I don't believe a word you're saying anyway,' Lisa said. 'Emma, she's just trying to lure you to her house so she can get her parents to have a go at you.' She sneered at me. 'OMG – d'you really think we're *that* stupid?'

I could answer that, I thought, *but I better not*. 'I swear on my brother's life that I'm not trying to set you up where my parents are concerned. They won't even be home. They've got something to do and they won't be back 'till late. If I wanted to get them involved to get you in trouble, I'd just go to the headmaster and grass you up.'

Emma's eyes narrowed suspiciously. 'Just tell me what this cool thing is and I'll decide whether I'll come or not.'

'Like I said, you wouldn't believe me if I told you,' I said. 'This needs to be *seen* to be believed.'

'Really?' one of the girls said, looking quite intrigued. 'Can I come and take a look?'

Lisa elbowed her in the side. 'Shut up, you idiot!' she snapped at her. 'Are you really so dumb that you believe her?'

'I'm not lying,' I said.

Emma was weighing me up: staring at me with her beady blue eyes whilst she decided how to respond.

Moving closer to her, Lisa said in a lowered voice, 'You're not seriously considering going, are you?'

Still weighing me, still staring me down, it was a few seconds before Emma replied with a slow nod of her head. 'Little Miss Snotty knows what'll happen to her if she's trying to pull a fast one,' she said in a menacing tone. 'Her parents won't scare me. *Nobody* scares me. And my dad would smash some heads together if I told him I'd been lured into a trap. So yeah, I'm going. I want to see what this "cool thing" is. And it better be cool as well, otherwise ...' She cracked her knuckles together to finish the threat.

Yessss! I thought. *Gotcha!* 'That's great news,' I said. 'Be at my house for five o'clock.' I wrote my address on a piece of paper.

Picking up her bag, Emma slung it over her shoulder and said to her friends, 'Come on girls, I've just remembered there's something I need to do. We'll come back for our dinner in a bit.'

As they were leaving the hall, they kept giggling to each other as they glanced back at me. And after they'd left I had a giggle to myself, because I knew what was coming.

A minute or so later, Kieran turned up and asked me how my day was going, so I explained to him that Emma would be visiting us this evening.

'She's coming to our house,' he said, surprised. 'Are you mad? Why would you invite her to our house?'

'Emma thinks I'm doing her homework for her,' I said, showing Kieran the book. 'But after this evening, none of them will bother either of us ever again.'

'Just what exactly have you got planned, sis?' He cocked his head sideways and gave me a cunning look. 'Whatever it is, I hope this doesn't backfire in some way. I mean, are you sure it was wise telling her and her friends where we live?'

'Trust me,' I said confidently, 'she'll be scared of her own shadow after today.'

'I hope you're right.'

I hoped I was right, too.

Fortunately, the rest of the day went smoothly enough. I didn't have any more lessons with Emma, or any of her nightmare friends. And I managed to avoid her at home time as well. When I saw her making her way across the field, I hung back and walked at a snail's pace. With what I had planned for her later, I was sure that this would be the last time I would have to avoid her. I was almost looking forward to it.

By the time I reached the road, Kieran had caught up with me and was looking happy enough.

'I take it you had a good day then,' I said.

'It was okay, yeah,' he replied, nodding. 'I made some new friends. What about you?'

I gave him a vacant sideways look. 'Oh, I had a great day, thanks.'

'No, I didn't mean that; I meant did you make any new friends.'

I told him about Debra and how she was really nice to talk to. 'Would have been good if she could have stood by me when Emma and her gang were threatening me. She just watched from a safe distance and never once tried to get involved.'

'To be fair, she hasn't known you for very long. Would you have jumped to someone's defence if you were in her position?'

'I'd like to think I would.'

'Well, you're probably braver than she is. You just need to appreciate that not everyone is as feisty as you.'

I gave my brother a searching look, trying to gauge if someone sensible had hijacked his body. 'You're beginning to scare me with all this intelligent talk of yours,' I said.

'Is that a compliment?'

'It's as close as you'll get to one from me.'

'Oh, okay, thanks sis,' Kieran said, giving me a goofy smile.

Twenty minutes later, we stepped off the number 46 bus and arrived at The Mystic Cove. It was a kooky old Victorian building with a large bay window which took up most of its frontage. Peering through the window, we browsed the shelves, which were full of items.

'Hey, there's a wand there, look,' Kieran said, pointing. 'D'you think it works? D'you think I'd be able to cast a spell with it?'

'You'd probably blow yourself up or something,' I responded. 'That's assuming you could use it at all. You might have to be a witch or wizard to cast a spell. I'm sure the woman in the shop will be able to tell us.'

Kieran spotted a cauldron. 'That's like the one in our cellar.'

'Yeah,' I agreed. 'Just like it.' Something occurred to me. 'Hey, I wonder if Maud used to come here. I bet she did. I bet this is where she used to get all her magical stuff, don't you think?'

'You're probably right,' Kieran agreed. 'Shall we go inside?'

'Yes, let's,' I replied excitedly.

A bell above the door jingled as we entered. There was no one behind the counter, so we browsed the narrow aisles, taking in all the weird and wonderful things on display. Kieran took particular interest in some broomsticks, which were lined up by the far wall.

'If I buy one,' he said, 'd'you think I'd be able to fly on it?'

'Probably not,' I replied. 'But, failing that, you could always use it to sweep the yard. I'm sure that'd impress Mum and Dad.'

'Only a powerful witch or wizard can ride a broomstick,' someone said from the back of the shop.

A short, plump woman with blonde, scraggly hair appeared before us, regarding both of us with an inquisitive look. She was dressed in long, flowing, colourful robes, which draped behind her as she shuffled towards us.

'A powerful witch or wizard?' Kieran said to her. 'Well, that's neither of us, and that's for certain.'

'Not you, no,' the woman said to him. 'But you, on the other hand,' she said, eyeing me closely through her wise, old eyes, '… you have power *seeping* from you.'

'I do,' I said, taken back by what she was saying.

'She does?' Kieran said, even more taken aback than me. 'How so?'

'I know a witch when I see one,' the woman said. 'Especially a powerful one.'

Kieran couldn't help himself. 'My sister a witch?' he said, laughing out loud. 'Oh my God, I've heard it all now. If she was one, I think I'd have noticed by now.'

I was concerned that the woman might be offended by Kieran's outburst, but she didn't seem to be.

'You can believe what you want,' the woman said in a cool manner, 'but you will know better soon enough. The fact that you're here, browsing this store, is an omen in itself, wouldn't you say?' She didn't wait for a reply. 'My name Willa Fernsby. How can I help you?'

I looked at Kieran and he looked at me.

'Erm ...' I said, wondering where to begin.

'It's okay,' Willa said. 'Just say what you've come to say, my dear; I've heard it all, you know.'

Scented candles were lined up on a cabinet by the counter. Making her way towards them, Willa produced a wand from beneath her robes and held it above the candles.

'Ignito Luxano,' she said, giving the wand a little shake.

I let out an 'Oooooh!' of surprise as the candles ignited with a whoosh. Then a musky aroma began to fill the air, which I found pleasantly calming.

'That's a nice trick?' Kieran said. 'How did you do it?'

'If you want to believe it was a trick, then you believe that,' Willa said coolly with a smile. 'But, as I told you just now, you'll know better soon enough. You've come here for a reason.

Something to do with *magic*. So I'll ask again – how can I help you?'

The question was mainly directed towards me, but Willa glanced at Kieran (more out of courtesy than anything, I'm sure).

'We've been having problems in our new house,' I explained. 'We're certain that it's been cursed by the lady that lived there before us.'

Willa did not look surprised by what I had to say. 'And what makes you so certain that your house has been cursed, young lady?'

Oh, sheesh, where do I begin? I thought. 'Well, there's black mould all over the place and we can't get rid of it. We rub it off and it comes back. There's bats in the roof. We had a specialist out to get rid of them and now they're back again. A tree in the garden came alive and whacked my brother so hard that it knocked him off his feet and broke his arm ...'

'It didn't break my arm,' Kieran said, interrupting me. 'But it did leave me with a nasty bruise.' He rubbed his arm and winced for effect. 'Still hurts now.'

'Can you *not* interrupt me, please,' I said, giving him an icy stare.

'I'm assuming the house you live in is an old one,' Willa said. 'Most older properties suffer from problems with black mould. I can see how bats would scare you. Hearing anything scratching around in your roof at night must be most unnerving, but I can assure you that those unwanted lodgers are quite harmless. As for being assaulted by a tree, are you sure that's what happened? Was it a windy day? Could a branch not have been moved by a sudden gust and caught you unawares?'

'There was no wind,' Kieran said. 'I didn't see the tree whack me, but my sister did.'

'The branch moved on its own,' I said, 'because the tree is *alive*.'

'All trees are alive,' Willa said.

'Yes, but not all of them can assault people,' I said.

Willa pursed her lips together, then asked us to describe the tree.

'There's a row of them by our fence,' I said. 'They have big, circular leaves and long branches with knobbly ends. And underneath there are small, spiderlike plants growing, which are pretty creepy.'

A look of recognition passed across Willa's face. 'This house you speak of,' she said, 'where is it?'

I told her the address. 'When we first went to view the house and I was standing in the street, I'm sure someone was watching me from the upstairs windows. And I'm sure that person has been watching me ever since. She's dead, but she still haunts Selby House. Her name is Maud? Have you heard of her? Has she ever been into your shop to get magical supplies? She must have, surely. This is the only shop around here of its type that I know of.'

Willa nodded. 'Yes, I knew Maud; she was a good friend of mine.' Willa paced slowly back and forth, continuing to nod. 'All that you've told me so far is beginning to make sense now. I'm sorry I sounded so sceptical when you were explaining everything to me, but I like to investigate things from a non-magical perspective before entertaining any supernatural possibilities.'

'She's a friend of yours,' Kieran said. 'That's great news. Can you come to our house and ask her to stop terrorizing us, please?'

Willa stopped pacing and regarded him with a sombre look. 'I don't think that would work, somehow,' she said. 'My old friend became quite bitter towards the end, even towards me. When she asked me to help her out financially, I didn't have the money to give her. Not the amount she needed. Selby House meant everything to her. So when the debt company took it from her, it sent her over the edge. How much do you know about Maud and what happened?'

I told her about Reg and everything that he'd told us.

'Is he the old man who lives nearby?' Willa asked.

'Yes,' Kieran and I said in unison.

'Ah, yes,' Willa said warmly, 'I've spoken to him a few times. He's a nice man.'

'He is,' I agreed. 'And he told us that we should get out of that house as soon as possible. Before it's too late.'

Willa nodded solemnly. 'That sounds like good advice.'

'Yeah, that's all good and well,' Kieran said, 'but we can't convince our parents that the house is cursed. And we're afraid that they won't realise what's going until it *is* too late.'

'Well, I could talk to them,' Willa said, 'but they wouldn't believe me. They'd just think I was a silly old kook.'

'Reg said the same,' I said. 'He thought that my Mum and Dad would think he was just some crazy old man and ignore him. But if we can't convince our parents to leave the house, what should we do?'

Willa began pacing back forth again in slow measured steps as she pondered my question. Then she stopped and gave me an answer. 'You are very much right about that house being cursed. 'Maud told me *exactly* what she was going to do and *exactly* which curse she was going to cast. No one will ever live happily in that house. Not until the curse has been lifted. The way I see it, you have two options: you either leave the house, or you attempt to lift the curse with a powerful incantation.'

'An incan ... what?' Kieran said, looking confused.

'It means the use of words as a magic spell, my dear,' Willa explained.

'Oh, right,' Kieran said. 'Can you come and do that for us, then, please? We'd be forever thankful.'

'I'm afraid I don't possess that kind of power,' Willa said. Her eyes lingered on me. 'The curse was cast by a powerful witch, so it will take a powerful witch to remove it.'

'You want *me* to cast an incantation?' I said, aghast at the idea. 'I wouldn't know where to begin.'

'Fear not,' Willa said, 'I will tell you everything you need to know and supply you with all the ingredients.'

'Ingredients?' I said. 'I thought an incantation was just saying words. Will I have to make a potion or something?'

'Yes,' Willa said. 'The black mould in your house spreads darkness, so you need to dowse that darkness – or smother it, if you will – with light.' She took the cauldron from the window display and placed it at my feet. Then she began taking random items from shelves and placing them in a bag. 'Dead Sea Salt ... Lemon Zest ... Black Sand ... Satan's Lilac ... Coffin Nails ... Scorpion's Venom ... Pumpkin Juice ...'

'Erm,' I said as she selected the last few items, 'we don't have any money to pay for these things.'

Willa gave us a dismissive flick of her fingers. 'There's no charge,' she said. 'Just make sure you bring back anything you don't use.'

I assured her that we would.

'We have a lot of magical ingredients in our cellar,' Kieran pointed out. 'And there's a book of dark spells which we found in a drawer.'

'Best leave those alone,' Willa said, issuing us with a stern warning.

She put the bag full of ingredients into the cauldron, then gave me something which made my heart flutter: a wand.

Sporting a goofy smile, I held it up and moved it around in slow arcs. 'It's so light,' I said.

'Yes,' Willa said, 'it's made from willow. Not cheap. Please be careful with it.'

I assured her that I would.

'There's one last thing you'll be needing,' Willa said. She shuffled away, out of view, with her robes draping behind her. Seconds later she reappeared, holding a book titled: *Spells and Potions for Great Magic.*

'The incantation you require is on page 34,' Willa said. 'You need to make the Liquid Gold potion, apply some to a wall in each room, then say the incantation every time.'

'Will it really work?' I said, still in awe of the wand.

Willa said, 'If you mix the potion properly and say the words clearly, then, yes, it will work.'

'Can't you just mix it for us, please?' Kieran asked her. 'You're an experienced witch, so you'll get it right.'

'The incantation will be much more effectual if the potion is mixed by the person casting the incantation,' Willa explained.

'Oh,' Kieran said, looking disappointed. 'Best get it right then, sis.'

'I will,' I said, not feeling confident.

Willa wished us good luck. 'And don't forget to bring back the wand, the cauldron, and any of the ingredients you don't use. That wand is especially expensive.'

'I'll bring everything back,' I said. *Assuming I'm still alive,* I thought.

As we were about to leave, Kieran had one last question: 'Erm, about that tree in the garden that hit me. Is there any way it could uproot and move around?'

'No,' Willa said.

Kieran looked relieved.

'But,' Willa said, 'the plants it's protecting *can* uproot and have a *nasty* nip.'

'The spidery plants?' I said.

'Yes,' Willa said as she explained with wide-eyed enthusiasm. 'The spider plants. They usually eat worms but could easily confuse a child's fingers for being fat, *juicy* worms.'

'Oh,' Kieran said, his eyes growing wide with terror.

'Don't worry,' Willa said. 'As long as you don't bother them, they won't bother you.'

'Thank God for that,' Kieran said with relief.

'Now,' Willa said, casting a glance towards a clock above the counter, 'if you don't mind, I have some business to attend to, which means I need to shut early.'

'Oh, okay,' I said, picking up the cauldron full of magical stuff. 'Thanks for all your help. We'll get out of your way.'

'Yes, thanks for all your help,' Kieran said.

'It's a pleasure, my dears,' Willa said, smiling warmly. 'Keep safe, both of you. If things don't go to plan, get out of that house. And whatever you do, don't get any of that black mould on you; it's evil stuff and it *will* possess you.'

It'll possess *me*, I thought, terrified at the prospect.

After Kieran and I had left the shop, all he wanted to do was hold my wand.

'Why do you want to hold it?' I asked him as we walked along the pavement. 'It's not like you can cast a spell with it or anything. You're not a wizard. You're not magical … like me.'

'Whether or not you're magical remains to be seen,' Kieran said, looking offended. 'I just want to hold the wand to see what it's like to hold one.'

'It's just like holding a stick, really. I can't exactly feel power coursing through my veins as I hold it aloft, you know.'

'Say wha'?'

'Oh for crying out loud,' I said, handing it to him. 'Please don't drop it or damage it in any way. I want to take it back to the shop in the condition I received it, thank you very much.'

'I'll be careful,' he assured me, but I did not feel assured at all.

Holding it in front of him, Kieran regarded the wand with a look of awe on his face. 'I can't *wait* to see you try and cast a spell,' he said. 'If it works, it's going to be the most awesome thing ever.'

'I can't wait either,' I said. 'Can't wait to get rid of the black mould and lift that curse so we can live normal lives.' The weight of the cauldron was already hurting my arm, so I asked Kieran if we could do an exchange.

'Okay,' he said reluctantly.

'We need to hide that lot. If we leave it in the house, Mum is bound to find it. And then the questions will start.'

'Where can we hide it?'

'In the woods.'

'Good idea.'

About ten minutes later, as we passed through the trees, I spotted a huge one with a hollowed-out trunk.

'Perfect,' I said, placing the wand in the cauldron.

'So, little sis,' Kieran said, tucking it over the back, out of view, 'what is this cool thing you want to show the big bully from school? What have you got planned for her?'

'Oh nothing too hair-raising,' I said, smiling. 'Just want to scare her a little, is all. Just enough so she won't bother me again.'

'And what exactly does that involve doing?' Kieran asked, all ears.

'You'll see,' I said, still smiling.

'Hey,' Kieran said as we arrived back home, 'what do you think Mum and Dad will make of you being a witch? D'you think they'll believe you when you tell 'em? Or are you even going to bother telling 'em?'

These were fair enough questions. Ones I hadn't given any thought to, if I was honest. 'Let's just deal with one thing at a time, yeah,' I said in response. 'All I want to be focused on is what's going to happen in the next hour or so.' *Is this going to work as well as I hope it will?* I thought. *Or is it about to backfire in some way …*

'How long 'till she arrives?' Kieran asked.

'About ten minutes,' I replied, checking my watch.

In the kitchen, we looked anxiously out of the window.

'And you think she'll turn up, do you?' Kieran asked.

I shrugged. 'Either she will or she won't. We'll find out soon enough.'

I'd finally succumbed and told Kieran what I had planned and he'd expressed reservations. But I was determined to go ahead with it because it was the easiest way to make Emma wary of me.

Grabbing a glass from the cupboard, I poured myself some water from the tap and took a few quick sips.

Kieran noticed that my hands were shaking and asked me if I really was that nervous.

'Yes,' I said. 'I am.'

'Are you *sure* you wanna do this? You know it's going to anger Maud, so you're gambling on what will happen.'

'It will anger her, yes. But not so much that someone will get seriously hurt.'

A loud knock on the front door made us both jump.

'Uh-oh!' Kieran said, looking as nervous as I felt. 'I think someone's here early.' He glanced out of the window. 'Yep, it's definitely her. I can't believe she's *actually* come.'

'Probably thought it would make her look like a scaredy-cat if she didn't,' I speculated.

'Right,' Kieran said, jigging about like his feet were on hot coals, 'where do you want me? Shall I go in my bedroom?'

'That's a good idea.'

'Okay. But if I hear her picking on you, I'm gonna come down and – '

'I'm sure that won't be necessary,' I said, holding up a hand and cutting him off. 'Trust me, I can handle this. I can handle *her*.'

Emma banged on the door hard enough to make it shake in its frame.

'Whatever you say, sis,' Kieran said, disappearing into the hallway. 'Whatever you say.'

I waited to hear the click of his bedroom door shutting, then went to let my arch enemy in.

When I opened the front door, Emma didn't wait to be invited inside. She shoulder-barged past me, into the hallway.

'Nice little house you've got here,' she said with obvious disgust. 'Or ... NOT!' Spittle flew from her lips as she spat the words at me.

'We haven't been here long,' I explained, noticing a new growth of black mould on the ceiling, in the corner. 'And we're going to be doing the place up.'

'Even when you have decorated this place, it still won't be as nice as our house. I should have made you come to my house so I can show you what a proper home looks like.'

'Maybe next time,' I said, trying to be as pleasant as possible – when all I wanted to do was sock her in the eye.

'Don't hold your breath,' Emma said with a snarl. 'Okay, so what's this *cool* thing you want to show me? Where is it?'

'Follow me,' I said, leading the way.

When I opened the cellar door, Emma leaned in and said, 'We're going down *there!* What could you possibly have to show me in a cellar that could be cool? This better not be a trap of some sort!'

'It's not a trap,' I assured her.

'Just tell me what it is. I'm not stupid. I don't trust you.'

'I could tell you, but you won't believe me. You just need to *see* it!'

'See *what!*'

I flipped the light switch, then led the way. Down the moss-covered steps I went, holding on to the rail. When I was halfway down I stopped and looked back up. 'Well,' I said, 'are you coming, or what?'

Emma stayed where she was for a few seconds, then rolled her eyes and followed me.

When we reached the bottom, she looked around and said, 'Wow – what a tip. This place makes the rest of the house seem like a palace.'

'Yeah, it is a mess,' I said. 'Follow me.'

I took her to the dark wood cupboard in the corner, opened the top drawer, then pulled out the book of magic. I showed it to Emma.

'Magic for the Dark Mind,' she said, reading the cover. 'Is this *it*? Is this the "cool thing" you wanted to show me?'

'Yes. It's a real book of magic. It used to belong to the witch who lived here before us.'

The way Emma was looking at me, I wasn't sure whether she was going to hit me or storm away in disgust. She did neither. 'You brought me here for *this!*' she said, slamming the book back into the drawer. 'You brought me all the way over here to look at some *KOOKY OLD BOOK!*'

'It's not just any old book,' I explained. 'And you shouldn't have done that; you've probably angered her now.'

'Angered who?'

'The witch who used to live here,' I said. 'The one who ...' Haunts this place, I wanted to say, but didn't.

'Are you trying to tell me that's a real magic book?' Emma said, beginning to cough. 'One with spells and potions that really work?'

'Yes.'

'Prove it.'

'How can I do that. I'm not a ...' I was about to say I wasn't a witch, but of course that wasn't the case, according to Willa at the shop. 'Just have a skim through the book.' I held it out for her. 'You'll see that it's real enough.'

Snatching it from me, Emma skimmed through the pages until she found a potion which interested her. 'This one makes you invisible,' she said, showing a moment of excitement which drained away immediately. 'Like anyone would be able to become invisible.'

Oh my God, I could have so much fun with that *potion,* I thought, brushing a cobweb away from my eyes. *I would troll some people so hard. And none harder than you, you big, fat bully.*

I opened another drawer and showed her the small jars of ingredients inside.

'These do look old,' she said, picking up a small, green one and examining it. 'But ... magic isn't real. Everybody knows that.' Emma coughed again, her eyes beginning to water. 'The air down here ... it's so dank. It's getting at my throat.' She noticed the cauldron in the recess. 'Wow – you've even got a cauldron down here.' There was obvious sarcasm in her voice. 'Don't tell me, that's the one the witch used to brew all her potions, right?'

'Yes, it is.'

'Oh, get lost will you!'

Emma was suddenly seized by another bout of coughs. 'Okay ... that's it ... I'm getting out of here.' As she was leaving, she put a hand on the wall for guidance. And placed her fingers in a large splodge of black mould. 'Errghh,' she said, pulling them away sharply. *'Ewwww!'* She held her hand out and looked at the mould, which appeared to be moving. *'Grosss!'*

'You need to get that stuff off you,' I said, 'and you need to get it off you now!'

She wiped her hand on her jeans.

'No,' I said. 'Not like *that!'* I grabbed her by the arm and tried to lead her up the stairs. 'You need to wash your hands thoroughly with hot, soapy water.'

Emma wouldn't move, though; she stayed rooted to the spot.

'Come on,' I said, trying to get her to move again. 'What are you waiting for? You need to get that stuff off you – *before it's too late!'*

Emma held her hand out to me and said, 'It's gone. I think …
it went into my skin.'

I checked her jeans, where she'd wiped her hand, and there
were no black smears.

'It's not on my jeans!' Emma said, going frantic. 'It's in my
SKIN! *I saw it happen!*' She coughed and spluttered, struggling to
breathe.

'Okay, enough,' I said, 'let's get out of here.'

This time when I grabbed Emma by the arm, she let me lead
her up the stairs and into the hallway. Bending over and putting
her hands on her knees, she continued to cough and splutter. So
I got her a glass of water from the kitchen, which she drank in
big, slurping gulps.

Next thing, I heard footsteps descending the stairs and Kieran
appeared. 'What's going on?' he asked me. 'Everything all right,
sis?'

I shook my head and gave him a grave look.

Emma continued to cough. 'I feel sick,' she said. 'Feel like I'm
gonna chuck.' Her complexion had turned deathly pale.

'What happened?' Kieran asked me.

'She touched the mould,' I explained.

'Oh,' Kieran said. 'That's not good. That's not good at all.'

'Perhaps you should put your head over the toilet,' I said to
Emma, placing a supportive hand on her back. *Mum and Dad will
do their nuts if they come in and there's sick all over the place*, I
thought.

'Need to get out of here,' Emma said, brushing my hand
away. 'Need … fresh air.'

She stumbled through the hallway and into the living room.

'No, not that way!' I said.

As Kieran and I followed her, I noticed new splodges of black
mould dotted around the place.

Emma went to open the patio door, so I stepped in front of
her.

'You don't want to go out there,' I said, barring her way. 'It's not safe.'

'I need to *Get OUT!*' she said, shoving me aside with enough force to send me to one knee.

Kieran tried to stop her as well, but even he wasn't strong enough. She shouldered him out of the way with ease.

Outside she went, with us following behind.

'Emma, please stop!' I said, trailing her down the steps. I could see what was about to happen and felt powerless to prevent it. 'You don't want to go anywhere near those trees ...'

Too late. As she brushed past some branches, a large bough looped around in an arc and hit her so hard that it knocked her off her feet. She went down like a tree that'd been felled, letting out an '*Oooomph!*' as she hit the ground.

'Oh Gawwwd!' I said, stopping dead in my tracks. 'That didn't just happen. Tell me that I imagined that and it didn't just happen.'

'It did,' Kieran said, looking on, aghast. 'It most definitely did.'

I moved a few steps closer, careful to keep out of striking distance. 'Do you think she's knocked out?' I asked Kieran. She was on her side, motionless.

'It certainly seems that way,' he responded, also careful to take a wide berth of the trees.

And then Emma sprang up like she'd been spring-loaded, scaring us both out of our wits.

'It hit me!' she said, scurrying away, holding her arm. 'That tree hit me!'

'I did try and warn you,' I said.

'It's a part of the curse on this place,' Kieran added.

'No it isn't,' I said.

'Curse?' Emma said, looking at Kieran like he was crazy. 'Curses aren't real, you *numnit!*'

'Neither are trees that hit you,' Kieran said. 'But one just did.'

Emma looked at us and then the tree. She shook her head. 'Maybe the wind ...' she said, trying to find an explanation, still shaking her head.

'There is no wind,' I said, wetting my index finger and holding it up. 'Barely even a light breeze.'

Emma seemed lost, scared, confused. And quite badly hurt. She rubbed her arm and grimaced, her cough forgotten.

'That tree hit me just like that,' Kieran said. 'Caught me on my shoulder.' He rubbed his shoulder for emphasis. 'Still hurts now.'

A rustling sound caught our attention.

'What was that?' I said.

'Probably the tree,' Kieran speculated.

'No,' Emma said, 'it wasn't.' She nodded towards one of the spider plants. '*That* was what moved. Please don't tell that they're going to start moving around as well.'

I leant forward to take a closer look. 'It's uprooting,' I said, backing away. 'They all are, look.' I pointed.

'Erm,' Kieran said, his voice quivering, 'I think now might be a good time to leg it.'

We all bolted at the same time – and collided with each other at the bottom of the steps. A brief scuffle took place, as we wrestled for who would be first. Even with her damaged arm, Emma was still able to push us aside with ease. Kieran followed her up the steps, with me trailing behind.

I didn't look back.

Only forwards.

Emma burst through the patio door, then closed it behind her. She put the latch down, locking us out.

'Hey!' Kieran said, banging on the glass. 'Let us in!'

Emma shook her head. She was terrified.

'Let us in!' Kieran said, banging on the glass so hard with his fist that I thought it would break. '*Let us in, dammit!*'

I glanced behind us to see if any of the plants were coming for us – but there was no sign of them yet.

'HEYYYY!' Kieran said, kicking the bottom of the glass. 'IF YOU DON'T LET US IN, I'M GONNA ...' He picked up a rock and readied himself.

'No, don't!' I said to him. 'Let me talk to her.'

'She isn't going to listen to talk,' Kieran said. 'All she's bothered about is herself.'

I pressed my face against the glass and pleaded with Emma to let us in.

She backed away and shook her head again. 'If I open the door, those things will get in.'

'You're not safe in there, though,' I said. 'Remember the black mould.'

Recognition sparked on her face. She looked around her, up at the ceiling and then the walls.

'Oh ... my ... God,' she said, 'there's *lots* in here. Where's it all coming from?'

'Never mind that!' I said. 'Just let us in – before it's too late!'

'Erm,' Kieran said, tapping me on the shoulder. 'I don't mean to alarm you, sis, but we've got company – and I don't think they're friendly.'

I turned to see three spider plants making their way up the steps, their long, wiry legs skittering over the concrete.

I was about to tell Kieran to go ahead and smash the glass, but then I heard a clicking sound and it opened. My brother and I didn't waste a second. We both tried to get through at the same time, though – and got jammed in the doorway.

'What the heck!' I said as we both squeezed through.

Then Kieran closed the door with a bang, put the latch down and tossed the rock aside. It clattered across the floor and disappeared behind the settee.

'D'you think that'll keep 'em out?' he said in a panic. 'Or d'you think they'll be able to squeeze under the bottom? Are all the windows shut, d'you know? The woman at the shop said that they might eat our fingers, didn't she? She did say that, didn't she? She did *actually* say that?'

'Stop bombarding me with questions!' I replied. 'And I'd forget about the spider plants for now. They're outside. That,' I said, pointing at all the black mould on the walls, 'is on the inside – and Emma swears it went into her skin.'

'It did go into my skin,' Emma confirmed, swaying back and forth like she was about to pass out. 'Oh ... ohhh ... I feel sick again. And my arm really hurts.' She gave it a wary rub with her fingers.

Kieran took no notice of her; he was too concerned with the mould. 'We need to get out of here,' he said, 'before it's too late.'

That sounded like good advice to me.

Something collided with the patio door – *thump!*

'It's those things,' I said. 'They're trying to get in.'

'If they do,' Kieran said, 'I'm gonna *stamp* on 'em!'

Emma stumbled sideways and would have fallen down had she not placed a hand on the settee to steady herself. 'I'm calling my Dad,' she said, pulling her mobile phone from her pocket. 'He's ... he's going to go mad when he gets here.'

I didn't doubt that would be the case. I tried to discourage her, but she ignored me. Plonking herself on the settee, she fingered the numbers.

While she was making her call I moved to one side with Kieran and whispered to him: 'I think I'd rather deal with what's in the garden than deal with him.'

'Yeah, me too,' he replied. 'Maybe we should just hide when he turns up.'

'When Mum and Dad find out what's happened, they're going to do their nuts.'

'I think they'll be too concerned with the mould and the finger-eating plants to worry about telling us off, don't you?'

'Oh I don't know, I think Mum would tell us off even if she was being attacked by ghouls and goblins.'

Another thump against the patio door made us all jump.

'Yes … yes,' Emma said with the phone cupped tightly to her ear, 'please get here as quick as you can – *I'm scared!*'

As she ended the call, Kieran said, 'Well, at least your cough has stopped.'

I shook my head at him. 'What a thing to say.'

'That's because I'm out of your hellhole of a cellar,' Emma said. She looked deathly pale. 'And now I'm going to get out of your hellhole of a house.' She pushed herself up off the settee – and then collapsed on the floor as if her body had turned to jelly.

Kieran and I both exchanged a worried look.

'Come on,' I said, grabbing her by the arm which hadn't been hurt, 'help me get her up.'

Kieran put his arms around her waist and we both tried to lift her.

'Damn,' he said, 'she weighs a tonne! We're never going to move her.'

'We have to,' I said, nodding towards the walls and ceiling, which were covered in even more black mould than a few minutes before. 'Soon we won't be able to get out of here because it'll be *everywhere.*'

The sight of it gave Kieran extra strength. He pulled her up on his own and began dragging her across the floor. I tried to help as best I could, but my brother was taking most of the weight. We were near the living room door when we heard a car pull on the driveway.

'Oh no,' I said. 'Please tell me that's not who I think it is. Please tell me they're not back early.'

Kieran let go of Emma and she slumped to the floor. He went to take a peek through the kitchen window and then came back.

'Yep,' he said, looking delirious, 'it's them. How are we gonna explain this?'

'We'll just tell the truth. Say that she came over so I could help her with her homework. She became queasy and collapsed. It's not a lie.'

'That's great – but whadda we do when fatso's dad turns up?'

I shrugged. 'Erm … hide.'

We heard car doors slam, footsteps on the driveway, and then the front door opened.

A few seconds later, Mum popped her head through the doorway. She looked at Kieran and me, then at the unconscious girl on the floor.

'What in the blues blazes is going on here?' she said.

'Erm, she's a friend from our new school and she, erm … collapsed,' Kieran explained. 'We're helping her to get outside so she can get some fresh air.'

I could see that Mum had a thousand questions boiling up inside of her, so I gestured towards the black mould. 'And there's also that, too,' I said. 'It's everywhere – and spreading!'

'Oh my!' she said, taking it all in with a gasp. 'Where has all *that* come from?'

'I warned you that there was something wrong with this place,' I said, 'but you wouldn't believe me.'

Dad poked his head into the room, all smiles. But his smile disappeared straight away when he saw what was happening. 'Oh dear,' he said. 'Who is this girl and what's happened to her?'

Thud! A spider plant hit the patio door. Harder than last time.

Skitter, skitter, skitter …

'And what was that noise?' Dad said. 'Is something trying to get in?'

'Yes,' I said, 'something *is* trying to get in, which is why we're trying to get *out*.'

'What is it?' Mum said.

'You don't wanna know,' Kieran said.

'We do,' Dad said, moving to the window so he could peer through. 'I can't see anything. What's out there, exactly? A stray cat? A dog? Or is it a fox?'

'Never mind that!' I said, nodding towards Emma, who appeared to be coming round. 'This is our biggest problem.' I gestured towards the black mould. 'And that too.'

'Oh yes,' Dad said, backing away from the walls in fear. 'I had noticed that. Now I will have to admit that that is not normal. Where has it all come from? And how has it formed so quickly?'

It's because the house is cursed! I thought. *I told you something was wrong with this place days ago but you wouldn't believe me. Well, maybe you'll believe me now. Maybe you'll* both *believe me.*

Suddenly, Emma's eyes opened and she looked up at me. I saw a flash of blackness in the whites of her eyes, but it was gone in less than a second.

'It really is inside of her,' I said, backing away.

'Inside of her?' Mum said, confused. 'What are you talking about, Ella?'

Emma got quickly to her feet and looked around at all of us. 'Where's my dad?' she said in a robotic voice. 'Is he here yet?'

A series of tapping noises from above made us all look upwards.

'What was *that?*' Kieran said.

'It'll be the bats that the experts were supposed to have gotten rid of,' I said.

'Maybe it isn't bats,' Kieran said. 'Maybe it's something else. Maybe the you-know-whats from the garden have got in.'

'What are these you-know-whats?' Dad said, becoming irritable. 'Just tell us, will you?'

'Needs to be seen to be believed,' I said.

'Right, okay then,' Dad said, storming towards the patio door …

'*Nooo!*' Kieran and I both said unison.

'Don't open the door!' Kieran pleaded.

'Okay, I've had enough of this silliness,' Mum said. 'I want answers and I want them right now. What in the blue blazes is going on here?'

'I'll tell you everything once we're outside,' I said. 'For now, we just need to get out of this house – before it's too late.'

'More cod's wallop,' Mum said, seething. She turned her attention to Emma. 'Are you feeling okay?' she asked her. 'You seem very distant and not with it, child. Would you like me to call a doctor?'

'No,' Emma replied calmly, 'I feel fine. My dad will be here soon.'

She looked at me and I once again saw a flash of blackness in her eyes. And then she smiled at me. I had never seen her smile before and it was a wicked thing to witness.

'I recognise you,' Mum said to Emma. 'You were at football with your dad on Sunday. He was the one creating a right kerfuffle.'

'I thought you looked familiar,' Dad said.

A loud banging noise from above made us all look towards the ceiling.

'I think something just knocked something over,' Kieran said.

'Okay,' Mum said, 'I'm going to see what's going on.' She disappeared into the hallway.

Skitter, skitter, skitter …

'And I'm going to see what's making *that* noise in the garden,' Dad said, striding towards the patio door.

'*No!*' I said, stepping in front of him. 'That's not a good idea.'

'Please move out of my way,' Dad said.

'No,' I replied, standing my ground.

'Either you tell me what's out there,' Dad said, 'or I'll pick you up and move you.'

I was about to reply but Kieran beat me to it. 'Plants,' he said. 'Flesh-eating plants.'

Dad chuckled. 'Oh kids,' he said, shaking his head, 'I've heard it all now.'

He put his hands on my shoulders and attempted to move me aside, but I wouldn't budge.

'We're not joking, Dad,' I said. 'It's part of the curse that's on this house: the curse that was cast by the woman who lived here before us. That's why *that* is growing on the walls.' I jabbed my finger towards a circle of black mould, which I was certain had spread since I'd glanced at it a few seconds before. 'There's an old book of magic in the cellar full of dark spells. And there's all sorts of potions down there, too. Go and take a look if you don't believe me. Actually, *don't* do that – there's loads of mould down there, so that wouldn't be a good idea.'

A bang on the front door was a welcome distraction. But then I remembered whom it would most likely be.

'That'll be my father,' Emma said, giving me a sly look. 'I'll go and let him in.'

As she went into the hallway, I whispered to Kieran, 'It's definitely inside of her. I saw it in her eyes.'

'Oh,' was all he could manage in response.

Dad entered the hallway to greet our visitor.

And that's when all hell broke loose.

Brian didn't wait to be invited inside. As soon as Emma opened the front door he burst into the house.

The look on my Dad's face said it all: I *really* don't want to have to deal with this man again!

'My daughter tells me she's been hurt,' Brian said, his cheeks flushing red with anger. 'So how has that happened and who's responsible?'

It was my dad who responded. 'Now look, I've only just got home myself, so I haven't been able to fully establish what's happened here. Your daughter seems fine now, though, so there's nothing to worry about.'

'I'll decide whether there's anything to worry about,' Brian said. He turned his attention to his daughter. 'Tell me exactly what's happened, Emma? Are you okay? You told me that you'd been hurt? Are you all right now?'

Emma shot an accusatory glance in my direction. 'It was *her*,' she said. 'First, she led me into the cellar to show me some weird magic book. The air is so bad down there that I almost choked to death in a coughing fit. And then she led me out in the garden and into a trap. As I was walking past one of the trees, she pulled a branch back and it hit me so hard that it knocked me down. Here, look.' She pulled her sleeve up to her shoulder and showed everyone a nasty bruise which was forming. 'It really hurts, Dad; I'm surprised she didn't break a bone.'

You lying cow! I thought. 'I did *not* lead her into a trap,' I said, protesting my innocence. 'It was the ...' I was about to blame the tree, but I realised how ridiculous that would sound.

Brian looked ready to punch someone. I was too small for him, however, so he focused his attention on my father.

'And where were *you* when this was happening?' Brian asked him. 'You told me that you've only just got home, so why weren't you here supervising these kids? What sort of a parent are you?'

Dad was lost for words. 'Well, I ... the thing is ... my wife and I ...'

'Were probably out doing something for yourselves, right?' Brian didn't wait for Dad to reply. 'To hell with the kids' safety, yeah. As long you and your wife are out having a good time, then that's all that counts. Never mind my daughter's safety, *aye!*'

I could see black mould forming on the wall by him. A small splodge, which was creeping out of the corner.

I said, 'Erm, I think we might want to le –'

But Dad cut me off, protesting his innocence. 'Now just hang on a minute. I didn't even know your daughter was going to be here. And my kids are old enough to look after themselves, thank you very much. One's eleven and the other's thirteen, for crying out loud.'

Brian had heard enough. He grabbed Emma by the arm which hadn't been hurt and marched her towards the front door.

We followed him into the hallway.

'What a dump this is,' Brian said, looking around and scowling. 'I remember coming here to evict the old lady that lived here before you lot. She was a strange old crone, that one. Nutty as a fruitcake. Only seems right that a new bunch of weirdoes should live here, I guess.'

'You work for the company that evicted Maud from this house?' I said, gobsmacked.

'I *own* the company that evicted her,' he said proudly. 'Price & Co: the finest finance company in the Midlands. I quite often go out with the bailiffs for evictions. Can't beat getting your hands dirty at ground level and it's always nice to see these scroungers who refuse to pay getting what's coming to them.'

Oh … my … God, I thought. *Well, if you want your revenge, Maud, now is your chance.*

Skitter, skitter, skitter …

'What's that noise?' Brian said, irritated.

'That didn't come from outside,' Kieran said, his eyes wide as dishes. 'I think they're *in* the house.'

Skitter, skitter, skitter …

'Where is that coming from?' I said.

'The living room, I think,' Dad said.

I went to take a look, but Kieran grabbed me by my arm. 'Is that wise?' he said.

'I'll be fine,' I said, shrugging him off.

I didn't pause, didn't hesitate – just stood in the centre of the room and listened.

Skitter, skitter, skitter …

And then I knew where the noise was coming from. Pressing my ear against the far wall, I said, 'They're in the wall!' I said. 'In the cavity!'

'*What* is in the wall?' Dad said. 'And don't give me any codswallop this time.'

'You've got rats,' Brian stated. 'And it doesn't surprise me.'

There was an air vent in the corner of the room, near the ceiling. Kieran and I both eyed it with concern because it didn't look very secure. The screws holding it in place were slightly loose. One hard whack and I was sure that it would ...

Suddenly, from upstairs, we heard a huge kerfuffle – and then a scream. With all the commotion since Brian had arrived, I had forgotten about Mum. She had gone to find out what was making the noise. As we heard her footsteps on the stairs, Dad moved to meet her. They bumped into each other as she reached the bottom.

'What on earth is going on?' Dad said. 'Are you okay?'

'*No!*' she replied as she bundled everyone through the living room door and then shut it behind her. 'No – I am *NOT* okay!'

A brief moment of recognition flashed across her face as she eyed Brian warily. But she was too concerned with whatever had scared her to give him any attention.

'What is it?' Kieran asked her. 'What's up there?'
She opened her mouth to reply – but then we heard them. Outside the living room door, flapping about.

'It's the bats, isn't it?' I said. 'The bats are out there?'

Mum nodded. 'Y-yes,' she said, her voice strained. 'But they're not normal bats; there's something wrong with them. I went in the attic to look around and found a huddle of them hanging from the ceiling in the corner. I shouldn't have approached them – I know I shouldn't – but curiosity got the better of me. And that's when some others appeared. They just came flapping out of the shadows, screeching their little heads off. I didn't think that bats were aggressive, but these are. I tried to close the door on my way out, but I couldn't do it; they were buzzing around my head like flies, their wings flapping in my face. How the heck could that guy from Renshaw's have thought that he'd gotten rid of all of them when the room is absolutely infested is beyond me. I'm going to have stiff words with that company in the morning, by gab!'

We could hear them flapping about frantically in the hallway.

I was quite sure I knew what was happening here. 'Is there any black mould up there?' I asked Mum. 'I bet there is, isn't there?'

'Yes, there's a lot,' she replied. 'I did notice that. But I was too scared to be concerned about it.'

'It's inside of them,' I muttered. 'Just like it's inside of ...' I looked at Emma and saw a flash of blackness in her eyes. A smile was playing at the corners of her mouth and she had an evil look about her.

Skitter, skitter, skitter ...

The air vent began to rattle.

'What's causing that!' Mum said. 'Don't tell me they've gotten into the cavities as well!'

'There is something in there,' Kieran said, 'but it's not bats.'

'What in the hell is going on here?' Brian said. 'What sort of loony bin are you lot living in?'

Mum looked at Dad and said, 'Like we haven't got enough to deal with here without him turning up.'

'For some reason, our daughter thought it would be a good idea to befriend his daughter and invite her to our house.' Dad said. 'But forget about that for now. We just need to concentrate on getting out of this house.'

That girl is no friend of mine, I thought.

The air vent continued to rattle.

Skitter, skitter, skitter ...

'Err, I don't want to alarm everyone to a panic,' I said, pointing to a particularly big splodge of black mould on the wall, 'but that's now spread even more.'

'Yikes!' Mum said, backing away from that area.

The bats continued to flap around in the hallway. The air vent kept moving as the spider plants tried to break through. The screws were now looking alarmingly loose.

'Let's go in the garden,' Mum said, making her way across the room.

I blocked her way. 'There's a good reason why I stopped Dad from going out there. That would *not* be a good idea.'

'Why?' Mum said. 'What's out there?'

'The same things that are trying to get through that vent,' Kieran said.

'Okay, I've had enough of this lunacy,' Brian said, grabbing Emma by her undamaged arm again and escorting her to the living room door. 'We're getting out of here.'

Shooting across the room like an Olympic sprinter, Mum positioned herself in front of them, blocking their way. 'You can't open this door,' she stressed. 'You'll let them in!'

'So what if I will,' Brian said, towering over her. 'They're just bats; they won't be able to hurt us.'

'Oh I think they will,' Mum said.

'Move aside,' Brian said. It wasn't a request; it was an order.

'Going out the back has to be a safer option,' Mum suggested.

'No it isn't,' Kieran stressed.

'Okay that's it!' Brian said, 'enough messing around – get out of my way, woman!'

He grabbed Mum by the shoulders and attempted to move her aside. But she was having none of it; she shrugged him off and pushed his hands away.

'Things are going to get rough,' Brian warned, 'if you don't get out of the way.'

'Things are *not* about to get rough!' Dad said. I'd never seen my dad truly angry before – but he was angry now. He took a step forward to show he meant business. 'Don't you *ever* touch my wife again.'

'And what are you going to do?' Brian responded. 'If I blew a kiss in your direction you'd fall over.'

'I'm tougher than I look,' Dad said.

Wow, go Dad, I thought, *never knew you had it in you.*

Brian shot a mocking look his way, then once again tried to move Mum aside.

'Get off me!' she said, resisting him. '*Get off me, you BIG OAF!*'

Then Dad waded in and all hell broke loose.

As the three of them wrestled with each other, I could see what was about to happen.

'The black mould!' I said. 'You're too close to it!'

But none of them listened. They were too caught up in the tussle to worry about anything else.

Emma didn't seem concerned that her father was wrestling with my parents. Quite the opposite, in fact; she found it amusing.

'I know it's inside of you,' I said in a low voice. 'I know that you're not *you* anymore.'

Blackness flashed in the whites of her eyes and she replied: 'You just need to shut your mouth, you … you little *witch.*'

'How do you know that about my sis?' Kieran asked her.

But she didn't answer. Just continued to watch the tussle.

Brian now had Dad in a headlock. Mum had taken off her shoe and was hitting Brian over the head with it.

'The mould!' I warned them again.

It was too late, though. Dad tried to get Brian off balance by lifting one of his legs, so Brian placed a hand on the wall – right in the mould.

'Eh, what the hell!' he said as Dad upended him and they both went down in a heap.

Mum was still hitting Brian with her shoe.

'Get your hands off me!' he bellowed, placing an arm over his head, trying to defend himself. 'Get your hands off me, you pair of lunatics!'

Dad took the opportunity to distance himself from the fight. He moved to the centre of the room with the rest of us. Mum, on the other hand, was not done dishing out punishment. She raised her shoe above her head and was ready to deliver another blow ...

'MUM!' I screamed. 'STOP! PLEASE STOP!'

She turned her head to look at me, her arm still raised above her head, shoe in hand.

'It's touched his skin!' I said, trying to make her understand. 'It's inside of him!'

She regarded me blankly, confused by what I was saying.

'He touched the black mould,' I explained, knowing that she would think I was mad. 'It's a part of the curse that's on this house – and now it's inside of him.'

I've never seen my mum lost for words. But she didn't know what to say at that moment. And neither did anyone else, either. We all just stood around for a few seconds, looking at each other blankly.

Meanwhile, while all this had been going on, the bats had been going wild in the hallway, no doubt trying to find a way to get to us. And the spider plants had been busy – skitter, skitter, skitter – trying to break through the vent so they could also get at us. The screws had now been loosened so much that the vent looked like it could pop off any second ...

'I don't feel too well,' Brian said, getting wearily to his feet. 'I think I'm going to ... *throw up*.' He was deathly pale, just like Emma had been after she'd touched the mould. 'Damn – what the heck is wrong with me.'

And that's when the vent popped off the wall. One of the screws hit Kieran on his cheek and he let out an '*Ow!*' of surprise.

'Uh-oh,' I said, backing away. 'Here we go.'

We all stared at the gaping hole where the vent had been, waiting to see what would happen.

'Maybe it was just the wind,' Dad said.

'Yeah, right,' Kieran said, also backing away.

Skitter, skitter, skitter …

The spider plants came flooding out of the hole, moving in different directions.

'*AGHHH!*' Mum yelled, holding her hands over her mouth whilst screaming.

Dad jumped onto the settee, as if that could somehow save him. 'What in the name of God are those things!'

'Spider plants,' Kieran said, batting one away with his hands. 'Don't let them anywhere near your fingers – unless you want to lose 'em.'

One landed on top of my head. I let out a shriek and pushed it off quickly.

'This house really *is* a loony bin!' Brian said. He put his hand on the door handle, ready to do the unthinkable. 'Come on Emma, we're getting out of here!'

'*No* – don't do that!' Mum said. 'You'll let them in ...'

But, by this time, it was too late. Brian had already opened the door and the bats were flooding into the room.

'*AGHHHH!*' Mum yelled again. Louder, this time. 'We need to get out of here!'

Brian didn't waste a second. Keeping his head low, he dragged his daughter into the hallway and they made for the front door.

Kieran lifted his foot high and then splatted a spider plant with his heel.

Bats were flapping around my head, so I picked up a cushion and fended them off as best I could.

Meanwhile, Dad was still on the settee, trying to defend himself from every angle. A spider plant jumped onto his shoulder and nibbled his ear. He howled in pain. '*Out out OUT!*' he said, jumping off the settee and gesturing for us all to get moving. '*Let's gooooo!*'

'Don't let the bats touch your skin!' I said, stamping on a spider plant as I made for the door, careful to keep clear of the wall with the big splodge of mould. Bats were flapping around my head and I was screeching like a banshee.

Kieran was first into the hallway, followed by Mum, and then me. As Dad followed behind us, he stepped on the back of my heel, making me fall forward. I collided with Kieran, who then collided with Mum, sending all three of us to the floor in a heap.

'Sorry,' Dad said, yanking each of us in turn to our feet.

Mum screeched, 'Close that door, for heaven's sake!'

Dad kicked away two spider plants that were advancing on us, then slammed the living room door shut.
As he was doing this, however, a few bats sneaked through. They flapped around our heads and we batted them away with our arms.

'Look at the walls!' I said, flicking one of them away like it was an annoying fly. 'All that black mould!'

'And don't touch any of it!' Kieran added, ducking out the way of a bat.

'Weirder and weirder,' Dad said, pushing us all towards front door.

Once we were all safely outside, Dad breathed a huge sigh of relief. 'What just happened in there?' he said. His question was levelled mostly at me, but he looked at everyone – including Mum – for answers. 'Have I slipped into an alternate dimension or something? Since when could plants move around like that?

And what was with those bats? I'm sure they're not supposed to be aggressive like that. Are they?'

'They've touched the black mould,' I explained. '*That's* why they've gone crazy. Which is what'll happen to any of us if we touch it, too.'

Mum was looking at me like she wanted to say something along the lines of: don't talk daft, girl – that sort of thing isn't possible. But, of course, she couldn't say something like that now. Not after what she'd just seen.

'I want to know everything,' she said. 'Tell me everything you know about what's going on here, Ella. Not now. When we're safely away from here. By God you're going to talk girl and you're going to tell it true.'

That's all I've done so far, I thought.

We could see the bats flapping about behind the glass in the front door. And we could faintly hear the spider plants skittering about, too.

'We need to get away from here,' Kieran said, 'before they all figure out how to get out.'

'They can't get out,' Dad said. 'Unless someone's left a window open. Are any of them open?'

'No,' I replied. 'The spider plants figured out how to get inside, so I'm sure it's only a matter of time before they get out. Probably through that vent they just busted through.'

'Oh,' Mum said. 'Best put distance between us and this house sooner rather than later then. And then we can call the police and let them know what's happened.'

'The police?' I said. 'What are you going to tell them? That we've been attacked by carnivorous plants and demonically possessed bats. They won't even bother turning up.'

'Of course I'm not going to say that,' Mum said. 'I'll just tell them that we've got intruders and they can take a look for themselves.'

A moaning sound from behind us made us all turn around. Brian and Emma were farther down the driveway, standing by a silver Mercedes. Hunched over, with his hands on his knees, Brian looked like he was about to throw up. He was also swaying back and forth as if he might pass out any second. And then he did. He fell sideways, hitting the tarmac with a *thud*.

'Oh great,' Mum said, rolling her eyes. 'I'd forgotten about *him*.'

Emma didn't react at all the fact that her father had just collapsed right in front of her. She just stood there, with a blank expression on her face, staring down at him.

'I suppose we better help him,' Dad said.

'I suppose so,' Mum said begrudgingly.

As we made our way towards them, Mum said to Emma, 'Don't worry, child, your father's just had a bad turn, is all. I'm sure he'll be okay in a bit, when he comes around.'

He really won't, I thought.

Dad went to one knee beside him, so he could get a better look. 'He's quite pale,' he said. 'Doesn't look good at all. Should we call an ambulance, do you think?'

'Let's just wait and see if he comes around first,' Mum said. 'People are too eager to call the emergency services these days, so it's no wonder they're strained. And we need to take stock of everything that's happened here before we involve any outsiders. I'm going to ring Jean. See what she's got to say about this. She always knows what to do when I'm in a pickle.' She sauntered away, out of view.

Jean was Mum's sister and I doubted she'd believe a word about the current pickle we were in.

'We really need to get away from here,' Kieran said.

'I know,' Dad said, getting back to his feet, 'but we can't just leave him here like this.' He turned his attention to Emma. 'I'm sure your dad will be okay in a minute. He'll be up and about in no time, you'll see.'

'They left us when we were in the living room,' I said, giving her a cold stare, 'so maybe we should *leave* them.'

Emma gave me a cunning smile. 'Oh we'll be just fine,' she said. 'It's you that needs to worry.'

'Why would we need to worry and not you?' Dad asked her.

'Because the black mould is inside of her,' I said, staring her out. 'It's inside both of them.'

'That's why she's acting weird,' Kieran added, staring at her as well.

'And it's going to be inside of you, too,' Emma said, reaching towards me with that cunning smile still on her face.

I took a few steps back, quick as could be. 'Don't let her touch you,' I said. 'Whatever you do, do *not* let her touch you.'

Kieran distanced himself from her, but Dad just stood there like a fool, appealing for us not to be silly.

'We're not being silly,' I assured him. 'Do NOT let that girl touch you. Otherwise the mould will be inside of you, too.'

Emma shook her head and smiled as she edged closer to Dad. 'Honestly,' she said to him, 'what is up with your children, Mr Tickles?' She twirled her index finger at the side of her head, indicating that we'd lost our marbles. 'I think they both need to get some counselling, if you ask me.'

Then she grabbed Dad by his wrist and squeezed hard.

'*NO!*' I said. '*Get your hands off of him!*'

Kieran moved forward to help, but Dad yanked himself free of her and backed away.

'What did you do that for?' Dad said to Emma as he rubbed his wrist. 'What sort of game are you playing, little miss?'

Emma just smiled a knowing smile. And then she began moving in my direction.

By this time, Mum had finished on the phone.

'Well, Jean thinks I'm losing my marbles,' she informed everyone as she walked towards us. 'Is everything okay?' She focused her attention on Dad. 'Why are you rubbing your wrist like that? Have you hurt yourself?'

'No, he hasn't,' came a reply. Everyone turned to see that Brian was back on his feet and not looking remotely ill at all. 'Your husband will be *jussst* fine … in a short while.'

He was too far away for me to get a good look at him, but had he been closer I was certain I'd see flashes of blackness in the whites of his eyes. 'Oh yes, everyone's going to be *jusssssst* fine soon enough.'

Mum gave him a wary look as she made her way towards the rest of us. 'I've informed the police as well,' she lied, her comment aimed more at Brian than anyone else, 'and they assured me that they'll be here quickly.'

By this time, Kieran and I had distanced ourselves from the others. We beckoned Mum to us, but she was too fixated on Dad to take any notice. He was still rubbing his wrist and had gone deathly pale, like I knew he would.

'Are you all right?' she said to him as her face filled with concern. 'You really don't look well.'

'Don't go near any of them!' I said, now frantically beckoning her to come to Kieran and me. 'And don't let any of them touch you. Not even Dad!'

But Mum was too concerned about Dad to heed any warnings. She went to him and took him by the arm, trying to steady him.

'You need to sit down before you fall down,' she said.

'Mum, watch out!' I said as Emma edged closer to her. '*Don't* let her touch you!'

Emma grabbed her by the wrist and squeezed hard. Mum shook her off immediately, but, of course, it was too late.

'What did you do that for?' Mum said, taking a few steps backwards.

I said to Kieran, 'Both of them have been touched by her now. They'll pass out soon enough, I bet. And then they'll come back changed. We need to be away from here before that happens.'

'What?' he replied, disgusted at the idea of fleeing. 'I'm not leaving Mum and Dad with those weirdoes. And what happens if those things get out of the house? They'll attack them and we won't be here to help.'

I glanced towards the house and saw bats flapping around in the kitchen. They were banging against the window, trying to get to us. The spider plants were on the kitchen top, banging their bulbous heads against the glass. I wondered how long it would be before it broke.

'Those creatures won't attack our parents,' I said. 'They're a part of the curse now as well.'

Putting his head in his hands, Dad began swaying back forth like he might pass out any second. 'Oh my word,' he said, moaning. 'I *really* don't recall ever feeling this ill.'

Mum gave Emma a hard stare as she put her arm around Dad's waist to prevent him from falling over.

'Come on,' Mum said, trying to coax him towards a big oak tree by the side of the driveway, 'park your backside on the floor and rest your spine against this trunk until I can get some help.'

Brian and Emma smiled confidently as they watched them struggle.

'Let's go,' I said to Kieran, 'while we still can.'

'But …' he said, still not happy at the idea of leaving our parents.

I could see that our opportunity to get away unnoticed would soon be gone, so I began moving briskly towards the trees, whilst beckoning Kieran to follow. He hesitated, so I beckoned him again, making furious gestures with my hands. *Come on, you fool!* I thought, willing him to move. *Let's gooooo!*

After a few more moments of uncertainty, he finally began to follow. As we moved away, I cast one more glance towards the house. A flicker of movement in one of the upstairs windows caught my eye. It took a few seconds for my eyes to adjust because the sun was low in the sky and bright in my eyes. Flattening my hand, I placed it above my brow to cut out the glare. And then I saw her, watching me from the shadows. And I wasn't the only one who was seeing this.

'That's her, isn't it?' Kieran said, also putting a hand over his eyes to shield them. 'That's the witch? Maud?'

'Yes, that's her.' I replied, filled with dread. I grasped Kieran's shoulder and kept us both moving.

Into the trees we went, disappearing from view. Through the undergrowth we jogged, stepping over fallen tree trunks and crashing past bushes. About five minutes later, when I was sure we were a safe distance away, I brought us to a halt by a stream.

Exhausted, I put my hands on my knees and took a few seconds to catch my breath.

'So,' Kieran said, breathing heavily with sweat glistening on his forehead, 'what are we gonna do now, sis?'

'We're going to go ... back,' I said, gasping for air, 'and we're going to ... lift that curse.'

'We're going back?' Kieran said, surprised. 'But we've only just left.'

'Not yet,' I said. 'There's someone we need to visit first.'

'Who's that?' Kieran asked. And then he figured it out. 'The old guy from the cottage? Reg?'

I nodded. 'I want to see what he's got to say about everything that's happened.'

'You think he might know something he hasn't told us yet?'

'Maybe. There's only one way to find out.'

Kieran thought things through for a moment, then said, 'Well, okay, but don't you think Willa from the magic shop would be the best person to talk to about this. I think she'd want to know about what's happened and I'm sure she'd tell us exactly what we need to do.'

'Couldn't agree more. But the shop isn't open at this time in the afternoon and I don't know where she lives. And she's already told us what to do and given us the things we need to do it.'

'You really think you can cast some magical spell that'll lift the curse?' Kieran said, not looking optimistic.

'Yes,' I said, truly believing that I could, 'I do.'

'Better get going then.'

When we had fled from our house, we'd gone in the opposite direction from where Reg lived. We hadn't cared about where we were going at the time – only getting away from danger.

'We'll need to go past our house to get to his, won't we?' Kieran said.

'Yeah. We'll have to take a wide berth. That's assuming we can find our way through these woods without getting lost, of course.'

About fifteen minutes later, we were quite sure that we were lost. Until we heard the distant rumble of car engines.

'That might be the road that goes past our place,' Kieran said.

So we went to take a look. Emerging by the side of the road, we glanced in both directions.

'I'm not sure if this is the one,' I said. I remembered that the road we lived near was called the B612, but that didn't help us much now as there were no clues as to whether this was the stretch we were looking for or not.

A small, red car was driving towards us from the right, so I waved it down. An old lady pulled up next to us and asked us if there was a problem.

'What road is this, please?' I asked her.

She pursed her wizened lips together as she gave it some thought. 'Hmm … I can't remember but I'd know it if somebody said it.'

'The B612?' Kieran chimed in.

'That's it!' the old woman said chirpily. Her eyes narrowed as she regarded both of us in turn. 'Say, are you pair lost or something? Is everything okay?'

No, everything is not *okay*, I thought. *Far from it.* 'Everything's fine,' I replied. 'We just need to know which way it is to get to town.'

The old woman pointed ahead. 'That's where I'm going,' she said. 'Would you like a lift? It's not safe to walk along a road such as this. There's no pavement and people tend to speed along here like it's a racetrack.'

'We don't need a lift, thanks,' Kieran said. 'And we'll keep back from the roadside, if it'll make you feel better.'

'It would,' the old woman said. She seemed reluctant to leave us on our own and then enlightened us as to why. 'About a quarter of a mile back, some loony walked out into the road and I would have hit him if I hadn't slammed on my anchors. He kept telling me to get out of my car, but I didn't. Then he told me to wind down my window, but I wouldn't. Then he came up with some wishy-washy tale about how he needed my help because someone was injured. I'm old enough and wise enough now to smell a lie when I hear one.'

'This loony,' I said, 'what did he look like?'

'He was tall and slim, with big tufts of brown hair on his head.'

'Was he wearing a brown jumper and blue jeans, by any chance?' Kieran asked.

'He was,' the old woman confirmed. 'Do you know him?'

Kieran and I exchanged a worried look.

'Yes, we do,' I said. 'Thanks for your help.'

I grabbed Kieran by his arm and began walking away with him in the direction we needed to go.

The woman got slowly out of the car and called after us: 'Do you think I should have called the police?'

So they can turn up at the house and get infected as well? I thought. *I don't think so.*

'Don't worry about it,' I called back to the old woman, 'that was my dad you were talking to. He is a bit weird but he's okay.'

The old woman seemed satisfied with my answer, so she raised her hand then got in her car and trundled away.

'You know what's gonna happen when our parents or the other two come in contact with other people, don't you?' Kieran said.

'More people are going to feel ill, then pass out, then turn weird and dangerous.'

'This thing could spread – and *quick*.'

'Only just figured that out, have you?'

We upped our pace, then began jogging.

About five minutes later, we arrived at Reg's and banged on his door. When he didn't answer, we banged again – louder.

'Knew yeh'd be back at some point,' we heard a familiar voice say. We looked to our left and Reg was standing there, regarding us with a curious expression. 'Now how can I 'elp yeh pair? Somethin' teh do with that 'ouse yeh've been foolish enough to move into, I'm guessin'.'

'Things are getting out of control,' I said.

Kieran began to blabber, motoring out words like a machine gun: 'The black mould's inside of our parents now and ... and ... they'll have turned weird like Emma and her dad. So anyone they touch will get infected. Those weird plants that were growing in the garden just attacked us and ... and ... so did some bats and we're supposed to do some incantation to make everything right. Which means we'll have to go back into the house where all those things are and ... *and* ...'

'*Whoa!*' Reg said, raising his cane in the air and waving it around. "Old yeh 'orses there, laddo. Let's take one thing at a time, ayuh. Nobody who panicked ever achieved anythin' meaningful. Let's get inside, make a brew, and yeh can tell me all 'bout it without the dramatics.'

'There's no time for tea!' Kieran said. 'This thing is gonna spread *quickly!*'

'There's always time feh tea,' Reg said, gesturing us both to enter.

In the kitchen, I put the kettle on and readied everything.

Whilst I was doing this, Kieran paced back forth, agitated.

'Take the weight off yeh legs,' Reg said, seating himself at the table.

'I'm okay, thanks,' Kieran replied, continuing to pace.

'Well, I'm not okay with yeh wearin' out my floor like that,' Reg said, 'so take a seat or wait outside.'

Reluctantly, Kieran took a seat across from Reg.

I finished making the tea as quickly as possible, then poured the old man a strong cup.

'Feel free teh 'ave a cup yehselves, why dontcha,' Reg said. 'An' grab some biscuits from the cupboard; I've jus' got some Custard Creams that might take yeh fancy.'

I thought that Kieran would say there was no time for biscuits either. How foolish of me. Of course there was time for them where my brother was concerned. Even the prospect of chaos and danger that lie ahead could not put a dampener on *his* appetite.

'Seeing as we could all be infected by some weird curse soon enough,' he said, retrieving the tin, 'I better fill my belly while I can.'

'That's a good attitude to 'ave,' Reg said, 'but don't go scoffin' 'em all now, will yeh.'

'Ov courth not,' Kieran said, grinning with a mouthful of biscuit.

'Now,' Reg said, focusing his attention on me, 'things 'ave obviously taken a turn feh the worst. So tell me – slowly an' calmly – what's got yeh all of a tiz?'

I took a deep breath, then told him everything he needed to know: about Emma and what'd happened in the cellar; about the spider plants and bats; about Emma's dad turning up and the revelation that his company had been the one responsible for Maud's eviction; about how Emma had touched her father and infected him with the mould; Last but not least, I told Reg about my parents and how they were now infected as well.

'Eh, you forgot to tell him about what happened at The Mystic Cove,' Kieran said to me.

'Now there's the best person teh speak to about this,' Reg said. 'The lady that runs that place will know *exactly* what teh do, so she will.'

'She already told us what to do,' I said, 'and she gave us all the things to do it as well.' I paused slightly, before resuming. 'Apparently, according to Willa, there's more than one witch in town. And a magical concoction will do the trick.'

Reg's large, bloodshot eye widened in surprise. 'Yeh' are a witch as well?'

I nodded.

'Well, blow me down,' he said, shaking his head in surprise. 'I bet that's come as a bit of a shock, eh?'

'You could say that,' I said.

'Yeh look doubtful,' Reg said to Kieran. 'What's up? Think it's a load-a hoopla, do yeh?'

'Let's just say I'll believe it when I see it,' Kieran replied.

Reg said, 'Yeh better 'ope yeh sister *is* a witch, otherwise things could go from bad teh worse real quick, from the sound of things.' He took another slurping sip of his tea, then licked his lips and focused his gaze on me. 'So, yeh've gotta mix some potion an' cast a spell or somethin' like that, yeah?'

'Something like that,' I said.

'An' are yeh confident yeh can do that?' Reg asked me.

'Not … exactly,' I said. 'But I'm going to give it my best shot.'

'That's not quite what I was hopin' teh 'ear,' Reg said. 'I want yeh teh tell me that yeh *can* do it an' that yeh gonna lift that curse no matter what.'

I wish I felt as confident as you want me to feel, I thought. But I told him what he wanted to hear anyway. 'I'll lift it one way or another,' I said, raising my chin as a show of strength. 'Whatever it takes.'

'Atta girl,' Reg said, sporting a toothless smile. 'So, what's yeh plan of attack? How are yeh gonna get into that 'ouse without gettin' touched by the baddies?'

'We need to give it a bit of time before we go back,' Kieran suggested. 'With any luck, they'll all have moved off when we get there. The spider plants and bats will still be in the house, though.' He shuddered at the thought.

I nodded, agreeing with this plan of approach.

But after fifteen minutes had passed, I became sick of listening to my brother crunching nervously on the biscuits whilst shifting restlessly in his chair.

My chair scraped across the tiled floor as I stood up and said, 'I can't wait here any longer; I need to see what's happening and I need to know if my parents are all right.'

'Me thew!' Kieran said through a mouthful of biscuit.

'Good idea,' Reg said, snatching the barrel away. 'Yeh pair best be gone before me laddo 'ere eats me out of 'ouse 'an 'ome.'

'We'll find a spot near the house where we can hide and spy on the place to see what's going on,' I said. 'And we can look in the magic book to see what needs to be done to cast the incantation.'

'Okay,' Reg said, liking the sound of this. 'But be *careful*. Any sign of trouble an' get away from there pronto. One touch is all takes from what yeh've told me, so don't take any unnecessary risks, yeh 'ear me.'

'I hear you,' I said.

'Me too,' Kieran said.

'I wish I could 'elp yeh,' Reg said, whacking his cane against the table leg in disappointment. 'But I'd be more of a 'indrance than anythin', yeh understand, ayuh?'

'We do,' I assured him.

Reg wished us good luck, then he saw us off at the door and watched us as we walked up the garden path.

'Keep your doors bolted and don't answer to anyone unless it's us,' I said to him.

'Like I need tellin' that,' Reg said. 'I'm 'idin' under the table as soon as yeh pair are outta sight.'

'I wish I could hide under a table,' Kieran said to me as we disappeared from view.

'Now is not the time for being a coward,' I said. 'I need all the help I can get.'

'I know. I was just joking.'

'Now is not the time for joking, either. We both need to stay alert and ready for anything. I don't want to become one of Maud's mould-infected zombie minions, but that's what'll happen if we're not with it. One touch is all it takes, remember. *One* touch.'

'Like I'd forget something like that.'

Back into the woods we went, our feet crunching on fallen twigs and leaves.

'D'you know what'd be really tragic?' Kieran asked me. He didn't wait for a reply. 'Imagine that we get to that hollowed-out tree trunk and all your magical gear has been nicked. What would we do then, eh?'

'Now that *would* be tragic,' I agreed.

But when we arrived at the trunk, the cauldron was still there, tucked away over the back, where we'd left it. Reaching in, I huffed and puffed as I pulled out the heavy cauldron, which still contained all the items I needed to perform the incantation.

I removed the bag and other items from inside and placed them gently on the ground. Then I sat cross-legged on the floor and opened the book at page 34.

'Don't you think we should scout the place out first, before we start making concoctions? You never know, we might not even need to bother with any of this magical silliness. The infection from the mould might have worn off by now and everyone might be back to normal.'

'They might be,' I agreed. 'But I doubt it.' I moved my finger down the page of text as I read what needed to be done. 'A pinch of Dead Sea Salt,' I said, selecting the correct jar and unscrewing the lid.

'What the heck is Dead Sea Salt?' Kieran said, plonking himself next to me.

'Err ... salt from the Dead Sea, maybe. Don't ask me what it is, because I'm as clueless as you. And I don't want three-hundred questions fired at me as I'm doing this, please. I need to concentrate because I don't want to get it wrong.'

'O-kay, soz. But I had no intention of bombarding you with questions.' He watched as I added the first few ingredients. 'Can I ... put some in? Or do I need to be a wizard to do that?'

'I have no idea, so it's probably best that I do it ... And without any further *interruptions!*'

Kieran shuffled away from me. 'Fine ... *fine*. Keep your hair on, why don'tcha.'

Composing myself and concentrating as hard as I could, I began adding more ingredients: two to three Coffin Nails; three to four slivers of Lemon Zest; a dash of Scorpion's Venom; one palm-full of Black Sand; a globule of Satan's Lilac ...

'That stuff looks disgusting,' Kieran said, watching me as I added it to the mix. 'Reminds me of snot.'

Ignoring him, I added in the remaining ingredients: two sprigs of Rosemary, two pinches of salt; three horse hairs; a clove of garlic; a dead fly (*yuk!*); four large mushrooms; some ginger root; and two spiders' legs (*double yuk!*) …

'Is that it?' Kieran enquired. 'Is that everything?'

'Not quite,' I said. 'We need some water.'

'Where are we gonna get that from? Our house?'

'No. I want it mixed and ready *before* we get there. We could go back to Reg's, I suppose. Or there's that stream we passed when we were lost.'

We decided that Reg's was closer and that there would be less chance of getting lost if we went there. The cauldron was heavy to carry, though. Even Kieran struggled to lug it (being careful to use his right arm as his left was still giving him twinges), whilst I carried the other stuff. And Reg was surprised to see us back so soon.

'Crikey,' he said when he answered the door. 'Yeh can't 'ave done what needed teh be done in the time yeh've been gone, I'm sure.'

Kieran held up the cauldron and explained what we needed.

Gesturing him to put it on the table, Reg then filled a jug with water. He handed it to me and I added in the correct amount.

'Needs a good stir now,' I said.

'Can I do it?' Kieran asked.

I couldn't see any reason why not. 'I suppose so,' I said.

Reg handed him a large wooden spoon and he began stirring the potion enthusiastically.

'Didn't the woman at the magic shop say that this stuff was called Liquid Gold?' Kieran said as he continued to stir. 'It doesn't look very golden to me. More like a light brown, if you ask me.'

''ave yeh added in the correct ingredients?' Reg enquired, his larger eye widening as he came in close for a gander. 'An' 'ave yeh put in the correct amounts?'

'I followed the instructions carefully,' I replied. 'But I haven't said the magical words yet.'

I once again opened the book at page 34 and read what needed to be done. 'Sounds simple enough,' I said.

'Nothin' is ever as simple as what yeh think it'll be,' Reg said. 'Yeh learn that when yeh get teh my age, so yeh do.'

I had a feeling this might be the case, but it turned out not to be so.

I was so nervous that my hand was shaking as I held my wand over the cauldron and said, loudly and clearly, the magical words: 'Luxio Magnis Clarandum!'

Please work, I thought, waiting for something to happen. *Please, please work!*

A few seconds passed and I started to get dismayed.

And then something *did* happen …

'Ooh, look,' Kieran said, stepping in for a closer look, 'it's beginning to steam and go yellow.'

The mixture hissed and bubbled as vapours began to fill the kitchen.

'Somethin's definitely 'appenin',' Reg said, wafting a hand in front of his face.

The steam filled the room so quickly that it was like a thick fog had descended within seconds. Reg opened the back door and a window to let it out.

A few minutes passed before the bubbling and hissing died away.

Reg was still wafting his hand around, even though most of the steam had disappeared by now.

'Ooooh, look,' Kieran said, with his head still over the cauldron and a goofy expression on his face. 'It's glowing now!' It was so bright that he had to move back and shield his eyes with his hand.

'The name of the concoction is Liquid Gold,' I said, 'so it's looking like I may have *actually* done this right.'

Reg put his cane aside and clapped his gnarly hands together, giving me a round of applause. 'Congratulations! Now yeh can get teh work. No time teh waste. 'eaven only knows what's 'appened since yeh were last at that 'ouse of yours.'

No time to waste, indeed …

Snatching everything up (apart from the bag full of unused ingredients, which we didn't need anymore), Kieran and I made for the door as Reg once again wished us luck with everything to come.

Off towards the trees we went, as fast as our feet would take us.

Kieran was struggling to carry the cauldron. 'This thing weighs even more now with the golden liquid in it,' he said, huffing and puffing, then complaining some more.

'Do you want me to help you carry it?' I said. I felt guilty because all I was holding was the book and wand, neither of which weighed much.

'No,' he said. 'I'll manage.'

As we passed through the woods, Kieran stubbed his toe on a rock and nearly fell over.

'Will you look where you're treading!' I said. 'The last thing we need is you spilling that stuff all over the place. We could need every drop, for all we know.'

Kieran glared at me. 'Sorry, sis; I'll try to be more careful. Okay?'

Grasping the cauldron handle with my free hand, I said, 'Together, yeah?'

'Together,' Kieran said with no protest.

Even with both of us carrying the cauldron, it was still a slog. We argued as we made our way through the trees and undergrowth. When I snagged my foot on a bush and nearly fell, Kieran was quick to tell *me* to be careful.

Nearing the house, we tried to be as quiet as possible. Not easy when you're in the woods and every step you take makes noise, no matter how cautiously you move.

Positioning ourselves behind a huge tree, we took turns peaking around it so we could see what was happening.

'I don't see anyone,' Kieran said. 'But that doesn't mean no one's there. They could be hiding in there, waiting to pounce on us as soon as we step inside.'

'Not only that,' I said, 'as we mentioned before, there's the bats and spider plants to worry about. Some might have found a way out, but there's bound to still be some in there.'

'I don't see any cars. That's a good sign.'

'Hmm ...' I said, giving it some thought. 'Maybe.'

'You think it could be a trap?'

'It's a definite possibility.'

Kieran began looking around.

'What are you looking for?' I asked him.

'Something I can use as a weapon.' He spotted a thick, heavy stick, then went to retrieve it.

Whilst he was gone, I began sifting through the book, looking for a spell that might be useful. I found one on page 211.

When Kieran returned, he crouched beside me and said, 'Rigidio Maximus: what does that spell do?'

'Freezes somebody on the spot,' I said with a smile.

'Cool. Now *that* could be useful. D'you think it'll work? D'you think you'll be able to do it?'

'There's only one way to find out,' I said as my smile widened.

'Err, you're not freezing me.'

'But we need to run a test.'

'Not on me, you're not.'

'You're the only person I can practice on. I can't exactly do it to myself, now, can I?'

'Knowing you, you'll get it wrong and turn me into a potato or something.'

'I just have to say two words whilst pointing my wand at you. What can go wrong?'

'I don't want to find out. And you might not be able to unfreeze me.'

'Again, all I have to do is say two simple words.'

Kieran shook his head. 'Thanks ... but no thanks.'

We haven't got time for this, I thought.

Glancing at the book, I made sure of the magical words, then I pointed my wand at Kieran ...

'No ... no, don't you dare,' he said, standing up and backing away.

'Rigidio Maximus!'

With his arms outstretched in a warding off gesture, Kieran froze on the spot like a statue. His stick dropped to the ground: *thud!* I looked at him for a moment, not sure whether he was toying with me or not. Any second now I was certain he'd spring to life and say, '*Ahah – gotcha!*'

But he didn't. I really *had* frozen him. Under less dire circumstances, I might have been tempted to toy with him a little – tickle his belly or something – but there was a task that needed doing. And it needed doing quickly.

Taking another glance at the book, I noted the magical words for unfreezing Kieran, then I raised my wand and said, 'Relaxus Rigidio!'

Kieran sprang to life with a start. 'Oh my God, that was weird,' he said, his eyes wide with either amazement or fear (or a combination of both). 'Please don't ever do that to me again 'cause it wasn't nice.'

'Sorry,' I said, keeping my distance just in case he tried to get revenge. But, of course, that wasn't going to happen – because I had a wand that was capable of doing amazing things and he was now very wary of that short, thin piece of amazing wood. 'At least we know the spell works.'

'Yeah,' Kieran said, still visibly shaken. 'And we also know that you're *definitely* a witch.'

I had got so excited about what I had just done that I'd forgotten why we were here and the dangers that could still be around.

'Get back behind this tree,' I said, gesturing my brother towards me.

Realising the dangers himself, he darted forward and positioned himself next to me. I leaned one way and he leaned the other as we both craned our necks, looking towards the house.

'Still seems all clear,' I said. 'No signs of movement.'

Kieran agreed with me. 'No signs of movement.'

Putting our backs against the huge trunk, we both looked at each other and nodded.

'No point in delaying,' I said.

'Let's do this, sis.'

Kieran picked up the cauldron and stick. I snatched up my book. Then off we went, walking towards the house at a brisk pace. Reaching the front door, Kieran put his ear to the glass pane at the top and listened.

'Can't hear anything,' he said in a low voice.

He pushed the handle down, then slowly opened the door, which creaked on its hinges. The hallway was clear: no signs of any bats or spider plants. And no signs of any two-legged foes either. All we could see, danger-wise, was the black mould. There were patches of the stuff everywhere, which was oozing and bubbling grotesquely. On the ceiling, it hung down in some spots, making me think of sinister stalagmites.

'Be careful,' I whispered in Kieran's ear. 'That stuff could drop on us.'

Next, we checked the kitchen, which was all clear too (apart from lots of the black stuff, of course). Kieran gave the downstairs toilet an inspection.

'Not good in there,' he said, closing the door with an unsettled look on his face. 'Not good at all.'

I was not tempted to take a gander.

'This seems a little too quiet for my liking,' Kieran whispered. 'What d'you reckon, sis? I've got a bad feeling in my stomach.'

I had that same feeling as well. 'We need to check every room before we start, so keep your wits about you.'

Next up was the living room, which was also clear of any people, bats, or creepy plants. Just more of the black stuff – *lots* of it.

'No way did all those bats and spider things find a way out of this house,' Kieran said. 'There *has* to be some here, somewhere. And if there are some here, where are they?'

'If we make some noise, we might just find out.'

'I can call out, if you like?'

I gave this some thought, then nodded.

Kieran cleared his throat, then said, loudly and clearly, 'Helllo! Is anybody here!'

No reply came. I expected to at least hear the flap of wings, or *skitter-skitter-skitter* of the spider plants as they reacted to the noise. But there was none of that. The only thing that greeted us was unnerving silence.

'Where d'you suppose Mum and Dad have gone?' I said. 'And Brian and Emma?'

Kieran shrugged his shoulders and shook his head. 'I dunno. Down to Macdonald's for some gut-busting food and a good chinwag.'

Even in this desperate situation – as nervous and scared as I was – I couldn't help smile at the idea of my parents socializing happily with two of the most obnoxious people I've met in my life.

'That's a nice theory,' I said, managing a smile, 'but you know that Mum can't stand that place.'

'That's right,' another voice said, 'I loathe that place with all my heart.'

Kieran and I turned to see Mum standing near the doorway with the other three behind her.

Gasping, I opened my mouth to say something, but the words caught in my throat and all I could manage was a whimper.

Kieran was so surprised that all he could mutter was: 'Mum!'

Putting his head over her shoulder, Dad grinned viciously and said, 'Hello, kids, have you missed us?'

Flashes of blackness appeared in the whites of his eyes.

This was a trap and we walked into it, I thought, angry with myself. *How stupid are we!*

'M-mum … D-dad,' I said. 'I didn't think you were here.'

'Of course you didn't,' Emma said from the hallway. 'That's why you're here with your pot of gold: to smear it all over the place and lift the curse.'

'But that's not going to happen,' Brian said from beside her, 'because we're here to stop you – and stop you we *will*.'

How do they know what we've got planned? I thought frantically. *How could they possibly know?*

And then it came to me: Maud.

She had anticipated what we would try to do and been ready. She had known that Liquid Gold would destroy the mould and was ready to defend against this happening. But had she known that it would be me who would try to lift the curse? Or had she just been prepared to deal with everyone or anyone who might attempt the deed? A flashback to being in The Mystic Cove gave me the answer: 'I know a witch when I see one.' That was what Willa had said to me when I was there. And if she knew a witch when she saw one, then Maud probably did too.

'Just one touch,' I muttered to Kieran. 'Remember, just one touch.'

His grip on the stick tightened as he readied himself. 'Stay back,' he said, issuing a warning. 'Don't come any closer!'

Mum, Dad and the other two ignored him. They edged slowly forwards, all of them grinning. The black mould on the walls began to bubble and move as if responding to this.

Time to issue a warning of my own. 'Stay back!' I said, raising my wand and pointing it at Mum. 'Stay back – *or else!*'

'You wouldn't hurt your own mother, now, would you?' Mum said, pretending to look sad.

'Or your father,' Dad said as he stood beside her. 'You wouldn't hurt your 'ickle daddykins, would you?'

'Mum, Dad, it's the mould that's making you act like this,' I said, pleading with them. 'It's the curse! You need to fight it – *please* fight it!'

They continued to advance, with Brian and Emma behind them. And the mould continued to move on the walls and ceiling. Any second now I was sure it would reach out to grab us. But that's not what happened. On the far wall, a small mass of it bubbled up and dropped to the floor. Legs popped out – six of them – and a head popped out of the top. And then I knew what it was.

'A mouldy spider plant!' Kieran said, cringing. 'As if they weren't bad enough before!'

More blobs of mould began plopping to the floor. Legs and heads began sprouting …

'That one's got wings, look,' Kieran said, pointing with his stick. 'Mouldy bats as well!'

Emma cackled. 'Oh dear, it's not looking too good for you, is it?'

Brian sneered at me. 'What are you going to do, zap all of us with that wand of yours?' He gawped at Kieran. 'And is that all you've got to protect yourself? A *stick!* I don't like your chances, kid.'

'Perhaps I should throw it at your head,' Kieran responded.

More spider plants and bats were emerging from the walls and ceiling: dropping to the floor and sprouting legs, heads, wings. One plopped down next to Kieran, so we backed away, fear gripping both us.

'Just put the wand down,' Mum advised, advancing a few steps towards us. 'Things will go so much easier if you don't resist.'

I pointed my wand at her, not sure if I could bring myself to use it on her. 'It's the curse, Mum,' I said, pleading with her again. 'It's the black mould! Fight it! *Please* fight it! I know you can. You're stronger than this – I *know* you are. Don't let it control you.'

For a moment – just a split second – she looked confused and I thought I was getting through to her. But then blackness flashed in the whites of her eyes and she glared at me with such hate.

'Nice try,' she said, 'but you're not … powerful enough.'

All the spider plants and bats had materialized from the walls and ceiling, it seemed. But they weren't attacking.
They were just on the floor, poised – as if waiting for someone to issue a command.

It occurred to me that my Mum and others didn't know what I was capable of. They knew I had a wand and that I was pointing it at them, but they didn't know that all I could do was freeze them. They were clearly wary of me.

There were only two ways out the living room: into the hallway (which was out of the question for obvious reasons) and through the patio door, which would take us into the garden.

Kieran was looking towards it, having the same idea as me.

'Do you really think you could get through that door before one of us touches you?' Mum said, throwing her head back and laughing out loud.

'What are we gonna do, sis?' Kieran muttered in my ear. 'Any ideas?'

'You're not going to do *anything*,' Mum said. 'Please put the wand down and make this nice and easy for everyone.'

'Do as your mother says,' Dad warned. 'You know you always do.'

From behind them, Brian and Emma grinned menacingly.

Not this time, I thought, levelling my wand at Mum. *I won't be hurting her*, I had to remind myself. *Just turning her into a human statue.*

As Mum took a step forwards, the mouldy creatures began to stir around us and advance.

'We're done for,' Kieran said, terrified. 'Absolutely done for.'

But then a knock at the door made Mum and everyone else stop in their tracks. She raised a finger and the mouldy creatures stopped their advance.

'Who the heck could *that* be?' Dad said.

Brian and Emma went to find out. We heard the front door open and then someone said in a loud, high-pitched voice: 'Rigidio Maximus!'

I looked at Kieran and he looked at me.

'Somebody just used the freeze spell,' I said.

Mum and Dad went to see what was going on. They stepped into the hallway, disappearing from view – and then …

'Regidio Maximus!'

Kieran and I looked at each other again, both asking the same question with our eyes: what is going on?

I had expected the mouldy creatures to respond to this commotion, to either advance on us or head for the hallway, but they didn't. They just stayed where they were, as if still waiting for an order.

'Well, yeh made short work of them, so yeh did,' we heard a familiar voice say.

'Reg!' Kieran and I both said in unison.

Careful not to touch any of the creatures, we went to see what had happened. In the hallway, my parents and the other two had been frozen stiff by someone using magic. Who had done this, I wondered? Not Reg, surely. He wasn't a wizard, as far as we knew. The voice that'd said the magical words had been familiar too. And then I realized whom it was.

'It's Willa from the magic shop!' I said, excited.

'It is indeed,' I heard her say in response.

We couldn't see her or Reg very well because of the bodies that were in the way, but we could hear them.

'Oh-mi-gosh, this place is infested,' Willa said. 'Be careful not to touch anyone or anything – and stand well clear.'

Kieran and I reversed into the living room.

'Motus Moblata!'

My parents began sliding across the floor to the left wall and the other two slid the other way, creating a gap.

'Don't worry,' Willa said, 'I haven't hurt them – just frozen them so they aren't a threat.'

'It's okay,' I said, 'I've used that spell, so I know what it does.'

'Casting magic spells already,' Willa said, impressed. 'And that's not an easy one to do either. You really must be as powerful as I thought.'

I looked at Reg and he raised his cane in acknowledgement.

'Thought yeh could do with a little bit of 'elp, so I did,' he said.

'You brought Willa with you?' I said.

'No, no,' Willa said, 'we just met up on the driveway. Looks like we both came to the same conclusion: that you'd need some extra help. I've spoken to Reg before a few times when I've visited Maud so it was a pleasant surprise to see him here again, given the circumstances. At first, I thought you would be able to handle this situation by yourself, Ella, with the power that's radiating from you. But, after you'd gone, the more I thought about it, the more I knew I had to be involved. This is a very powerful curse that's been cast here and you will need assistance, given your novice status.'

'I can't do much,' Reg said, shrugging his bony shoulders, 'but I felt like I needed to be 'ere too. Even if it's jus' to be a distraction.'

'Well, you're just in time,' Kieran said, ''cause they were about to swarm all over us. But now they're not gonna be swarming over anyone,' he added, standing in front of Emma, goading her, ''cause they can't move – *heh heh heh!*'

'I wouldn't get too confident,' Willa said, sweeping past us in her colourful, flowing robes. 'There's a lot of work to be done here before any celebrations can be had, I can assure you.' In the centre of the living room, she looked around, taking in everything. Black mould was bubbling and creeping about on the walls. The spider plants and bats were still rooted to their spots. 'Hmm ... poor, unfortunate creatures.'

'They were about to attack us, but then you showed up,' I explained. 'My mum put her finger in the air and they all stopped dead. I think her and the others can command them.'

'You're right,' Willa confirmed, 'they can.' She raised her wand and said some magical words. 'Haerio Herasco!'

All the creatures sucked together to form a huge, writhing mass in the centre of the room.

'Whoa,' I said, amazed. 'What did you just do?'

'I bound them all together,' Willa explained.

From the hallway behind me, I heard another, '*Heh heh heh!*'

Kieran was still standing in front of Emma, taunting her.

'Now, now,' Reg said, giving him a tap on the head with his cane, 'enough of that, kiddo. Yeh'll keep your distance if yeh know what's good feh yeh.'

Willa said, 'What part of "stand well clear" did you not understand!'

'Sorry,' my brother said sheepishly as he edged away from Emma. 'Won't happen again.'

'We must work quickly now, before it's too late,' Willa said. 'Smear Liquid Gold on a wall in each room of the house, like I told you to do. There aren't many areas that the black mould hasn't covered, so time is of the essence here, you understand?'

I did. Retrieving the cauldron, I found an uninfected part of the wall, then smeared Liquid Gold with my fingers. The effect was immediate. Radiating outwards, the glowing substance began to do its job. And then the house began to tremble as if a tremor had hit the area.

'Maud, old friend,' I heard Willa say, 'please leave the people of this house in peace and go on your way without trying to cause them any further harm. I know what happened to you has driven you to distraction and I understand your need for vengeance, but what you're doing here is evil ...'

Willa gave me a sharp look because I had stopped what I was doing so I could listen to this plea.

Kieran appeared at my side and picked up the cauldron. 'C'mon – next room, sis.'

We both moved into the hallway with Reg and he shut the door, leaving Willa on her own.

Clicking his gnarly fingers together, Reg gestured me to continue what I was doing.

I found a clear patch that wasn't near any of the frozen people, then set to work again. The golden substance dripped from my fingers as I smeared it onto the wall.

'That's amazin' stuff,' Reg said as we watched it radiate outwards, slowly eating away the mould. The house trembled again. Even worse this time. 'Somebody's not 'appy, an' that's feh sure.'

As we moved into the kitchen, I could hear Willa talking, still making her plea, but I couldn't make out what she was saying. *For all our sakes*, I thought, *I hope your friendship with Maud still counts for something.*

Next up, after we'd finished in the kitchen, was the downstairs toilet.

'Every time you put that stuff on a wall, the tremors get worse,' Kieran said. 'I just hope the house is still standing by the time we finish.'

'Ayuh, what yeh waitin' feh?' Reg said to me. He gave me a tap on the arm with his cane. 'There's not a second teh waste, so there ain't.'

Kieran placed a hand on my shoulder as he stepped in close because he knew how much this room scared me. 'Don't worry,' he said, 'we're right here with you and we've got your back.'

Giving him a nod, I went to open the door and noticed that my hand was shaking. *Keep it together*, I thought. *You've got two people watching out for you: an old guy who can barely move and your brother who's packing a deadly ... stick.* Despite everything, this made me giggle.

'One second you're scared out of your wits and next you're cackling to yourself,' Kieran noted. 'What gives?'

Suddenly, from in the living room, we heard a commotion. Because Willa had raised her voice we could make out what she was saying quite clearly.

'No, *no!*' she said, issuing a warning. 'Stay back! If you ever valued our friendship then *please* stay back!' We heard another commotion and then Willa issued another warning: 'I mean it! Don't make me do it, Maud! I understand your anger, believe me, I do, but what you're doing here is madness. No – NO! Stay *BA –*'

A strange voice said one word, 'Disarmamentius!' and then another: 'Subduviosa!'

'*Errghh!*' we heard Willa say in Frustration. 'That's a cheap trick! I should have known to expect as such!' Willa sounded like she was struggling somehow. 'Oh the indignity! Get these ropes off me! Release me! *Release MEEEEE!*'

The others and I had heard enough. Kieran flung the door open and it hit the wall with a *bang!* In the centre of the room, Willa had been bound by long, thick rope, which was snaked around her body like a Boa constrictor. Her wand was on the floor, beside her.

Wide-eyed and frantic, she looked towards us and said, 'Be careful – she's in the mould.'

Putting the cauldron and book down, I rushed to her and tried to free her. I couldn't loosen the rope, though; it was bound tightly by some invisible force. Kieran tried to help as well, but it was no good. Even with two of us pulling as hard we could, the rope stayed bound in place, unmovable.

'You're wasting your time,' Willa said. 'Only magic can free me from this bind.'

She edged sideways, tripped over the carpet and went down on her side with a thud. She grimaced as her head hit the floor.

'The counterspell is in the book,' she said through harsh breaths. 'Page eighty-six.'

Grabbing the book from the hallway, I quickly turned to the correct page and noted the magical words. Then I pointed my wand at Willa and said, 'Subduviosa Reversum!' But nothing happened. Willa stayed bound by the rope.

'It's all in the pronunciation,' Willa said. 'You must give the A in Subduviosa some oomph and the first R in Reversum must be drawn out, rolled: rrrrrr!'

I raised my wand to try again, but a flash of movement to my left caught my eye. About a third of the room had now been cleared of black mould by the steadily spreading Liquid Gold, but from the far wall, which was still covered in the stuff, a blob began to form, protruding outwards.

'That's her!' Willa said. 'Free me – *and quick!*'

Concentrating hard, I levelled my wand at her and pronounced the magical words exactly as she'd told me. 'Subduvios*a* Rrrrreversum!'

The rope loosened around her. As Kieran helped her up, it slid to the carpet in a loose bundle. Willa picked up her wand

and pointed it at the blob, which was now sprouting long pointy bits.

'Are they fingers?' Reg said, aghast.

'Yes, they are,' Willa confirmed. 'They're *hers*.' She gestured towards the hallway. 'Go on, you lot, get the job finished. And no matter what noises you hear coming from this room, do *not* attempt to help me. I will deal with this and I will do it on my own. Just spread that Liquid Gold all over this house and lift this curse. Do it – *now!*'

We didn't need telling twice.

As we left the room, the door slammed shut behind us, making us all jump.

'I think she means business this time,' Reg said.

Mum, Dad and the other two were still frozen, which was good (kind of). It hurt to see my parents in such a way, but I knew they hadn't been harmed. And I also knew that they would try to harm me if they could.

The Liquid Gold was busy doing its thing around us and also in the kitchen.

'What are you waiting for, sis?' Kieran said. 'Let's do this.'

Tucking my wand down the front of my jeans, I picked up the cauldron and went back to the small toilet. I paused outside the door.

'We're with you,' Kieran said, giving me a reassuring nod.

'Ayuh,' Reg added, 'we're with yeh, girl.'

I counted in my head – 1 … 2 … 3 … – then eased the door open and looked inside. It was as bad in there as I suspected it would be. But there were still spots on the walls which were mould free. The room was so small I didn't even need to enter to do what needed to be done. I spread some on the nearest clear spot, then closed the door with a snap. The house shook again.

'Only two rooms left to do downstairs,' Kieran said. 'The cellar and the games room.'

'We'd have to go past Maud and Willa to get to the games room,' I said.

'The cellar, then,' Reg said.

'It'll be really bad down there,' I said. 'Even worse than the toilet. Can we leave that 'till last?'

'Whatever!' Kieran said. 'Can we just get on with it!'

From the living room, we heard Willa issue a warning. 'I'm giving you one last chance to give it up, Maud, and then the gloves are off. No more tricks, you hear me! *No MORE!*'

Picking up the cauldron, Kieran said, 'Forget that – *let's move move move!*'

I led the way upstairs and others followed. Reg struggled, even with the use of his cane. He told us not to wait for him.

First, I did the landing. Reg made it up to us just as I was finishing. Red-faced and out of breath, he supported himself as best he could with his cane and gripped the bannister with his spare hand for extra support.

'Perhaps you should sit down,' I suggested.

'Never mind me,' he replied, wheezing, 'yeh jus' get on with what yeh doin'.'

Next up was my bedroom. The last time I had been in here there had only been a few spots of black mould. Now every wall was covered with the stuff and not much of the white paint was visible.

I was about to set to work when someone – probably Willa – yelled something downstairs. This was followed by a loud bang, which sounded like something crashing against a wall and shattering to pieces.

Mum is not *going to be happy about the state of this house after this fiasco is over*, I thought.

'Why are you smirking?' Kieran asked me.

'Just thinking about Mum, that's all.'

'Her being frozen and unable to move is funny?'

'No, I wasn't thinking about that. It doesn't matter. Let's just concentrate on what needs to be done.'

After we'd finished up in my bedroom – and more tremors had shaken the house – we heard another commotion downstairs. A loud thunderclap of noise shook the floor beneath us and someone cried out in pain.

'I hope that wasn't Willa,' Kieran said.

'I want to go down there and help,' I said, pulling my wand out and eyeing it confidently, 'but I know that wouldn't be a good idea.'

'You only know one spell,' Kieran pointed out.

'An' Willa is distractin' Maud so yeh can do what yeh doin',' Reg said from the doorway.

I wasn't sure what shocked me most: the state of my brother's bedroom, or the amount of black mould that was in there.

I made short work of the remaining rooms upstairs, however, which left just the cellar and games room to sort.
The Liquid Gold was steadily doing its work. It was eating away the black mould and brightening the house so much in places that I thought I would soon need sunglasses.

Meanwhile, downstairs, the battle between Willa and Maud raged on. Lots of strange words were being shouted: spells being cast, I assumed. Lots of weird noises could be heard: fizzes and bangs and even a loud wailing sound at one point. They really were slugging it out in there. *Really* going for it. I'm sure it would have been quite a spectacle to behold, had I been able to watch.

Next up, however, was the cellar. I was even more afraid to go down there than I had been to go in the toilet. It was where Maud had stored all her magical items and where the most black mould was in the house. I dreaded to think how bad it was down there now. But, as things turned out, we never got that far.

Kieran and I had to leave Reg behind again as he struggled to get down the stairs.

From inside the living room, someone yelled something, there was a fizzing sound – and then a loud thud, as if something, or someone, had just collapsed on the floor.

Please don't let that be Willa, I thought again.

Silence filled the house.

'What d'you think just happened?' Kieran whispered in my ear. 'Sounds like someone lost the fight to me.'

'That could be the case,' I whispered back. 'But was it Willa or Maud?'

Kieran knew what I was thinking. 'There's only one way to find out. I know she told us not to go in there, no matter what we hear, but if she's been taken out, we're not gonna be able to do what we're doing.'

I agreed with him. As I manoeuvred past my parents and the other two, I reached for the door handle and someone behind me coughed, 'Ahum!'

That's my dad or one of the others, I thought, fear gripping every part of my body. I'd forgotten that Reg was with us.

'Now whaddaya think yeh doin', yeh pair?' he said. 'Do I need teh remind yeh again about what Willa told yeh teh do an' what she told yeh not teh do? Two rooms left an' yeh two are wastin' time, not followin' instructions again, so yeh not.'

'Did you hear what just happened?' I asked him.

Reg leant to one side, supporting himself wearily on his cane. 'I 'eard a kerfuffle. But that doesn't mean yeh should go investigatin'. Keep spreadin' that golden stuff and don't waste another second, yeh 'ear me!'

This was the first time I'd seen even a spark of anger from the old man. Even he was beginning to panic now.

'He's right,' Kieran said, giving me a nod. 'There isn't a second to waste.'

'Absolutely right,' I replied, nodding agreement.

Not hesitating in the slightest, I opened the door and entered the room. From behind me, I heard Reg let out a wheeze of frustration, but this didn't concern me. What *did* concern me was the body on the floor, lying motionless and prone.

'Oh no,' Kieran said, gawping over my shoulder. 'This is bad – this is very, *very* bad.'

'Yes,' I agreed, fear welling up inside of me. '*Very* bad.'

'Is she … dead?' Kieran asked.

I moved a few steps closer to get a better look at Willa. 'No,' I said with relief, 'she's breathing. She's just been knocked out.' Her wand was next to her, broken in two.

There was no one else in the room, as far as we could see.

'She'll be in the black mould,' I warned, 'so keep an eye on the walls and ceiling.'

There wasn't much mould left in the living room, however; the Liquid Gold had eaten about two-thirds of it away.

From behind Kieran, Reg put a hand over his eyes to shield them from the glare, which was becoming blinding.

'Ah,' the old man said, 'that's not what I was 'opin' teh see.'

'At least she's on her side,' Kieran commented, 'in the recovery position.'

Upon entering the room, I had been fearful that the writhing mass of creatures might have been set free – but they were still all bound together: the mouldy spider plants and bats. I had a feeling that this would not remain the case for long, however, now that Willa had been defeated.

From behind us, in the hallway, we heard a noise: a kind of gurgling, gloopy sound.

'What was *that*?' Kieran said.

'I don't know,' I replied, 'but it doesn't sound good.'

The strange voice we'd heard before said two words: 'Relaxus Rigidio!'

Reg hobbled to the doorway to see what was happening, then immediately began retreating with a look of terror on his old, wise face. 'Oh Gawd,' he said, 'she's unfrozen 'em, so she 'as.'

Then Mum entered the room, sporting a fearsome glint in her blue eyes.

'Oh dear,' she said, grinning, 'your witch friend seems to have taken a fall.'

'What a terrible shame,' Dad said, appearing behind her.

And then, of course, came the other two.

'*Heh heh heh!*' Emma said, focusing her attention on Kieran. 'You're not laughing now, are you?'

Her father did not look pleased as he fanned into the room with the others. 'How dare you laugh in my daughter's face,' he said, glaring at Kieran like he wanted to kill him (which may well have been the case). 'Nobody does that to my Emma, you hear me! *Nobody!*'

'S-s-sorry,' Kieran said, stammering. He was still holding the stick. His grip tightened around it as he took a step backwards.

Reg said, quite calmly and clearly, 'Don't s'ppose there's any chance of negotiatin' our way out of this, is there?'

Mum shook her head.

Shifting his weight uncomfortably, Reg raised his cane and said, 'Thought yeh might say that.'

Mum focused her attention on me. 'I'm going to ask you this once more and just once,' she said. 'Put the wand down … or else.'

My response was immediate: 'No.' I pointed my wand at her and issued my own warning. 'Take one step closer and I'll … I'll blow you all to smithereens.'

'Really?' she said, looking surprised. 'Your own mother? Know how to do that, do you?'

'*Yes,*' I replied without hesitation, fixing her with a hard stare.

'*Noooooo,*' a strange voice said, seeming to echo out of nowhere. It was the same voice we'd heard before: the one we were sure belonged to Maud. '*Nooo* – she does not.'

I moved to my left, glancing past Brian and Emma, so I could see what was happening in the hallway. Just like the living room (which was now nearly clear of black mould, I noted), the hallway was glowing brightly because of the Liquid Gold. But by the front door, there were a few big splodges of mould remaining. It was from one of these that a tall, dark figure was emerging: a figure covered from head to toes in the black stuff. I watched in horror as Maud – yes, I was one hundred percent sure it was her – stepped sideways, freeing her arm with a gloopy slurp.

'What's happening?' Kieran enquired fearfully.

'It's her,' I replied. 'It's the witch.'

Careful to stay clear of the writhing mass of creatures, I edged back towards Reg and my brother: safety in numbers and all that.

And then we readied ourselves for battle. I held my wand up, ready to cast the only spell I knew. Kieran drew his arm back, ready to strike out with his only weapon: the stick. Reg raised his cane, eager to swing it.

'Are you three serious?' Emma said, smirking. Glints of blackness flashed in the whites of her eyes. 'Just give it up, why don't you.'

'Yeah,' Brian said, sneering. 'Give it up.'

'*Never,*' I replied through gritted teeth.

Mum and Dad took a softer approach. They tried to appeal to Kieran and me as if they were still our parents. On the outside they were. But on the inside they were bad, corrupted, *evil.*

'Daughter, darling,' Mum said, wearing a forced smile, 'do the right and put the wand down.'

Darling! I thought. *When have you ever called me darling before?*

'Sweetheart,' Dad said to me with a puppy dog expression, 'no harm will come to you. Just give it up with this silliness. I give you my word as your father and someone who loves you dearly.'

It hurt to hear him call me sweetheart. 'You were threatening me a few minutes ago and now you love me dearly. I don't think so.'

I looked down at Willa, who was still out cold. *Please come round*, I thought. *We could* really *do with your help.*

As I focused my attention back on my parents, they and the other two parted to make way for Maud. She oozed into view, black mould dripping from her body like hot wax from a candle. Her shoulders were stooped, her movements slow and ponderous. It was like watching a walking shadow – except that *this* shadow was gloopy through and through. Her eyes were black protrusions, her mouth a gaping, dripping hole.

One touch, remember. One touch …

'Put that wand down,' Maud said, her words an oozing command. 'I will not ask again.'

'No chance!' I replied. 'The Liquid Gold is eating away your black mould.' I glanced around the room, squinting because of the glare. 'There's none left in here now and the whole house will be clear soon.'

'Wrong!' Maud said. 'You have not smeared it in every room, so you have *failed*.'

'Not yet, we 'aven't,' Reg said defiantly. He pleaded with her: 'We used teh be friends, you an' I – *good* friends. Stop this madness, Maud, an' stop it now. You must know that this isn't the way, so yeh must. Or 'as 'atred blinded yeh so much that it's wiped any common sense out of yeh?'

Ignoring him, she slowly raised her arm, then levelled a dripping finger at me and said one word: 'Disarmamentius!'

Even though I was gripping my wand tightly, it slipped through my fingers, pulled by some invisible force. Up in the air it went, twirling, twirling, twirling towards Maud, who caught it in her mouldy hand.

She doesn't need a wand to do magic, I thought, shocked.

Maud handed the wand to Brian, who snapped it across his knee, then threw the pieces aside.

'Uh-oh,' his daughter said, 'not so confident now, are you?'

Mum and Dad found this particularly funny.

I wanted to say I wasn't that confident anyway, but I said nothing because I'd been shocked to silence.

Maud looked to my right, at the writhing ball of creatures – and I knew what she had planned. I also knew something else: that I had to do something drastic quickly, or we were all about to end up like my parents. But what could I do? I'd lost my wand – my only means of self-defence – so what *could* I do?

Glancing towards the cauldron, a flash of inspiration ran through me. I looked at Kieran, hoping that he was thinking what I was thinking. He nodded. Good. *Great*. For once, we were on the same wavelength.

Don't hesitate.

Don't think.

Just act ...

Scrambling towards it, we picked it up and swung it towards Maud, covering her in Liquid Gold.

'*NOOOO!*' she yelled in surprise. 'What have you done? What have you *DONE!*'

'Pulled the weed out at the root,' I said coolly.

The effect was immediate. The golden substance began to glow brighter and brighter – until the glare was so intense that I had to look away. Both Kieran and Reg shielded their eyes with their hands and looked away as well.

Meanwhile, Maud was screaming and cursing, thrashing about in a blind panic. She collided with Mum, knocking her to the floor. Mum noticed that she'd got some of the Liquid Gold on her arm and tried frantically to brush it off, but the stuff stuck to her like glue. The others just looked on, frozen, not knowing what to do.

'*NOOOOO!*' Maud yelled again. She continued to thrash about, colliding with furniture and knocking things over. '*You little witch! You EVIL little witch – NOOOOOOOO!*'

Me, evil? I thought. *Me!*

I wanted to watch what was happening, but Maud was glowing so brightly that all I could do was shield my eyes with the inside of my arm. Attempting to look at her now would have been like trying to look at the sun.

Her screams of rage and agony continued for about half a minute more. One last surge of brightness filled the room. And then that was it, the brightness faded away and I was able to see again. Well, kind of. The Liquid Gold had dazzled me so much that it'd burned a rainbow of colours into my retinas. After a few seconds, however, the rainbow began to fade and I was able to see.

Of Maud, there was no sign. Amidst a mess of broken ornaments, Mum, Dad and the other two had collapsed to the floor, unconscious. Or, at least, I *hoped* they were just unconscious. Kieran and I raced to our parents and knelt beside them.

'Dad,' I said, giving him a shake, 'are you okay?' When he didn't respond, I gave him another shake. More vigorous this time. 'Dad, are you all right? Please tell me that you're all right!'

Kieran took hold of Mum's wrist and checked for a pulse. 'She's alive,' he said with a smile.

Calming myself a little, I could see that Dad's chest was rising and falling, which meant he was breathing. Kieran noticed this too and we exchanged a look of pure relief.

We heard movement behind us and turned to see Willa stirring, her eyes slowly opening. Reg hobbled to her side and, with some difficulty, went to one knee beside her.

'Try not teh move too much or too quickly,' he advised. 'Yeh've 'ad a nasty fall, so yeh 'ave.'

'Oh my,' Willa said, giving her head a shake as she propped herself up on one chubby elbow. She looked at Reg, then Kieran and me. 'What's happened? Where is Maud? We need to stop her before it's too late.'

I explained what had happened and Willa let out another 'Oh my'. She was still groggy, not quite with it. She gave her head another shake, her jowls quivering – and then she noticed her wand. Both parts of it. Her face dropped.

Kieran said. 'Yours isn't the only one that's been broken in two.' He gestured towards mine on the floor. I'm sure my face must have dropped too when I looked at it. 'You do own a shop full of 'em,' Kieran went on, 'so getting a replacement isn't going to be a problem for you, is it?'

'Getting a "replacement" would be impossible,' Willa said with some irritation. 'Once a wand is broke, it's broke. There is no spell that can repair one. And that one had been handed down through three generations of our family. My mother would be bereft with remorse if she could see what had happened to it, may she rest in peace, God bless her soul.'

'Oh,' Kieran said awkwardly. 'Sorry.'

'You do say the most stupid things at the most stupid times,' I said to Kieran.

'I apologized,' he said, glaring at me.

It was then, as I looked around the room, that I noticed what had happened to the creatures. Like everything else in the house, they were no longer covered in black mould. And they were no longer bound together as a writhing mass, either. They were lying motionless on the carpet, in a pile. I thought I saw one of the spider plant's legs twitch and a shudder ran through me.

Willa noticed what I was looking at and said, 'It's okay; they won't harm you now that the curse has been lifted. Bats are not aggressive creatures by nature and the same can be said of spider plants, as I'm sure I told you before. They can be quite loving little things, especially if they take to you.'

Heaven forbid, I thought with another shudder.

Holding out a hand, Willa said, 'Okay, I've had enough of being down here. If someone would kindly help me up, please.'

Reg's knees popped as he got awkwardly back to his feet with the aid of his cane. He shuffled aside, making way for Kieran and me.

I positioned myself to one side of Willa and Kieran positioned himself on the other. We each grabbed a hand and began to pull. At first, I didn't think we'd be able to do it. But then, with one almighty effort, we yanked Willa to her feet.

'Thank you,' she said, giving her multi-coloured dress a brush off with her hands. 'It feels so much better to be upright.'

The others began to stir. Emma came round first. She looked around the room, confused. She gave me a baleful glare (with no glints of blackness in the whites of her eyes, thank the Lord) – and then she noticed Brian beside her, who was propping himself up on one elbow.

'Dad,' she said, 'are you okay?'

'No,' he replied grumpily, 'I am not.'

Meanwhile, Mum was pushing herself up off the floor and making her way towards Dad, who was groggiest of them all.

'Oh my life,' he said, looking like he might throw up – and then he did.

Screwing up her face, Emma sprang to her feet and said, '*Oooooh!* Did you have to do *that* right near me?'

'Like he could help it,' Mum said, placing a supportive hand on Dad's arm.

'Fear not, people,' Willa said, 'any danger there was has passed now. And any sickness you're feeling will soon pass, too.'

'Who, exactly, are you?' Brian said as he stood up next to his daughter. 'And what the heck just happened here? What the heck just happened to *me*?'

I couldn't think of where to begin with an explanation. My head was still too overloaded with everything that'd happened, so I said nothing.

'For now,' Willa said, appealing for calm, 'all we need to do is concentrate on checking that everybody is okay and well. How much can any of you remember?' She looked at each of them in turn, but her question seemed more directed at Mum than anyone else.

'All of it, unfortunately,' she responded, shaking her head. 'It was like half of me – the good half – was trapped inside my own body whilst another evil half took over. I was powerless to stop what I was happening. I've never felt so helpless. It was so infuriating – and scary.'

'That's what it was like for me,' Dad said, wiping drool from his bottom lip.

Emma screwed up her face again, so I shot her a dirty look.

Then Brian banged his forearm against the wall, making everyone jump. 'Stop pussyfooting around and tell me what just happened to me! I don't want to hear any codswallop about how anyone feels – I just want to *KNOW* what happened to *ME!*' His face was flushed purple with anger and his hands were balled tightly into fists.

Reg levelled his cane at him. 'Yeh better calm down, yeh big brute,' he said, showing no fear whatsoever. 'Like everyone 'ere ain't been through enough already without yeh kickin' off.'

'Don't think that your age will protect you from a good slap,' Brian warned him.

'Okay, I've heard enough,' Willa said. She snapped her fingers at him – 'Pleasantzium Temprataz!'

For a second he just stood there, a mixture of hatred and confusion covering his face. And then he smiled at everyone. It was a big, toothy smile, which appeared so abruptly that it made me smile as well.

'Feeling happy now, are we?' I asked him.

'*Yessss!*' he said, his eyes bright with an enthusiasm I'd never seen in him before. 'Very happy – *verrrry* happy indeed.'

Now it was Emma's turn to look confused. 'Dad, are you all right?' she asked him. 'You don't quite seem yourself.' Before he could reply, she directed her next question at Willa. 'What did you just do to him? You cast a spell on him, didn't you? I remember all the thoughts that woman was putting into my head – that *witch*! And you're just like her. You're a witch, too!'

'Indeed I am,' Willa said. She clicked her fingers at Emma – 'Pleasantzium Temprataz!'

Just like her father, Emma went from nasty to nice in the flip of a switch. She gave me such a warm, glowing smile that I couldn't help but chuckle.

'You put a spell on them to make them nice,' Kieran observed.

'I most certainly did,' Willa said.

'And you didn't need a wand to do it,' I observed.

'A lot of spells can be done without the use of a wand,' Willa informed me.

'So why do yeh even need one? Reg enquired.

'Some spells are too powerful to be done without a wand,' Willa explained. 'It also focuses and intensifies a witch or wizard's power, making spells and charms easier to cast.'

Dad was still on the floor, looking on with a blank expression on his face.

'You should have believed Ella when she told you that something was wrong with this place,' Kieran said to him and Mum. 'And I should have believed her when she first told me, too. Sorry I doubted you, sis.'

'There's nothing to be sorry about,' I said. 'What's done is done. And, to be honest about it,' I looked at my parents, 'I'd have been sceptical in your position as well. I fully understand why you didn't believe me.'

'We have a lot to talk about,' Mum said to me. 'A lot to talk about indeed.'

'I love talking,' Emma said, grinning. 'It makes me happy to chat to people.'

Really? I thought. You've got to be kidding me, right?

'I love talking to people, too,' Brian added, positively beaming.

'Oh my life,' I muttered under my breathe.

Mum helped Dad to his feet and then he gestured towards the pile of creatures, which were thankfully not covered in mould anymore. 'Erm, I don't mean to alarm anyone,' he said, 'but some of those things are *moving*.'

'It's okay, they're just coming around and none of them will hurt you now that Maud has gone,' Willa reiterated.

'You told me that spider plants had been known to nip fingers off,' I said.

This bit of information got everyone moving away from the creatures quickly.

'Adult spider plants have been known to nip off fingers, yes,' Willa said, appealing for calm, 'but these are just babies. As I told you before, now the curse has been lifted, you have nothing to worry about; they will not harm you.'

Mum pointed at a bat that was flapping its wings, getting ready to take flight. 'And what about them,' she said, 'are they harmless as well?'

Several took to the air at the same time, flying frantically around the room, colliding with things.

'*Ha-ha!*' Brian said as one landed on top of his head and pooped on him.

Kieran, on the other hand, did not seem so happy to have one around him. He ducked out of the way and fled to the other side of the room, with the bat following him.

One of the spider plants scurried over to Reg and he hobbled away, grunting unhappily.

As more of the creatures began moving around, the room descended into chaos. Spider plants scurried around, freaking everyone out (everyone apart from Willa, of course). And the bats took to the air, flying around the light fitting, dive-bombing people.

'Erm, is there anything you can do about this?' I asked Willa, swiping one away from my shoulder. 'Because this is getting a bit out of hand now.'

'Yes, yes,' she agreed, struggling with one herself, 'this is getting a bit out of hand, I'll grant you that.' She clicked her fingers together and said, 'Rigidio Maximus!'

The spider plants froze where they were, their many legs no longer scurrying. The bats dropped to the carpet, one after another, their wings no longer flapping. Everyone, apart from Brian and Emma, breathed huge sighs of relief.

'Well thank Gawd feh that,' Reg said, clutching at his chest. 'I thought I was goin' teh 'ave a coronary, so I did.'

'Apologies,' Willa said to him, 'I should have anticipated that.'

'Why did you freeze them?' Emma said, smiling. 'I haven't had that much fun in a long time.'

Kieran said, 'Is she and her dad gonna be permanently like that?'

I wasn't sure which was more annoying: the old them or the new.

'It'll wear off,' Willa said. 'Eventually.'

She looked quite sad and I guessed why.

'I'm sorry things came to what they did between you and your friend,' I said to her. 'It must have been hard to fight her like you did.'

'It was,' Willa said, nodding solemnly. 'But I shall always try and remember her as the woman she used to be and not the woman she became.'

After a moment's silence, Mum looked around the room and shook her head. 'There's a lot of cleaning up to do here,' she said. 'And, like I mentioned before, there's a lot to talk about as well.'

'What about this golden stuff on the walls?' Dad asked Willa. He squinted because of the glare. 'Will that fade or will we have to scrub it off?'

'It's already beginning to fade and will be gone within a few hours now that its job is done,' Willa replied. Any black mould that hasn't been touched by it will die anyway now that Maud is gone. And with regards to this place looking a mess, I can easily sort that for you.'

She clicked her fingers together and said some magical words: 'Mudos Servatus Reversum!'

All of a sudden, the room began tidying itself. Ornaments on the floor levitated up and back to the shelves they'd fallen from. Bits of furniture began sliding across the floor, straightening themselves like they had minds of their own. A glass lamp that'd been broken gelled itself back together and then repositioned itself next to the fireplace. A clock picked itself up off the floor and put itself back on a shelf. Everyone watched the spectacle in amazement. But none of us was more amazed than my mum.

'Wow!' she said. 'I need to employ you as a full-time cleaner.'

'Alas,' Willa said, 'that's not a post I'd be interested in taking on.'

I looked on with wonder and excitement filling every part of me. 'I can't *wait* to learn how to do magic,' I said.

For the third time, Mum said, 'A lot to talk about ...'

EPILOGUE

(Five days later...)

It was Saturday morning. My parents had just nipped out to do some shopping. I'm not sure who was more eager to see them go: Kieran or me. Racing towards the patio doors in the living room, he gestured me to get my broomstick and get a move on.

'They're going to be gone for a good few hours,' I said, picking it up, 'so we've got plenty of time.'

'I know,' he replied, 'but I can't wait to see you do this. It's gonna be the most awesome thing ever!'

'I wouldn't get too excited. I might not even be able to do it. And I'm a bit worried that I could fall off.'

'Just don't go too high then.'

'What if a neighbour sees me?'

'We don't have that many neighbours near us. There's only Reg – who'd probably have a chuckle to himself – and those two houses across the way.'

'But what if I go up and can't get back down,' I said, genuinely worried that such a thing could happen.

'If you're as powerful as Willa says you are, then I'm sure that won't be the case.'

Something in the corner of the room, near the ceiling, caught my eye – and my heart sunk.

'What's up?' Kieran asked. He followed my line of sight and noticed what I was looking at. 'Oh no,' he said, shaking his head. 'Tell me that's not what I think it is. Tell me that the black mould isn't back.'

I moved closer, so I could get a better look. Then I breathed the biggest sigh of relief ever. 'It's just a smudge of dirt,' I said.

'Are you *sure*?' Kieran asked me as he edged closer. 'Ah, yeah, you're right – it is just dirt.' He mimicked wiping sweat from his brow. 'Flippin' 'eck, I was getting ready leg it then.'

'Yeah, me too.'

'C'mon, let's get outside.' Kieran went to the patio door and peered out towards the sky. 'Those clouds look dark, so I think it's gonna rain soon.'

On the way out, we gave the trees by the fence a wide berth, because we didn't fancy getting clobbered. There were still some spider plants growing beneath them, so the trees would be protective. The ones that'd invaded our house had been taken away by Willa, so she could care for them (they make good pets, she'd told us – rather you than me, had been my response). As for the trees, my parents wanted to chop them down and have them removed. But Willa told them that that would be bad luck. Plus there was the (not so) small matter of who would chop them down and how they would do it without getting their head taken off.

As for the bats in the roof, Renshaw's had visited the day before and removed all of them. An expert from the company assured us that the bats wouldn't come back this time and Mum, above everyone else, hoped that they were right.

Standing in the middle of the overgrown lawn, I looked towards the house, then shook my head. I still couldn't believe everything that'd happened in such a short space of time and how much it would change my life.

'What's up, sis?' Kieran asked. 'You're not still worried about anything, are you? Willa assured us that it was over and Maud won't be coming back, so you can relax, yeah. Why are you smiling?'

'I keep thinking about Brian and Emma. That spell that made them both nice should have been permanent. I can think of a few other people who I'd use it on, if that were the case.'

'Are you referring to Mum here? She wouldn't be her if she wasn't a bit of a grump.'

'No, not her. Just other people I've met before.'

'Talking about Emma, did she given you any trouble at school yesterday?'

I shook my head. 'No, she's keeping her distance. Even though Willa wiped her memory of everything that happened that day, she still seems wary of me. I think she knows now that she needs to be careful around me, but she doesn't know why.'

Willa had erased Brian's memory, too. A quick click of Willa's fingers and a magical word – Meminus! – had done the trick.

'Let's just hope she stays wary,' Kieran said, eyeing me mischievously, 'or you might have to give her a zap with your wand. You could hang her upside down or something and we could take turns throwing eggs at her head.'

I shook my head again. More vigorously this time. 'Willa warned me about not practising magic until I've had some training. I could mutter the wrong word or mispronounce a spell and kill someone. It's serious stuff.'

Kieran gave me a sideways glance, with a smile playing at the corners of his mouth. 'Your classes don't start 'till the beginning of September. Are you trying to tell me that you're not gonna do any magic over the next few months? Not one spell – not *one* little spell!'

'That's exactly what I'm telling you,' I replied. But I couldn't keep a straight face as I said it.

The day before, I had visited The Mystic Cove to take back the items I'd promised to return. But Willa had been reluctant to accept them and informed me that I would probably need them. When I asked why, she'd told me about the Bostwick School of Magic:

'I know the man who runs it and I think it would be in your interests to attend classes, so you can learn about the craft.' She'd asked me if I would like to attend and I had answered yes with no hesitation at all. I'd grinned at the prospect and eyed the broomsticks lined up near the wall.

'You will need one of those for your lessons,' she had said. 'I suppose you could take one now, free of charge. After everything you've been through, I think you deserve it. There is one condition, however: you don't attempt to ride it until you've attended classes and received some instruction. Can you give me your word on that?'

'*Yes!*' I had said, again without hesitation.

'Good,' she'd said. 'I'll be around your house in a few days to collect Maud's things from the cellar. In the meantime, don't be tempted to go down and meddle with any of it. Heaven knows what you might stumble upon down there.'

I gave her my word that I wouldn't. At least I'd been able to keep my word with regards to *that*.

'Are you gonna give it a go then, or what?' Kieran said, urging me to get on with it.

'I've just remembered that I didn't tell Mum and Dad about the school trip to the farm for our class, which is in a few weeks.'

'Stop delaying and just get on with it.'

'I feel guilty about doing this because I gave Willa my word that I wouldn't.'

'And how's she's going to find out. I'm not gonna tell her. Are you?'

'That's not the point. I gave my *word*.'

Kieran let out a noise of frustration. 'You can't just bring me out here, get me all excited, and then back out. C'mon, sis, just give it a little try. Just a *little* ride, yeah?'

I looked up towards the ever-blackening sky and a few spots of rain hit my face. The leaves on the branches of the trees near the fence rustled as the wind began to pick up a little. If I was going to do it, I needed to do it soon, before the heavens opened up and drenched us both.

I put the broomstick between my legs.

Kieran blurted out: '*Yes!*' He backed away and fist-pumped the air. 'Lezzz go! You remember what the book said, yeah?'

'Yes.'

There were no magical words. I just need to concentrate and imagine myself hovering up into the air. So that's exactly what I tried to do. Closing my eyes, I concentrated hard – but nothing happened. I tried again – but nothing happened. I stayed grounded.

'Perhaps you're trying too hard,' Kieran said. 'Maybe you should relax a little.'

'Perhaps I'm not as powerful as Willa thinks I am. She said only a powerful witch or wizard can fly a broomstick.'

'You can do this,' Kieran said, giving me an encouraging smile. 'I *know* you can.'

Closing my eyes, I took a deep breath. And then another. I imagined my feet leaving the ground and me floating up in the air. Floating, steadily floating, with my eyes still shut. I stayed like this for a while. But then I soon opened my eyes when I felt the ground fall away beneath me. Looking down, I was delighted to see that I was hovering three or four feet above the grass.

'*Woo-hoo!*' Kieran shrieked. 'You did it! You *actually* did it!'

'I did,' I replied, just as amazed as him. '*Woo-hoooo!*'

I looked at Kieran and he looked at me. That mischievous look was on his face, so I knew what he was thinking.

Guiding the broomstick upwards, I rose to a height of about fifteen feet. I couldn't see anything of interest because of all the trees around me though, so I kept moving upwards until I could.

'Wow!' I said as I hovered above the treetops, taking in the view. 'Just … *wow!*'

In the distance, I could see the top of the church spire in the town. Just beyond this were hills of rolling yellow and green fields. A row of thatched cottages lined the road which snaked up to the darkening horizon. Closer by was Reg's house. Tendrils of smoke were spiralling from the chimney on the roof. I made a mental note to visit him soon, then turned my attention back to what I was doing.

Big raindrops began splattering my face as I looked upwards, but I was having too much fun to care.

'Sorry Willa,' I said, 'but this has got to be done.'

Angling the front end of the broomstick skywards a little, a big grin spread across my face as I shot forwards through the air, picking up speed ...

Made in the USA
Middletown, DE
24 October 2022

13214039R00126